"BONES, CAN YOU TELL ME WHEN HE DIED?" KIRK ASKED.

"And also," he continued, "anything about the weapon that did it."

McCoy looked over Kirk's shoulder and his expression turned grim. He gulped and gave the body a quick examination. "I'm surprised Security didn't catch the killer in the act; he's been dead only a few minutes."

"That short a time, how could we have missed him?"

McCoy simply shrugged. "I'll do a complete autopsy when Security is through recording the mess, but as a first guess, I haven't got a clue about what happened here." The doctor shook his head in bewilderment. "Those cuts are deep and parallel, like giant claw marks—though anything with claws long enough to do that much damage would have to be one *hellaciously* big monster."

Look for STAR TREK Fiction from Pocket Books

STAR TREK®

ENEMY UNSEEN

V. E. MITCHELL

POCKET BOOKS

New York   London   Toronto   Sydney   Tokyo   Singapore

An *Original* Publication of POCKET BOOKS

POCKET BOOKS, a division of Simon & Schuster Inc.
1230 Avenue of the Americas, New York, NY 10020

STAR TREK is a Registered Trademark of
® Paramount Pictures.

This book is published by Pocket Books, a division of
Simon & Schuster Inc., under exclusive license from
Paramount Pictures.

ISBN: 0-671-68403-5

First Pocket Books printing October 1990

10 9 8 7 6 5 4 3 2 1

POCKET and colophon are registered trademarks of
Simon & Schuster Inc.

Printed in the U.S.A.

to Jon

for believing I could write this—and for reading all its incarnations more times than he cares to remember

Historian's Note

This adventure takes place shortly after the events chronicled in *Star Trek: The Motion Picture*.

Chapter One

Captain's Log, Stardate 8036.2: While on a routine star charting mission, the *Enterprise* has been ordered to report to Starbase 15. When we arrive, we will receive orders for a short-duration, high-priority mission. We will also be dropping off First Officer Spock so he can rendezvous with a transport to Vulcan. He will be taking a two-week leave to attend the Vulcan Academy of Science's Invitational Conference on Extreme-Energy Physics and the Fine-Scale Structure of the Universe.

Personal Log, Supplemental: While I would not normally envy Mr. Spock a leave on Vulcan, in this case I suspect he is getting the better part of the deal. I greatly fear our new assignment will be a diplomatic one. I also have grave doubts about the temporary First Officer that Starfleet has promised me. All I have been told is that this is his final training assignment before he is assigned as First Officer to the deep-space exploration vessel USS *Challenger*, which is to be commissioned next month.

LIEUTENANT COMMANDER UHURA acknowledged an incoming call and turned to Kirk. "Captain, I'm receiving a message from Starbase 15. It's Admiral Chen."

"On screen." Kirk straightened in his chair. He remembered Chen from Starfleet Academy, and she had always been a stickler for appearances. She also had a reputation for taking pleasure in handing out unpopular assignments. This time, Kirk was determined to remain impassive, no matter how unpleasant the mission.

A small-boned woman of Chinese extraction appeared on the viewscreen. She began speaking immediately. "Captain Kirk, as you have no doubt surmised, your ship is being assigned to transport the Kaldorni delegation and a Federation negotiating team to the diplomatic planetoid, La Paz. Detailed information is being transmitted to you now. Your passengers will be ready to beam aboard when you arrive. Chen, out."

"Still gives orders like she was on the frontier," the navigator, Ensign Yeshua ben Josef, muttered, directing the comment toward his navigation console as he rechecked the coordinates for the final approach to Starbase 15.

Lieutenant Commander Sulu glanced away from the helm controls and flashed ben Josef a wide grin. "It pays. Sometimes you only have power for two minutes of long-range transmission. You have to make every word count."

Kirk ignored the exchange. "Mr. ben Josef, how long till we arrive?"

"Fifteen minutes, sir."

Kirk stood. "Mr. Sulu, you have the conn. Inform me when we arrive. Commander Uhura, relay Admiral Chen's information to my quarters. I'd better find out what's so hush-hush *before* we get to Starbase 15."

"Jim! Wait!" McCoy was still adjusting the collar of his dress uniform as he hurried down the corridor to join the captain. "What's this about a diplomatic mission, Captain? Tell me it isn't true."

Kirk paused outside the transporter room. "Sorry about that, Bones. For the next few days, we're the diplomatic shuttle service in this quadrant."

2

"More precisely, Captain, the *Enterprise* is one-half of the quadrant's diplomatic shuttle service." Spock, carrying a small duffel bag at his side, arrived from the opposite direction. "The Diplomatic Service's cruiser, *Juan Martinez,* is the other half."

"And just how do you know so much about this?" McCoy said, bouncing on his toes. "You're not even going to be on the ship for the next two weeks."

"That is correct, Doctor. However, I still read the briefing tapes. I consider it my duty to keep informed on the ship's assignments."

"And just what is our assignment?" McCoy gave Kirk a look that said "Let's see just how good he is." Hiding a grin, Kirk turned away from them and entered the transporter room.

"The *Enterprise* has been assigned to transport a delegation from the United Worlds of the Kaldorni Systems to La Paz for negotiations with their counterparts from the Beystohn Amalgamated League of Planets. While en route, a Federation negotiating team will work with the Kaldorni to establish the protocols for the actual negotiations." Spock followed Kirk and McCoy through the door without missing a beat. "Both the Kaldorni and the Beystohnai have appealed to the Federation to prevent a war between them over the rights to settle the planet Yagra IV."

"Never heard of it," McCoy muttered, glaring over his shoulder at the transporter room door as it whisked shut behind him. He was already sorry he'd started the discussion. From Kirk's amused expression, McCoy suspected the captain was enjoying his discomfort.

Spock ignored McCoy's interruption. "Yagra IV is a high-gravity, tropical world located in the Epsilon Carinae system. It is approximately halfway between the Kaldorni and the Beystohn home planets. Neither group considers Yagra to be an ideal planet. Its gravity is much higher than the Kaldorni homeworld, while the climate is uncomfortably hot and humid for the people accustomed to the subarctic climate of Beystohn. However, Yagra IV is one of the few planets available for colonization that is within reach of the spaceflight technologies of the Kaldorni and the Beystohn League."

"Was all that in the briefing tape?" Kirk asked in surprise.

"I did some supplemental research, Captain. The information is flagged for your attention."

"Thank you, Mr. Spock. I'll check it as soon as I can."

"Captain, I have a request to make. In my spare time, I have been working on the prototype of a program that is intended to provide logical advice for those who need it. It is based on an experimental artificial intelligence system that promises to revolutionize the way our computer systems operate. Though the system is far from complete, it would greatly facilitate the next set of revisions if someone other than myself tested the program."

"Just what this ship needs." McCoy rolled his eyes toward the ceiling. "A programmed *Vulcan-in-a-box.*"

"The program is not designed for this ship," Spock countered. "The ideal use for such a system would be to advise personnel on small scout vessels that do not carry the broad range of specialists found on the *Enterprise.* And I hardly think that the description *Vulcan-in-a-box* is appropriate, Doctor. To date, I have worked on the program for only 17.34 hours. That is hardly enough time to provide it with the data links to support a knowledge base equivalent to that possessed by a very young human. I merely wished to ask the captain if he would test the program's operation so that I can make the modifications necessary to optimize performance."

"Thank you, Spock. I will see what I can do." Kirk turned to the Transporter Chief. "Status report, Mr. Rand."

"Starbase reports our passengers are ready to trans-

4

port, on your command," Transporter Chief Janice Rand replied. "Mr. Spock can beam down when he's ready."

Spock crossed the room and stepped onto the transporter pad. "With your permission, Captain Kirk."

"Enjoy your conference, Mr. Spock." Kirk nodded to Rand. "Energize. And then start bringing our—guests—aboard."

The familiar whine of the transporter filled the room. Spock dissolved into shimmering energy and disappeared. Rand reset the controls and beamed up the first contingent from the base. Five people materialized.

A tall, heavyset man in his late fifties that Kirk recognized stepped off the transporter pad first. Joachim Montoya was dressed entirely in black, except for the silver Federation insignia on the left side of his tunic. His dark eyes and his black hair shot with silver at the temples emphasized his somber outfit. His gaze flicked around the room before settling on Kirk. Montoya extended his hand to the captain. "You must be Captain Kirk," he said, smiling. "I've heard a great deal about you. It's a great honor and privilege to finally meet you."

"Thank you, Commissioner." Kirk's response was guarded. The heartiness of Montoya's greeting set his nerves on edge. "The *Enterprise* and I are honored to be at your service."

Montoya's smile never wavered. "Thank you, Captain. May I present the rest of my party?" He gestured toward two men and a woman who wore Federation insignia. "My aides, Kristiann Norris, Devlin Vreblin, and Paul Zayle." As Montoya said their names, each nodded to the captain. Norris was a slight woman of average height, with medium brown hair, hazel eyes, and plain features. Vreblin was short and wiry, with a scar across his cheek and upper lip that twisted his mouth into a permanent sneer. His dark hair and eyes appeared to match his dour expression, and Kirk hoped he would never quarrel with the man. Zayle was tall, blond, and endowed with enough good looks to make up for the shortcomings of his co-workers. Kirk decided Zayle's qualifications were more in his muscles than in his brains, but conceded those credentials were impressive.

"And my wife of three months, Cecilia Simons." Simons, obviously accustomed to making grand entrances, glided forward and dropped her traveling cloak. It billowed to the floor and spread into a puddle of plum and crimson. Zayle scowled as he retrieved the discarded garment.

Simons was tall and slender, with cascades of midnight-black hair that tumbled off her shoulders. Her scarlet dress flickered as she moved, and her feral sapphire eyes positively glowed. She flowed across the room and extended her arms to Kirk.

"But, Yonnie," she purred, "there's no need to introduce me to Captain Kirk. Jimmy and I are *old* friends."

Kirk stiffened as he recognized her. *Cecilia Simons?* he thought. *Is that what she's calling herself these days?* "It's been a long time . . . Cecilia." *But not nearly long enough,* he added savagely to himself. "I wasn't expecting to see you."

"But I was expecting to see *you.*" Her voice throbbed with passion. "I couldn't wait when Yonnie told me the ship we were traveling on was commanded by my old friend."

I'll just bet. Kirk bit his tongue to keep from saying the words aloud. He wondered what she wanted that was worth such an act. To keep from thinking about that now, he turned to Montoya. "Commissioner, I'll have a yeoman show you to your quarters."

Montoya nodded. "Thank you very much, Captain. My aides and I will wait for the Kaldorni, but my wife wishes to get settled as soon as she can."

"Of course." Kirk issued the order and as they

waited for two crewmen to load the party's luggage on an antigrav pad, he was aware of Simons studying him. The calculating expression on her face increased his apprehension.

As soon as Simons left, Rand transported the first of the Kaldorni. Four bronze-skinned men wearing full leather battle armor materialized. Their lacquered and burnished brass chest plates and arm pieces gleamed brightly. They carried a vicious-looking knife in each hand. Kirk sized up their tall, muscular frames, and thanked his lucky stars they were from a low-gravity planet. In a fight, the difference in gravity adaptations would tip the battle against the Kaldorni.

"Would you mind explaining, Mr. Commissioner?" Kirk pointed toward the Kaldorni and their drawn knives. The sight of so much weaponry did nothing to improve his feelings toward the mission.

"An honor guard, Captain. No high-ranking Kaldorni travels anywhere without a suitable escort." Montoya flashed Kirk another of his wide smiles. "The knives are purely for ornamental purposes."

Kirk scowled inwardly. The knives looked *extremely* functional to him. He wondered what other details had been omitted from the information Chen had given him on the Kaldorni. "I hope you're right," he grumbled under his breath.

The four Kaldorni came down the steps and lined up facing the transporter pads. "Energize," one ordered in a deep, strongly accented voice. Kirk nodded to Rand.

The transporter whined and six Kaldorni males, dressed in heavy, floor-length cloaks, materialized. Beneath their cloaks, the diplomats wore richly decorated robes made of brightly colored fabrics. The guards clanged their knives together above their heads, then knelt before the Kaldorni ambassador. Their weapons sliced forward in swift arcs and came to rest, crossed, at the ambassador's feet.

The ambassador was short and heavy, with a round

face and full, sensuous lips. His gray eyes seemed pale and colorless against his dark skin. With his slightest movement, the ambassador's ornate jewelry jangled. He gave Kirk the impression of being someone who relished life extravagantly.

Kirk spoke first. "I'm Captain James T. Kirk. Welcome aboard the *Enterprise.*"

The Kaldorni ambassador nodded curtly and one of his aides moved to his side. "Ambassador n'Gelen l'Stror Klee accepts your welcome for himself and those who attend him. I am the ambassador's mouthpiece, k'Vlay t'Stror, and will speak his thoughts to you."

"The Kaldorni consider it improper for a person of high rank to speak directly to a person of lower rank," Montoya explained to Kirk. "By definition, non-Kaldorni are of inferior rank until their actions prove otherwise."

Kirk scowled and nodded an acknowledgment. Had Chen sent him *anything* of importance about these people? A group of status-conscious diplomats was the last thing he needed—or wanted—aboard the *Enterprise!*

"The ambassador requests that all nonessential personnel please leave the room," t'Stror said. "He wishes to bring his wives aboard now, and it is not proper for an outworlder to look upon them."

As if searching for extra people, Kirk looked around the transporter room. Satisfied that a troop of Klingons had not beamed in while he was watching the Kaldorni, Kirk replied, "The only people I see are senior Federation representatives here to welcome you. We're hardly 'nonessential personnel.'"

"It is not proper for an outworlder to look upon the ambassador's wives," t'Stror repeated. "You will all leave this room now."

Kirk swallowed a retort. Spinning on his heel, he led McCoy and the Federation diplomats from the room.

"This mission is starting to sound like trouble,"

McCoy said as the door closed behind them. Kirk gave the doctor a sharp look; McCoy's comment echoed his own doubts.

"Would you explain this business of armed bodyguards and not speaking to persons of 'inferior rank'?" Kirk made no attempt to hide his anger from Montoya.

"It's just their way of doing things, Captain." Montoya smiled. "Their culture is deeply rooted in the militaristic traditions of their past. The Kaldorni are extremely proud of preserving their customs as they reorganize their society to conform with the demands of the future. In this, they are much like the Japanese in the seventeenth century, if you remember your Earth history. I think you'll really like them, once you get used to how they do things."

Kirk's frown was skeptical. "And I have two weeks to 'get used to them,' as you put it?"

"I'm certain it won't take that long, Captain."

A work party appeared with an antigrav pad just as the door opened. The six Kaldorni women were bundled in dark cloaks and heavy veils; their only visible features were their uniformly wide, pale gray eyes.

"Escort the ambassador and his party to their quarters," Kirk ordered. A dark-haired woman separated from the work party, acknowledged the order, and started down the corridor with the Kaldorni delegation. Kirk turned back to Montoya. "If you're ready now, I'll have someone show you to your quarters." He signaled for another crewman.

"We would be most grateful, Captain."

"Then if you'll excuse me, Commissioner, I have some business on the bridge."

"Of course, Captain."

By the time he reached the bridge, Kirk had relaxed considerably, although he was still irritated at the inadequate background material he had received. He headed for the communications station. "Uhura, get me Admiral Chen. I want to speak with her immediately. I'll be in my quarters."

"Aye, aye, Captain." Uhura's reply bounced off Kirk's retreating back. As he entered his cabin, the intercom whistled. He palmed the switch. "Kirk here."

"I have Admiral Chen, sir."

"Put her on." As Chen's face appeared, her proud, stubborn bearing reminded Kirk of her steely determination and indomitable will. Somehow, he doubted that he would like her answers to his questions.

"Admiral, may I request additional information on our present assignment?"

"What would you like to know, Captain?"

"The information you sent us completely lacks pertinent sociological and cultural data on the Kaldorni. We need more information if we are to avoid seriously offending these people."

Chen's mouth twitched as if she were suppressing a scowl. "Commissioner Montoya is perfectly capable of supplying all the information you require. However, to make the mission run more smoothly, we have prepared a supplemental briefing tape for you. It is being sent over with your Acting First Officer, and should arrive shortly."

"Thank you, Admiral. By the way, who will be my First Officer while Spock is on leave?" Kirk hoped his question sounded casual. So far, his attempts to find out whom he was getting had met with no success, and he was beginning to feel extremely frustrated.

Chen acted as if she had not heard the question. "Captain, I cannot overemphasize the importance of your mission. We believe someone is trying to sabotage the negotiations between the Kaldorni and the Beystohn League. Also, there may be a spy in the ambassador's party. You must prevent anything from disrupting these negotiations. The stability of this quadrant depends on it."

"Admiral, may I point out that the *Enterprise* is an *exploratory* vessel. We are not properly equipped for this kind of diplomatic assignment."

"Objection noted." Chen started to say more, then signaled to Kirk to wait. She spoke at length with someone off screen. "Make that confirmed, Captain," she said, turning back to Kirk. "Base Security has just found a body. It's Kaldorni, but we don't know yet if we will be able to identify the individual. So it's verified—there is a spy aboard your ship masquerading as a member of Ambassador Klee's party."

"I see, Admiral." Kirk gritted his teeth. This mission was sliding down the disposal chute in a big hurry. "I also want to talk to you about Commissioner Montoya's wife. On an assignment this sensitive, I do not feel my officers should be distracted by having uninvolved civilian passengers aboard. I request that Ms. Simons be beamed back to base before we break orbit."

Chen shook her head. "That's out of the question. Commissioner Montoya insisted on having her accompany him. In addition, she has a daughter serving on the *Enterprise*. A lieutenant named Whitehorse. You wouldn't want to deprive your crewwoman of her mother's company, would you?"

"I'm sure she'd never forgive me." Kirk thought the sarcasm in his voice was unmistakable, but Chen did not react.

"If that's all, have a good day, Captain. Chen out."

"Kirk out." He palmed the screen off and slumped in his chair with a huge sigh of frustration. "Lovely. Just lovely," he grumbled to himself. Two weeks of being a shuttle jockey for an ambassador who refused to speak to him; the delicate chore of finding a spy and murderer among said ambassador's staff; and, to top it off, no escape from Cecilia Simons. McCoy's prediction of trouble was starting to sound like a forecast for radiation from a supernova. Kirk flipped on the intercom; it was time to put out the blast warnings. "Uhura, inform Geologist Whitehorse that her mother is on board."

"Yes, sir. And, Captain, the transporter room reports that the Acting First Officer has just beamed aboard."

"Very well, Uhura. Have him report to my quarters at once."

"Aye, aye, sir."

Within minutes, the door buzzer sounded. Kirk looked up from the reports Spock had flagged for him. "Come."

The door opened, revealing a short, wiry man with a shock of bright red hair. The newcomer paused in the doorway, his green eyes twinkling like a mischievous leprechaun.

"Patrick!" Kirk bounded to his feet and rushed to greet his old friend and classmate. Commander Patrick Eugene Brady, his face split by an ear-to-ear grin, swept Kirk into a bearhug. "Patrick, how did you manage it?" Kirk asked when he had recovered from the surprise. The last Kirk had heard, Brady had been serving on a small exploration vessel at the edge of Federation space. The grapevine had said the assignment was at least partly punitive—that Brady's flair for practical jokes, second at the Academy only to the legendary Finnegan, had been the reason for his exile. The rumor went on to say that Brady's scientific genius was all that had saved his career. Apparently, Starfleet had been reluctant to lose a man of Brady's talents, in spite of his disrespect for proper discipline. Kirk was sure the story had grown in the telling, but knowing Brady, he suspected it was based on fact.

Still grinning, Brady dropped into a convenient chair while Kirk returned to his seat. He flipped a briefing tape across the desk to Kirk. "A man's got to learn his job somewhere. Some of the top brass don't like my methods, but they've decided I've earned another chance." Brady shrugged. "They say I need a month's training on a Constitution-class cruiser before the *Challenger*'s commissioned next month. "So Captain, I'm here to learn."

"This is a switch—you admitting there's something you don't already know." Kirk laughed. "You know, I think I might enjoy teaching you something, for a change."

"Oh, I wouldn't go that far. I do already know you're expecting trouble on this mission. Want to tell Uncle Patrick about it?"

"How much do you know?"

"Beyond the basics? I was in Admiral Chen's office when she found out about the spy. What else I should know?"

"Commissioner Montoya brought his wife with him. I am—somewhat—familiar with the woman. She always brings trouble with her by the cargo pod."

"Is this the person McCoy said gave you such a warm greeting? She must be some lady."

Kirk snorted. "She's no lady," he shook his head. "I don't know what she's up to this time. That's always the problem; you never know until it's too late." He picked up the briefing tape. "I suppose I'd better look at this. As your first assignment on the *Enterprise,* arrange a briefing for all department heads in two hours to discuss our assignment. In particular, we need to review the information Starfleet sent us about the Kaldorni, discuss its impact on ship's operations, and decide how it will affect the welcoming dinner this evening. After that's arranged, report to Sickbay so McCoy can do a physical for your medical records. I'm sure you didn't let him do that earlier."

Brady rose. His face was a study of wounded virtue. "I plead innocent, Captain Kirk. Do I look like the kind of person who would disobey regulations and skip my required physicals?"

"Brady." Kirk's voice rose in warning.

"Aye, aye, Captain." Brady managed to imitate a scared midshipman almost until he reached the door.

Chapter Two

MUCH TO KIRK'S SURPRISE, the formal diplomatic dinner for the Kaldorni went off well—after the seating arrangements were adjusted to conform with their standards of propriety. Ambassador Klee required his own table, since the Kaldorni refused to accept anyone aboard the *Enterprise* as Klee's equal. However, by arranging small tables around the ambassador and by placing Klee's spokesman in a central position, the required social forms were observed while maintaining a convivial atmosphere.

The ship's dietitian and her staff outdid themselves to create a menu that fulfilled the requirements of a formal affair while observing the dietary restrictions for individuals of three different species and a dozen cultural backgrounds. In addition, the briefing room had been redecorated on short notice to resemble the terrace of a Kaferian villa. Someone had found several murals that suggested distant mountain scenery. Sulu had raided Hydroponics for two dozen ever-flowering nightplum bushes, which were banked against the walls. The blossoms filled the air with their sweet, heavy fragrance. Tiny pinlights decorated the bushes, lighting the room with a dim golden radiance. Simulated candles, powered by larger pinlights, picked out gleaming highlights on the plates and tableware.

The setting seemed to relax the mixed party of Kaldorni, diplomats, and ship's officers. Kirk could not remember when he had been at such a lively and entertaining formal event. Halfway through dinner, he even found himself discussing the Kaldorni custom of avoidance with Ambassador Klee. Most of Klee's remarks were in Kaldorni and were translated by his "mouthpiece" t'Stror, but sometimes the ambassador bypassed his interpreter. Even then, Kirk noticed, Klee still spoke as if t'Stror were repeating his words.

"Would t'Stror indicate to Captain Kirk that he has taken an unnecessarily limited view of our practice of avoiding direct speech with those of inferior rank. One must retain the respect of one's inferiors, and how can one do so if one is too familiar with them?"

"I haven't noticed any lack of respect among my crew, and by definition, the captain of a starship is the highest ranking person aboard. . . . t'Stror, would you please relay that?"

"But t'Stror will convey to Captain Kirk that he does not keep his crew for life. He is permitted to dismiss a crew member who is unnecessarily disrespectful. When one is born to a ruling position of one's people, one has charge of one's people for their entire lives. So one must demarcate who is leader."

"t'Stror, please tell the ambassador I'll consider his point, but I prefer to talk with my people."

Klee's response was in Kaldorni, and t'Stror had to think before he translated it. "The ambassador says your system may work for you—though he seriously doubts it—but we have all the time we need for discussion on Kaldorn. And if we used your system, what would happen to all the younger sons of younger sons, who have no employment? Besides being born to rule on Kaldorn, one must protect one's status through useful service. If this person could not serve

Ambassador Klee and be his humble mouthpiece, where would he be?" t'Stror paused before adding, "With the honor comes the responsibility to serve. He is correct; were I not his mouthpiece, I would be nothing—lower than the lowest no-caste because I would lack a means to serve."

"I'll think about what you've said."

Kirk took a mouthful of his dinner and scowled at the flavor. It tasted like twice-heated, unflavored soya base. He knew that Starfleet Medical had recently recommended a new food base for the synthesizers, lower in fat and higher in protein than the old base, and that Dr. McCoy had offered to field-test it on the *Enterprise.* Kirk sighed. Every time the food bases were changed, the dietitian had to recalculate the flavoring and supplement balances for each item prepared by the synthesizers. Obviously, the program for Kirk's *veal aristini* would have to be modified again. Kirk glanced across the room at McCoy, who was engaged in a spirited debate with Lt. Tenaida, the Deltan Science Officer-in-training. McCoy appeared oblivious to the problems the captain was having with the new food base.

Kirk grimaced and took another mouthful of his dinner. The health of starship crews on long voyages was a perpetual concern for Starfleet Medical, and they were constantly modifying their dietary and exercise recommendations to assist all personnel in maintaining optimum physical condition. An occasional "off" meal was small price to pay for progress, Kirk supposed, but sometimes he wondered why the new food bases were not supplied with fully tested recipe databases instead of just formula guidelines. The ship's dietitian insisted that it was because each individual food processing system had a personality acquired from long-term exposure to the preferences of its users, but Kirk sometimes wondered if that wasn't how Starfleet's dietitians assured themselves of job security.

To take his mind off his dinner, Kirk looked around the room. Opposite him, Patrick Brady was listening to Cecilia Simons with an interest he usually saved for practical jokes or his next shore leave. Kirk felt a momentary twinge of jealousy at the sight of someone paying so much attention to Simons. It was a reflex habit he had thought was long gone. Of all the women Kirk had ever known, few had affected him as deeply as Cecilia Simons—both for good and ill. She possessed an uncanny, erotic magnetism, an almost psychic awareness of every man's deepest desires, and her manner promised immeasurable fulfillment. Half the men in the galaxy would gladly surrender their souls for a few hours of Simons' company; a large majority of the other half, Kirk was sure, already had.

Cecilia Simons liked handsome men, fancy clothes, expensive jewelry—and anyone who would provide her with them. If she had restricted her activities to her personal entertainment, Kirk would have worried less. However, Simons reveled in political intrigue, and Kirk knew her current involvement with Commissioner Montoya boded ill for the mission. He was confident some interested faction had purchased Simons' services, although he wondered who could afford her price. Even if he knew, Kirk would have trouble preventing Simons from interfering; she worked by indirection—a subtle word here, a convenient encounter there. When everything was analyzed, the evidence showed only that she was present at key times and places before a disaster. If a twenty-year string of coincidences ever became grounds for conviction, Cecilia Simons would be sentenced to spend the rest of her life in rehabilitation. Even then, Kirk was certain she would seduce her way to freedom in less than six months.

The dinner ended early when the Kaldorni ambassador excused himself to spend the rest of the evening in his quarters with his wives. Commissioner Montoya took the opportunity to leave with Simons, although to Kirk she appeared reluctant to retire so early.

"The captain knows the lady Simons?"

Kirk looked around, startled. "Oh—t'Stror. I thought you left with the ambassador." He took a deep breath, trying to put aside the disturbing memories. "I knew her a long time ago. She hasn't changed much."

"She has been—how do you say it?—most cooperative in helping me to learn the human language and customs. I could not serve my ambassador and my people nearly so well without the lady's help." The interpreter punctuated his words with quick, rhythmic gestures that sketched patterns in the air before him. Kirk watched his hands, trying to isolate the subliminal cue the movements suggested. t'Stror's body was shaped like one of the algae globes in Hydroponics, squat and shorter than any of the Kaldorni except the ambassador himself. He moved easily and appeared to have little difficulty in adjusting to the *Enterprise's* gravity field, even though it was much stronger than that of his home planet.

"Are your quarters satisfactory?" Kirk asked. "Is the heavier gravity bothering anyone? I'm sorry we didn't have enough warning to equip your living quarters with independent gravity fields."

"We understand the difficulty, Captain, and we find the accommodations to be most excellent. The ambassador in particular is pleased with the arrangements provided for himself and his wives. I believe the ladies are finding it troublesome to move with the greater gravity on *Enterprise,* but they will learn. Myself, this is my seventh trip off our planet, and I have learned to enjoy the change muchly." t'Stror's smile was guileless and his green-gray eyes beamed with pleasure. "Now I must excuse myself so that I may be available if my ambassador needs me." He bowed his head slightly, while extending and rotating his left wrist in a gesture of leave-taking.

Brady joined Kirk as t'Stror moved away. "You got over your distrust of the Kaldorni in record time, Captain."

"You know, as much as I hate to admit it, Montoya was right about them. They really aren't so bad once you get to know them. That avoidance thing looked like it was going to be a real headache, but the ambassador explained how it fits into their society. It isn't just a matter of status consciousness."

"Tenaida said that some of the North American Indian tribes used to practice a form of avoidance between married men and their mothers-in-law, if that brings it a little closer to home." Brady fell into step with Kirk, and they left the room.

"Tenaida told you? When did he come up with that, I wonder? It seems a little out of his field."

"Apparently, he did some supplemental research after the briefing this afternoon."

"That's interesting." Kirk's features relaxed into a smile. The young Deltan was turning into a Science Officer worthy of the confidence Spock placed in him. Too often, trainees for such positions took a long time to realize just how broad their responsibilities were. "And speaking of Tenaida, where is he? The dinner ended so early, we could get in a short poker game before bedtime." Kirk chuckled. "He asked what we humans saw in the game, so McCoy and I have been teaching him. Want to join us?"

"Sure. But I don't know where he went. He disappeared as soon as the ambassador left. Oh, there he is." Brady pointed down the corridor. The Deltan's slender form pushed through a cluster of people talking in the corridor. Tenaida was carrying a tray of food.

"I thought you just finished dinner, Tenaida." Brady greeted the Deltan scientist with a sardonic grin as the two senior officers caught up with him. "If you keep eating like that, the doctor will put you on a diet."

Tenaida was shorter than Kirk and moved with the powerful grace of a highly trained athlete. The corridor's lights gleamed off the olive skin of his bald head. At Brady's words, he lifted one thick eyebrow in a gesture copied from Spock. His dark eyes danced with amusement as he tilted his head to look at the Acting First Officer. "I doubt that the doctor will pay much attention to my food consumption, Commander Brady. My latest physical was well within the norms for my race and age."

Kirk scowled. Sometimes Tenaida was a little too human. If he neglected the minor physical differences —the completely hairless skull, the almost subliminal muskiness of Deltan pheromones, the too-muscular movements of Tenaida's slender body—Kirk would swear Tenaida was human.

"In addition," Tenaida continued, "the food is for Lieutenant Whitehorse. She has been working since midafternoon on developing a model to account for the discrepancies in the data we obtained for the Shansar system. I promised to help her with the computer simulations when the dinner was over."

"I wouldn't think she'd need help with the computer," Brady said. "Her record file says she's half computer herself!"

"She *is* an extremely able scientist. However, the Shansar readings are unusual, and we had completed only the preliminary scanner runs of that system before the ship was called to Starbase 15."

"Are you sure it isn't the girl you find interesting? You're even taking her dinner." Brady turned to Kirk, his eyes twinkling. "What do you think, Captain? Doesn't it look like he's gone soft on her?"

"Enough, Mr. Brady." Kirk knew Brady's teasing was not serious, but he doubted if Tenaida understood the rules of the all-too-human ritual. Tonight, the dinner, although enjoyable, had taxed his own patience for the bantering. At the moment, he did not even feel up to pursuing the usual debate on the definition of *preliminary,* a term he had found most scientists used until they had studied a phenomenon for at least three decades. He turned to Tenaida. "Good luck with your simulations. If your results are interesting enough, perhaps Starfleet will let us make an additional survey of the Shansar system after we finish this assignment."

"That would be most satisfactory." Tenaida nodded farewells to Kirk and Brady, and strode away, balancing the tray with absent-minded grace. Kirk suspected that Tenaida's mind was already lost in the realm of higher mathematics.

"Jim, I know I haven't been on this ship all that long, but he seems to be spending a lot of time in the geology lab. I've always wondered about the Deltans and their celibacy oaths. You don't think he's making a move on Whitehorse, do you?"

Kirk shrugged. "Romance isn't against the regulations. Besides, he probably enjoys speaking his own language for a change."

"What's that got to do with it?"

"Dr. Chapel mentioned it the other day. She said Whitehorse is the only other person aboard the ship who speaks Deltan without an atrocious accent."

"Is that so? I suppose it would be hard for him to always have to speak a foreign language." Brady ran a hand through his thick, red hair. "When most of the crew is human, sometimes it's hard to remember that the others don't share our common heritage. At least, not from birth."

"And Tenaida speaks English so well, you don't remember it's not his native language." Kirk sighed. "Well, it looks like we won't be playing poker tonight. McCoy prefers to play with a larger group."

The two officers headed down the corridor and separated to go to their respective cabins. As his door closed, Kirk felt a sense of relief wash over him, as if he had just locked out the day's problems. He supposed he was being optimistic to think he could avoid all of them until morning.

The door to the geology lab swished shut behind Tenaida. The room lights were off, except for a single spot of brightness over the workstation in the far corner. He paused while his eyes adjusted. The lab was a crowded, irregularly shaped room with inner and outer walls curved to match the space available. The room was about seven meters square, but most of the space was occupied. Storage cabinets down the lab's center divided the space into two narrow work areas; loose specimens and sample crates dotted the floor in random piles. Four computer stations occupied the forward and aft walls, and the outside wall was filled with the daunting array of processing equipment needed to prepare samples for geochemical analysis.

Janara Whitehorse bent over her computer console, entering data and running simulations to check the accuracy of her model. When Tenaida entered, she looked away from the screen, unwrapped her legs from the central column of her chair, and dropped to the floor. She was a small, compact, olive-skinned woman with dark hair twisted and piled on top of her head. Her black, loose-fitting jumpsuit was covered by a blue-gray overtunic, and her boots leaned against the far wall. Janara padded across the room, neatly avoiding the piled specimen containers, and took the food tray from Tenaida. He watched her carry the tray back to her station, thinking that her walk reminded him of the controlled prowling of a half-sized *nahgre.*

She pushed the tray onto an empty stretch of counter and levered herself up to sit beside it. Tenaida joined her, nibbling on a green apple, while she devoured the rest of the food.

"Thank you, *kai,*" she said when the last bite was gone. "I needed a break." She dropped to the floor and stretched. Without her boots, the top of her head was even with Tenaida's shoulder. "Let's see how the latest simulation came out. I still haven't been able to write a function that describes the observed density profiles."

"Did you account for the chemical anomalies in the outer planets?" When they had discussed the problem yesterday, Janara had just gotten the results of the second batch of analyses. The numbers had agreed with earlier results, ruling out the possibility that there had been an error in their scanner data.

"That's the problem. It's almost as if I have two separate solar systems here. If I model the deviations in the outer system correctly, the *mu* factor increases without limit for the inner planets. And if I limit the term to fit the observed data for the inner system, I can't get a reasonable fit for the outer planets. I was just about to scrap the whole thing and start over. Why don't you look at it first?"

She entered a command and the lines of Vulcan script began marching across the screen. Janara had spent almost two weeks programming the human-designed computer to accept the Vulcan symbology, and afterward Tenaida asked himself why he had neglected the project. No one had yet found a way to program Federation computers to operate with the intuitive, multiphasic structures common to Deltan systems. The rigid and logical structure of the Vulcan system, and its mathematical precision, allowed for a limited approximation of the Deltan phase-logics and aided in the solution of otherwise intractable problems. However, translating a problem into the appropriate Vulcan constructs often seemed as difficult as solving it in the imprecise human system. Tenaida shook his head; the reason he had not reprogrammed the science banks was that he knew he would be reassigned when his training was completed. He had not felt he should take the liberty of reprogramming the computers unless he was permanently assigned to the *Enterprise,* especially when the ship's Vulcan Science Officer had not already done it.

Tenaida studied Janara's equations, searching for errors in her model. Finally, he froze the screen on a set of fourth order differential equations. "Are these the terms that are causing the difficulty, *kaia?*"

Janara nodded. "Depending on the limits I impose on those equations, I can force any answer I want. Except the right one."

"I'll examine your equations more carefully and explore ways of restricting those terms. Would you reexamine the data for possible modifications in the equations themselves?" When she nodded again, he scrolled to the beginning of the file and started working on the first equation.

"Enter."

The door slid open and McCoy entered. He held one hand behind his back. Kirk palmed off his viewscreen.

The doctor crossed the room and held out a bottle of Saurian brandy. "How about something to wash away the taste of the diplomatic courtesies?"

"Doctor's orders?" Kirk grinned and reached for a couple of glasses. McCoy uncorked the bottle and poured. Picking up his half-filled glass, Kirk slid downward in his chair and stretched his legs out, relaxing. The brandy exploded in his mouth and slipped smoothly down his throat. As a pleasant warmth spread through him, Kirk felt the tensions of the day recede.

"I was listening to Commander Brady talking with your friend, Cecilia Simons, over dinner. She's— quite a lady."

Kirk turned the words over in his mind, trying to guess what was behind the implied question. "That's one way of putting it."

"I'd be interested to hear your story. You seemed upset when she came aboard."

"Upset?" Kirk shook his head. It took more effort than he expected to keep his tone casual. "Surprised, maybe. I haven't seen her for a long time, and I certainly didn't expect her to beam aboard my ship."

"How long, Jim? Long enough so it won't affect your judgment? My interest is professional—anything that affects the captain of this ship is my business." McCoy smiled to soften his words.

Kirk gulped a mouthful of his drink. "So that's why you're serving the fancy anesthetic." He toasted McCoy with his glass. "All right, Bones, this round is yours.

"Cecilia Simons and I were lovers—I'm sure you guessed that. It was a long time ago, and I was young and foolish. So young and foolish I thought someone who had just been promoted to second officer of the scout ship *Aeolus* might have something to offer a woman who was celebrated as one of the most beautiful and fascinating females in the galaxy.

"You know, even then, she was known for that. . . . But what I wanted and what she was after were two entirely different things. We were chasing some Aldebaran pirates, and she came on our ship as a courier. Only, it turned out that she had—shall we say—an interest in the Aldebarans, and interfered with the ship's operations at the wrong time."

Kirk fell silent, reliving that long-ago night on the *Aeolus*. It had been early morning, about 0100 ship's time, and the watch should have been his. Instead, Kirk was in Sickbay, incapacitated by stomach cramps and nausea. He and Simons had spent the evening together, savoring a romantic dinner. The dessert, served just before Kirk was scheduled to go on duty, was his special favorite—brandied chocolate cheesecake topped with Cerian cherries, whipped cream, and fudge sauce. Before he had finished his serving, Kirk began vomiting. Within minutes, he was so sick he had to be carried to Sickbay. The doctor diagnosed the cause of his illness as a fast-acting virus that had somehow gotten into the food synthesizers. When he recovered, Kirk tried to learn more about the cause of his illness. He discovered that the virus resembled oncs that had been developed to inject malignant cells with anticancer drugs, but the pathologist's report indicated this particular strain had been modified to deliver a severe, extremely fast-acting strain of influenza. By the time Kirk was supposed to be on the bridge, he was completely incapacitated.

Meanwhile, the bridge was staffed with a skeleton crew for the night shift. In spite of their orders, the mission so far had been uneventful, and boredom was diminishing everyone's alertness. The duty officer, guessing how Kirk's evening had started, decided not to disturb him when Kirk failed to appear. He thought Kirk would be grateful and could return the favor at a later date. When the sensors picked up the first anomalous readings, the bridge crew wasted precious seconds trying to reach Kirk. The young doctor who was treating him had not thought to notify the bridge of Kirk's condition until she heard the duty officer page him.

At first, no one on the bridge could interpret the sensor readings. As they finally identified an alien vessel off the ship's starboard side, the intruder opened fire. By the time the *Aeolus* responded, her shields were severely strained. The captain arrived in time to save his ship, but the intruder escaped.

Kirk sighed, returning to the present. "We almost lost the ship because of her, Bones. I was the only officer with previous deep-space experience assigned to that watch, and somehow Simons knew it. Later, I found a life support belt hidden in her luggage. I don't know what her escape plan was, but she was prepared for the ship's destruction.

"Of course, we couldn't prove it wasn't coincidence, but such coincidences follow her like a *sehlat* after prey." Kirk downed the last of his brandy. "Does that answer your questions about my sordid past, Doctor?"

McCoy stared into his glass for a long moment. "I reckon it does. Although I don't rightly see how Miz Simons could be as schizophrenic as you describe her."

"Maybe she's just a good actress." Kirk picked up his empty glass, examining it as if it held McCoy's answer. "Actually, Bones, I've been asking myself that one for a *long* time. If you figure it out, let me know."

"Certainly." A slow grin spread across the doctor's face. He climbed to his feet and reached for the bottle. "That's the right attitude, Jim. A healthy dose of questioning always keeps things in perspective."

"Always, Doctor?"

At the door, McCoy paused. "Well, almost always." He made good his escape before Kirk could pursue the subject. Kirk stared at the closed door, wondering if he really had fooled McCoy. He doubted that he had the proper perspective on Cecilia Simons. He wondered if he ever would.

After a moment, he reached over and flipped on his computer. He *had* promised Spock he would test his program; he could hardly devise a more *human* test for its logic than consulting it about Cecilia Simons. It took him a few moments to locate the file. When he accessed it, Spock's image filled the screen.

"Captain, since you are viewing this, I will assume you are about to test my program. It is designed to function as a decision-making aid, and to provide information and logical advice to those who require it. I must emphasize that this version is extremely preliminary, and that I have not had time to implement all of the features I wish to include in the final program. In addition, I have not yet integrated all of the real-time response modules into the program design. Therefore, some of the *Enterprise*'s information systems are not yet available to the program because I have not had the time to modify their access formats to accommodate the new artificial intelligence system. However, I will be most appreciative of any comments you wish to make. The program is activated by the word 'Assistant.'"

For a moment after Spock's image faded, Kirk just stared at the screen. He had not realized how much he depended on Spock's advice until he watched the tape. Then he straightened in his chair. "Assistant, access computer files on our passenger, Cecilia Simons. Question: Does her presence on this ship endanger our current mission?"

A series of messages flashed across the screen, telling Kirk which files the computer was accessing. After a minute or so, the word "Done" appeared. "No information found to connect Cecilia Simons with our current mission. Past record indicates a 67.3 percent probability that such a connection exists but cannot be proven. There is a 97.45 percent chance of her disrupting the ship's normal operation in some way."

"How will she accomplish this?"

"Insufficient information. Data indicates a random factor in her behavior and methods that cannot be predicted by logical means."

"What can I do to prevent this?"

"Your options in this matter are extremely limited, and all have a high probability of resulting in unfortunate consequences to you personally."

"What?" Kirk stared at the computer in disbelief. Controlling Simons would result in unfortunate consequences for *him?* Clearly, the program had more problems than Spock had thought. "Assistant, please elaborate on your last statement."

"Option 1: Confine her to her quarters. Option 2: Have a Security guard accompany her at all times. Option 3: Confine her to the brig. Option 4: Return her to Starbase 15 by shuttlecraft. With any of these options, unless you have solid proof that she has done something to justify your suspicions, you will antagonize her husband. Commissioner Montoya will complain to his superiors and to Starfleet. The most probable outcome is that you will be relieved of command and severely disciplined."

"Wonderful. Just wonderful." Kirk stared at the computer for a moment, shaking his head. Spock's program seemed to have included every possibility in that list. Then a thought occurred to him. "By the way, Assistant, did you consider murder in your list of options?"

"I did not." The computer's voice sounded mildly offended, and Kirk wondered if it was only his imagination—the program sounded suspiciously like Spock. "Murder is illegal and no civilized being would consider it an option. In addition, you would be sentenced to a thirty-year term in rehabilitation for your crime."

"I see." Kirk reached over and turned off the computer, wondering what grade he should give Spock's program for that test. *Probably the same one I give Spock when I don't like his advice—"A" for effort, "F" for pleasing the captain.* He allowed himself a rueful grin, realizing that difference was exactly why Spock's abilities complemented his own so well. Any decision that satisfied them both would be the best decision possible in a given situation.

The woman rose silently and checked the sleeping man on the bed. The drug was strong; he would sleep for several more hours. Satisfied, she slipped from the room and padded down the deserted corridor to keep her rendezvous.

The alien fascinated her. Though his passion matched hers in their physical joining, she remembered no male who was so indifferent to her attractions outside the sleeping chamber. She returned to him as a moth to the flame to learn the dangerous secret of his immunity.

Except for the sounds of fingers coding data into the computer or the occasional verbal command, the geology lab had been quiet for hours. Tenaida and Janara were immersed in the intractable equations and spared no energy for conversation.

A low moan broke Tenaida's concentration. Janara was slumped over her console, massaging her forehead.

"*Shan* Janara, is something wrong?" When she failed to answer, he repeated the question with more urgency in his voice, trying to penetrate the distraction.

She straightened, fingers still rubbing her temples. Slowly, her eyes focused on Tenaida. "Something . . . a wild animal, maybe. A predator, prowling the ship." Her fingers rubbed harder, as if the pressure would focus the image. "It wasn't clear enough to isolate."

"How long has it been there?" Tenaida asked. Janara's telepathic powers were formidable, but largely untrained. When the Deltan Mentors had recognized the synergistic potential of her combined human and Deltan genome, they had monitored Janara's development carefully. Her powerful psychic abilities had given her an exceptionally keen awareness of others' physical and mental ailments, and she had been marked for possible training as a healer. That changed when her mother took her and fled Delta Four just before the girl's seventh birthday. Janara spent the following years learning to suppress her abilities enough to function around nontelepaths, and to control her half-Deltan physiology sufficiently to keep from disturbing those around her. The turning point came when the legal guardianship of the thirteen-year-old girl passed to her maternal grandparents. Ursula and Tom Many-Sleeps Whitehorse provided the stability and security missing from the girl's life since her departure from Delta.

Tenaida knew that, since joining Starfleet, Janara had spent most of her leave time among Deltans, learning more about herself and her unique gifts. Even so, Tenaida doubted if more than half a dozen people on the *Enterprise* suspected her true heritage. Her long dark hair—whether engineered at fertilization or implanted after birth, Tenaida did not know—was an effective camouflage. No human expected her sober mien to conceal the strongest telepath born on Delta Four in the last fifty years.

"How long?" she echoed Tenaida, shaking her head to clear it. "I'm not sure. It slipped up on me. Several hours, I think. It's still there, in the back, but not as strong as that one flash." Janara shrugged. "I guess it's just someone in a dreadful mood."

She stared at her screen. Tenaida watched her for a few moments, then returned to his equations. She would have to solve the problem in her own way. He was again immersed in high-order differential equations when she interrupted him.

"*Shan* Tenaida," she asked, her voice barely above a whisper, "do you have any *boretelin?*"

His eyebrow lifted in a questioning gesture. "*Boretelin?* My mother sent me a substantial quantity last month." Tenaida's empathic rating had been in the lowest percentile-grouping for his age-mates. As a result, he had been surprised when he opened the last box of Delta-produced nutritional supplements his mother had sent him. In addition to the usual items, he had found several bottles of the psi-suppressant, *boretelin,* a drug developed on Delta Four to aid untrainable psi-sensitives in blocking the inputs they could not screen out.

Janara took a deep breath. "Please thank your mother for me the next time you speak with her."

Tenaida nodded as he understood his mother's reason for sending the drug. Janara's mental powers

31

combined the normal Deltan ability to receive images from other minds with a rare and powerful, though erratic, human ability to sense thoughts or feelings. At times, Janara needed *boretelin* to cope with the mental distress of constant input from untrained minds. "I'll return with your medicine."

"Thank you, *Shan* Tenaida." She lowered her head to the counter, shielding her eyes and ears with her arms. He left the lab, heading for his quarters.

It took him fifteen minutes to return with the medicine and Janara wondered why it was taking him so long. This far into the night shift, the corridors and turbolifts should be virtually empty.

Finally, the door opened. Tenaida crossed the lab and set a small, square bottle on the counter beside Janara. He noted that she did not appear to have moved in the time he had been gone.

"*Shan* Janara," he said. When she did not respond, he shook her shoulder to get her attention. She stirred and sat up, looking around the room as though only partially aware of her surroundings.

"*Shan* Janara, snap out of it," he ordered.

Janara rubbed her hand across her eyes, trying to clear her mind of the impressions that flooded it. Her hand groped for the bottle and she fumbled two brown, oval tablets from it. She swallowed the pills, washing them down with the last mouthful of cold tea from the cup sitting on the counter by her workstation. Tenaida watched the tenseness melt out of her slight frame as the medicine took effect. Janara picked up the square bottle and turned it over and over in her hands, rubbing the rough surface with her fingers. Finally she set it back on the table. "Normally, I can shut them out. Why is it I hear them so strongly tonight?"

"Perhaps you require additional training, *kaia.*"

She sighed. "Perhaps, *Shan* Tenaida. Perhaps." She reactivated her computer console and resumed work on the geochemical data for the individual planets. At first, her keystrokes were slow and stumbling, but as Tenaida listened, her speed gradually returned to normal. With a sense of relief, Tenaida turned his attention to the equations on his screen.

The woman stole into the deserted briefing room. Although the room was dark, she ordered the lights down again when the sensors detected her presence and increased the illumination. She felt her way to the table and slid into a chair, pulled out her compact comm set, and entered a command. The set squirted a brief pulse containing her message. Moments later, the red "Receiving" indicator lit up. She held her breath for the interminable few seconds needed to receive the high-speed transmission. When the light went out, she hid the comm set under her clothing and left the room. Unless the night-shift communications officer was monitoring the planetary broadcast frequencies, no one on the *Enterprise* should detect the transmission. However, she had no intention of waiting there to be caught. Later, when she knew she would not be interrupted, she would decode the transmission and discover its contents.

The door opened and the slender figure of the Deltan Science Officer marched onto the bridge. The night shift bent to their tasks, trying to appear more diligent than the available work justified. Although Tenaida was only temporarily assigned to the *Enterprise,* Captain Kirk would listen to his reports of any shortcomings as carefully as he listened to Spock. The evening shift bridge crew wanted Tenaida to give Kirk a flawless report.

The Deltan glanced around the bridge. The command chair was occupied by a black male of medium build. The navigator was a slender male with dark, curly hair and pale skin, and the communications officer was a chunky, olive-skinned female. Tenaida took his seat at the science station and activated the sensors. After ten minutes of checking his displays, he stiffened. He tapped the control pads, transferring the information to the main screen. A swirling glow, twisted in angry patterns, filled the viewscreen. "Lieutenant Jacobs, my sensors are detecting a previously uncharted gas cloud. I recommend that we change course to bypass it."

"Navigation, do you confirm that?"

"Negative. —No, wait. I'm getting dopplers on something now. I've never seen readings like this before."

"Recommend that we change course to the heading the computer is feeding to navigation," the Deltan said.

Jacobs clenched his suddenly sweaty hand around the arm of the command chair. In his experience, unexplained phenomena usually created more problems than suggested by first impressions. He double-checked the readings on the viewscreen. He had only moments to decide what the *Enterprise* should do. "Laysa, where's Captain Kirk?"

The communications officer signaled Kirk's quarters. After a moment, she said, "He is not responding to his intercom." She entered another command. "The circuit appears to be malfunctioning."

Jacobs checked the screen again, estimating how long until they reached the gas cloud. The distance was shrinking fast. "Ensign Carly, change course to Lieutenant Tenaida's heading."

"Aye." The navigator entered the command into his console. The scene on the viewer slid to one side as the *Enterprise* moved off on its new heading.

Tenaida entered a string of commands into his console. Then he pulled a tape from its slot and stood. "I have ordered the computer to take additional readings on that phenomenon. For now, my observations are complete. I'll report to the captain and tell him what happened."

"Thank you, sir. Lieutenant Laysa, tell Engineering

to trace the malfunction and reroute Captain Kirk's communications. Also, have them check the intercom unit in the captain's quarters as soon as he comes on duty in the morning."

"Maintenance order logged," she said, her voice mingling with the sound of the door closing behind Tenaida.

Chapter Three

Janara and Tenaida pored over the output from the latest version of their model. Condensed to a few lines of mathematical symbols, their night's work seemed insignificant. They had improved the fit between theory and observation, but both scientists felt they were far from solving the problem.

"That term still increases without limit if we use anything approximating the actual data." Janara tapped the troublesome equation with her forefinger. "I just don't see what we've missed."

Behind them, the door whisked open. Neither looked to see who entered.

"Copy that file to my work queue and I'll study the problem later, *kaia,*" Tenaida said. "However, I am on duty in twenty-seven minutes."

"Of course," Janara replied. Tenaida's unspoken message was that he needed the remaining time before his shift for his personal needs. When he turned to leave, Cecilia Simons was standing in the doorway.

"Excuse me, madam." But Simons did not move and Tenaida had to squeeze around her to get out of the room. As he passed her, she gave him a look of pure hatred.

After the door closed behind Tenaida, Simons sauntered forward. Her face wore an exaggerated smile.

"Janie, darling, aren't you going to say hello to your mother?"

Janara's back stiffened. She had not expected Simons to look for her while she was on duty. After a deep breath, she turned to face the older woman. "Mother, I had no idea you were on the ship."

"I left twenty messages in your mail file. You'd have known if you'd bothered to read them."

Janara counted slowly to ten in Deltan, Vulcan, and finally Apache before she replied. "I've been working on a problem since yesterday afternoon and haven't had time to check my mail."

"But surely, darling, they must let you sleep sometime."

"I work the night shift, Mother. I prefer it." Janara clenched her hands into fists behind her back, trying to control her impulse to throw something.

"I suppose you also prefer to associate with that Deltan *animal*. And encourage him by speaking the inhuman mumbo jumbo they call a language." Simons shook her head and rolled her eyes with the melodramatic exaggeration of a third-rate actress. "My only daughter. What's the universe coming to? I tried to bring you up right, but you reject everything I ever taught you."

Janara ignored her mother's theatrics and replied in a monotone. "*Shan* Tenaida is the acting science officer on this ship, and therefore my superior. I will speak whatever language I choose. You've told me often enough your experiences on Delta Four were not the most exciting of your life, but I don't share your distaste for the planet. The last time I visited Delta, *Shan* Tenaida's parents were gracious enough to ask me to stay with them." She paused, remembering the warmth they had shown her and how much she wished she could have grown up in so loving an atmosphere. There were still many aspects of the Deltan half of her heritage that she did not understand, but Tenaida's siblings and cross-cousins had been eager to help her. Not for the first time, Janara found herself wishing she could be part of such a close family group.

With a shake of her head, Janara pulled herself back to the present. She parted the hair on the side of her head, revealing the scars from the implant surgery. The surgeon Simons had hired to alter her daughter's Deltan appearance had been neither especially skilled nor especially careful. "Finally, Mother, you may think you tried to bring me up properly, but you're the only person in the galaxy who does. If you had cared for me at all, you would have left me with my father on Delta."

"How dare you!" Simons hissed. "You ungrateful monster! If you have any shred of decency or respect for your mother left, you'll request an immediate transfer to another ship!" She paused to regain control of herself. Forcing her most disarming smile, she continued in a soothing tone, "I'm only trying to do what's best for you, darling. Won't you please humor your dear mother in this?"

"No."

"Jane, I'm warning you—"

"Mother, would you please leave? I'm still on duty and you're interfering with my work."

"Darling, I'm only trying to protect you from that Deltan monster. Transfer off this ship."

Janara separated the strands of her dark hair to emphasize the scars. "In case you've forgotten, Mother *dear,* I'm part Deltan, too."

Simons' hiss of indrawn breath told Janara she had gone too far. Her mother's fist caught Janara on the side of the face and knocked her head against the edge of the console. She slumped to the floor, unconscious. Simons stormed from the room without looking back.

Kirk was humming a lively tune under his breath as he strode down the corridor. He *knew* it was going to be a good day. The Kaldorni delegation and Commissioner Montoya's negotiating team had settled into the briefing room with a minimum of trouble. To assist them, Kirk had assigned a yeoman to record the proceedings and retrieve needed information from the ship's computer. The only glitch was when the Kaldorni refused to allow a Universal Translator in the room. Kirk sympathized with Montoya on that issue, but on the whole, he was relieved to have fulfilled his diplomatic responsibilities so easily.

Kirk was feeling thoroughly pleased with himself as he stepped onto the bridge. Although he was a few minutes early, the people assigned to the day shift were already at their stations, getting briefed by their counterparts who were going off duty.

"Status report, Mr. Jacobs?" Kirk descended the stairs and crossed to the command chair, still smiling. He looked up at the main viewscreen and froze. "What's our course?"

Jacobs touched a couple of switches. "Bearing 124 mark 5, at warp factor six—as per Lieutenant Tenaida's orders, to avoid that uncharted gas cloud. He reported that you confirmed the new heading, sir."

A cold finger of uneasiness poked through Kirk's cheerfulness. "Give me a full report, Jacobs."

"Lieutenant Tenaida came on the bridge to check the sensors. After a few minutes, he began picking up some strange readings. We changed course to avoid a previously uncharted gas cloud. Then, when you didn't respond to your intercom, Lieutenant Tenaida carried a full report to you. He later relayed your approval for our current heading and speed."

"When did this happen, Lieutenant?"

"About 0330 hours, sir."

Behind them, the turbolift opened and Tenaida entered the bridge. Kirk turned, beckoning to the scientist. "A word with you, Tenaida, if you please."

Tenaida came down the stairs and stopped beside Kirk. "Yes, Captain?"

"Why did you tell Lieutenant Jacobs you had reported the course change to me, when you hadn't?"

Tenaida's forehead wrinkled with a puzzled frown at Kirk's tone. "What course change are we discussing, Captain?"

"Lieutenant Jacobs reports that you changed the ship's course last night to avoid an uncharted gas cloud. And that you then reported this to me and got my approval for the new heading." Repeating the accusation made Kirk feel as though he were talking to a computer with faulty inference circuits.

"I took no such actions." The Deltan's frown deepened, and his face flushed with agitation.

"Begging your pardon, sir." Jacobs straightened to attention. "You came on the bridge to check your equipment, discovered the gas cloud, and fed the new course information into my navigation console, sir."

"That is not possible, Lieutenant Jacobs. I have not been on the bridge since late yesterday afternoon."

Kirk studied the two men. Neither appeared to be lying. He knew Tenaida's agitation was a sure sign of his veracity and Jacobs' conviction blazed like a navigation beacon. There was only one way to settle the problem. Kirk turned to the communications station. "Commander Uhura, pull the ship's log for 0330 hours this morning."

"Aye, aye, sir."

"Let's take a look at the evidence."

Kirk and Tenaida crossed to the communications station. Uhura played the log extract on the display screen above her console. They watched the scene, then Kirk reran it. After the second time, he stepped back, shaking his head. The images left little room for doubt. "Tenaida, it looks like you. And it sounds like you. Can you explain?"

"No, Captain. Until twenty-five minutes ago, I was in the geology lab with Lieutenant Whitehorse, working on the mass distribution equations for the Shansar system."

"Will she verify that, Tenaida?"

"Yes."

"Uhura, run an identity check on that log extract."

"Yes, sir." Uhura activated the program. A series of graphic displays, curved lines, and varicolored bars chased each other across the screen. The final image was a jagged amber histogram. Uhura tapped it with her finger. "Inconclusive, sir. The computer says it may or may not be Lieutenant Tenaida."

"Run it again, Uhura. A dozen times, if you have to, but get me a definite answer. And find Lieutenant Whitehorse. I want to speak with her immediately."

"Yes, sir."

"Captain?" Tenaida's voice sounded strained and his face was a dull beige from the shock of seeing the log extract.

"Yes, Tenaida?" Kirk had to struggle to keep his voice level. Something he did not understand had happened on his ship, and he did not like the answers he was getting. He did not know Tenaida well, but Spock did. And Spock spoke as highly of Tenaida as Kirk had ever heard the Vulcan speak of anyone. Kirk trusted Spock's judgment implicitly, but the contradictory evidence was beginning to raise doubts in his mind.

"Do you wish to confine me to my quarters until this is resolved?" The Deltan stood rigidly at attention, as if Tenaida were fighting his own battle between appearances and reality.

Kirk felt the decision click into focus. He believed Tenaida when he said he had been in the geology lab. But if the Deltan were up to something, Kirk wanted to be able to keep an eye on him. "No. Carry on with your duties, Tenaida."

"Thank you, Captain."

"Mr. Sulu, change our course back to our original heading and reduce speed to warp two."

"Aye, aye, Captain." The helmsman entered the command. The stars slipped across the viewscreen as the great ship swung to its new heading.

Kirk dropped into his chair, scowling. The "top-of-the-universe" feeling he had had when he entered the bridge was gone, leaving him let down and irritable. He was still trying to account for the computer's indeterminate answers when Uhura interrupted his thoughts.

"Captain, Dr. McCoy wishes to see you in Sickbay. He says it's about your request to see Lieutenant Whitehorse."

"What does he want, Uhura?"

"He didn't say, sir. Just that he needed to see you in Sickbay."

"Tell him I'm on my way." Kirk heaved himself out of the command chair. "This had better be good," he muttered to himself as he left the bridge.

"All right, Bones. What's this all about?" Kirk's grim expression told the doctor all he needed to know about his captain's mood.

McCoy pointed toward the examination room. Kirk walked to the door and looked over at the figure on the bed, not believing what he saw. When McCoy entered the room to check his patient, Kirk followed.

Janara Whitehorse's slight form seemed lost under the blue thermal blanket that covered her. Kirk shook his head to dispel the illusion and moved closer to the diagnostic bed. Janara was unconscious. The left side of her face was swollen and a large bruise covered her eye; the other side of her face was also scraped and discolored.

"What happened?"

"The lab technician found her when he went on duty. She's got a mild concussion and assorted bruises and scrapes. As for what happened," McCoy shrugged, "your guess is as good as mine. I could wake her up and ask, but I'd prefer to let her come out of it on her own. Her hybrid physiology responds unpredictably to most of our drugs."

Kirk gave the patient a long, accusing look and strode into McCoy's office. For the moment, the timing of Janara's injury felt like a personal affront. He needed her testimony to support Tenaida's story, and this accident could not have happened at a worse time. "How soon will she regain consciousness?"

McCoy shrugged. "Could be fifteen minutes. Could be five hours. It's hard to tell with this type of injury. Is it important, Jim?"

"Perhaps." Kirk glared at the door of the examination room, willing Janara to waken. When that produced no results, he reached for the intercom.

"Tenaida here," the Deltan's voice replied from the speaker.

"Tenaida, was Lieutenant Whitehorse alone when you left her?"

"No, Captain. The commissioner's wife was with her."

"I see." Kirk felt a cold suspicion starting to grow.

"Is something wrong, Captain?"

"The lab technician found her unconscious when he arrived for his shift. She looks as though someone tried to put a fist through her cheekbone." Kirk gave Tenaida a few seconds to respond to the news, then concluded, "Kirk out."

He sprawled into the chair by McCoy's desk. "Bones, you tell me. In the middle of the night, someone who may have been my Acting Science Officer enters the bridge, detects an uncharted gas cloud, and alters our course to an arbitrary heading to avoid it. Tenaida claims he wasn't on the bridge last night, but the only person who can verify his story is unconscious when I go to question her. Should I feel paranoid?"

"It sounds like you've got the grounds for a case. Are you going to ask Ms. Simons what happened?"

Kirk closed his eyes. Just the thought of confronting Simons made him feel tired and depressed. He shook himself to break the mood. "I'll ask, but I'm not sure it will do any good. She'll just lie, if it suits her purpose."

"That sounds like you think she's the one who hit Lieutenant Whitehorse." McCoy kept his tone neutral.

"It wouldn't be the first time, Bones. As far as her daughter is concerned—well, Ms. Simons may tell the truth on some rare occasion, but I haven't heard of it yet."

"Her daughter? Am I following you, Jim?"

"I think you are. Cecilia Simons, or Deirdre Connell, or whatever other name she calls herself, is Janara Whitehorse's mother. And there isn't a female more unsuited to motherhood in the entire galaxy!"

"If Whitehorse's injuries are evidence for your conclusion, I'd agree with you. But what are you going to do about it? And how do you know so much about the situation?"

"Do about it?" Kirk gave a short laugh. "First, I'd have to have something more than my suspicions to go on. As for how I know so much about the situation— remember how she almost caused the destruction of the *Aeolus?* Well, our captain had had—shall we say—previous dealings with Ms. Simons, and he told me about them to explain why he wasn't going to put the incident in my record. His story included how he'd gotten the courts to declare Simons an unfit guardian for her thirteen-year-old daughter. Physical abuse had a lot to do with it."

"But you don't have any hard evidence to back up your suspicions."

"That's right." Kirk gave the doctor a tight, humorless grin. "But I'll bet you a bottle of Saurian brandy that Simons shows up here any minute with a story about Tenaida knocking her 'poor little daughter' around, and about how she got lost trying to find someone to help." Kirk stood, stretching his arms over his head to ease the tension in his back muscles. "I'm going to get some coffee. Call me the minute Whitehorse regains consciousness. And she's not to have any visitors until after I talk with her." He smiled to apologize for his next words. "I'm afraid that's an order, Bones."

As Kirk was leaving Sickbay, Patrick Brady fell into step beside him. "Why so worried, Captain? Didn't the little geologist confirm Tenaida's alibi?"

Kirk shook his head. "McCoy won't say when she'll be able to talk to us, either."

"And meanwhile, you'll act as though Tenaida's innocent, in spite of the log extract?" Brady lifted an eyebrow in a perfect replica of Spock's favorite gesture.

Kirk shrugged, wondering if Brady had ever met the Vulcan. "Let's say I'm keeping an eye on him for the moment. Besides, we couldn't get a positive identification from that recording. And a man is presumed innocent until proven guilty."

"I grant you that. But I looked at the recording, too. I'd say it was as close to proof as you're likely to get."

"The analysis disputes that. Unless Uhura's gotten a better determination while I was in Sickbay."

Brady shook his head. "If anything, her later results were even worse. She was muttering at the computer in Swahili when I left. At least, I guess it was Swahili, though I heard an occasional 'malfunction' or 'reprogram.'"

"Swahili? That sounds like real trouble. Which also means that log extract isn't *proof*. Or anything close to it. Uhura should have gotten a 99 percent certainty level on her first identity check. We've got Tenaida's complete files, and it was a clear recording. Something fishy is going on."

"Why are you so sure your acting science officer isn't behind it?"

Kirk paused for a moment. "I'm not sure. I don't have enough information to guess what's going on *or* who's responsible. At this point, it could even be one of your practical jokes." Kirk grinned to show the suggestion was made in jest. "So, until I get more information, I want to keep all my options open."

"Then that's why you didn't put Tenaida in the brig."

"Well, partly. Besides, like I said, I need evidence. Why don't you help Uhura with that log extract? If she's swearing at the computer in Swahili, things are serious. Somebody better get up there before she decides to reprogram the computer one circuit at a time."

"Is that 'reprogram' as in 'disassemble'?" At Kirk's nod, Brady's eyes widened in mock fear. "I'm on my way, Captain. Starfleet's computer systems are unreliable enough when the Vulcans have been working on them. I'd hate to see them after they've been worked on by someone who speaks Swahili with such viciousness."

"Let me know what you find, Mr. Brady. And the sooner, the better."

"You got it, Captain." Brady broke into a trot to catch up with a crewman who was approaching the turbolift. Kirk watched, shaking his head, then turned in to the recreation lounge to get his coffee.

Much to Kirk's relief, the rest of the morning passed without incident. When lunchtime came, he was more than ready to turn the bridge over to Sulu. On his way to get lunch, he stopped by Sickbay to check on Janara, but McCoy reported no change in his patient's condition.

"She's still unconscious, Jim. What I said before still goes. I'll give her a stimulant if you absolutely insist, but—"

"But you'd prefer not to." Kirk sighed. "Let me know when there's any change, Bones."

Kirk entered the dining area and punched his order into the food synthesizer. The machine hummed for an unusually long time as it searched its instructions. Finally, the door slid open, delivering a tuna salad labeled with Kirk's name. Frowning, he dropped the plate onto his tray. The label was the dietitian's way of telling him that she intended to see that he followed his prescribed nutritional schedule.

"You don't look like you care for salads, Captain." The speaker was Kristiann Norris, who was removing her lunch from the adjacent dispenser.

Kirk gave her a wry grin. "Well, let's just say there are other foods I prefer."

"I know what you mean. The worst thing about traveling on a spaceship is that my diet card always calls for exactly what I should have." She laughed. "Who wants to eat only what's good for them?"

Kirk found himself smiling in response to her cheerfulness. "You're right, of course."

Kirk pointed to an empty table on the side wall. Norris nodded, and they worked their way across the crowded room to reach it. "How are the negotiations going?" Kirk asked when they were seated.

She answered between mouthfuls of her cheese-and-sprout sandwich. "Don't know. Of course, it's really too early to say yet, and all we're supposed to do right now is establish protocols and agendas for the actual peace talks, but—" She took a sip of her juice. "Well, you get a feeling for these things, and this one feels like we're getting absolutely nowhere. Like trying to pin down a handful of fog."

Kirk found himself attracted by Norris' friendly, open manner. He realized his initial evaluation of her, based on her plainness, had been mistaken. "May I ask what you do on the negotiating team?"

"A little bit of everything, actually. Mostly, I work with computers. I try to find the relevant information in the reports covering the situation we're working on. Or run simulations to see how a particular course of action would turn out. Also, I work with languages and computer translators."

She took another bite of her sandwich. "It bothers me that the Kaldorni don't want a Universal Translator in the room. I can't quite explain it, but I get the feeling we're missing something important about the whole situation. Maybe the translator would give us the key.

"Hey, I'm being terribly rude, jabbering away about my job and not letting you get in a word edgewise."

Kirk grinned and shook his head. "I asked the questions, remember? But if you insist, I'll give you the captain's tour of the *Enterprise* this evening, so I can have my turn."

Norris' face lit up with a big smile. "I'd love it. Are you sure you've got the time?"

"I'll make the time." Kirk started to say more, but was interrupted by an intercom page. He went to the panel and pressed the control.

"Kirk here."

"Kirk," Uhura's musical voice floated from the speaker, "Dr. McCoy said you wanted to know when Lieutenant Whitehorse regained consciousness."

"Tell McCoy I'm on my way. Kirk out."

He returned to the table, looked at his half-eaten salad, and drained his coffee cup. "If you'll excuse me, Ms. Norris, duty calls."

"Only if you promise to call me Kris, Captain," she said, giving him another warm smile. The remark should have sounded flirtatious, but she made it sound sincerely friendly.

"All right, Kris. Until this evening."

"How do you feel?" McCoy asked his patient. He checked the diagnostic panel above Janara's head and saw the readings he had expected.

Janara winced at the sound and raised a hand to probe her swollen cheek. "Head hurts," she murmured, exploring the injury with a feather-light touch.

"I'm not surprised. You got a nasty knock there. What happened?" McCoy looked from the monitor panel to Janara's face. The hard line of her mouth told

McCoy that she would not surrender her story willingly.

Janara's fingers, still checking her injuries, circled down to her jawbone. "Ran into a wall."

"More like pushed, I'd say. Is there a law against talking to your doctor?"

A hint of annoyance crept into Janara's voice. "Just ran into a wall."

McCoy's exasperation sharpened his tone. "Lieutenant Whitehorse, I don't mean to go throwing my weight around, but I need to know who hit you."

"I'm clumsy. I tripped and fell over some specimens," Janara replied with more spirit.

"I've seen you do vari-grav gymnastics. Deltans make very poor liars. Almost as bad as Vulcans."

"So, I'm only half Deltan."

This time McCoy was sure of the twinkle of amusement in Janara's eyes. Realizing she could continue the verbal fencing for an hour, McCoy feigned a show of resignation. "You're right. You don't have to tell me. But don't you think Maintenance should replace that section of wall with one that isn't so mean?"

Janara's mouth twitched with the beginning of a smile. Finally, unable to control her reaction, she started giggling. The movement jolted her injuries. She winced and grabbed for her temples. "Ooooo, I don't think I want to do that."

"You're going to have a headache for a while, I'm afraid. So just lie there and be careful."

"Then you certainly don't want to hear about the wall that hit me, Doctor. It might raise my blood pressure." Janara's voice was calm, but her face had gone stiff from her efforts to control a sudden flare of anger. The heart monitor pulsed more rapidly.

McCoy made a big show of examining the diagnostic panel. "Your blood pressure's so low it barely registers."

"My normal reading."

McCoy gave the controls an unnecessary adjustment. "Look, Janara, you don't have to tell me, but if I don't know what happened, I can't help you prevent it from happening again."

Janara heaved a sigh that seemed to start from the soles of her feet. She turned her head away, studying imaginary patterns on the ceiling panels to keep from meeting the doctor's eyes. McCoy had quit expecting an answer when Janara finally spoke. "I had a fight with my mother." She fingered the bruise on her cheek. "As usual, I lost."

McCoy thought about several responses, but they all seemed inappropriate. Finally, he just waited for Janara to continue. Eventually, she did.

"Mother tried to pull a concerned parent act and Ptell me how bad off I was having a Deltan as my superior. So I reminded her of some basic facts she conveniently forgets."

"She hit you because of *facts?*" McCoy had to struggle to keep his incredulity from registering in his voice. "I think I'm missing something here."

"Hardly." Janara's voice was flat. "There's not much to it. After my mother married my father, she discovered certain peculiarities of Deltan culture. Like the fact that Deltans place a high value on honor, loyalty, family obligations—respectable things like that. Expediency is more my mother's style, and she's addicted to her pleasures. . . . Anyhow, she got bored when she found that life on Delta Four involved more than an endless orgy. Of course, she couldn't accept the responsibility for having made the wrong decision when she hooked up with my father, so she converted her resentment into hatred of anyone who reminded her of him. Which is to say, all Deltans.

"I reminded her that I was half Deltan and she hit me." Janara grinned ruefully. "You'd think I'd learn, wouldn't you?"

"You're taking this very calmly." In Janara's place,

McCoy figured he would have tossed Simons out an airlock years ago.

Janara gave a short, humorless laugh. "What would you have me do, jump up and down and throw a temper tantrum? My mother is a sick, twisted woman, and for that type of person, the worst reaction is no reaction. Besides, Doctor, I spent seven years growing up in her sole custody. You may not believe this, but there just aren't many ways left for her to hurt me."

"I still think something should be done, if the situation is as bad as you say."

"Name me something that hasn't been tried, Doctor." The sudden bitterness in Janara's voice surprised McCoy almost as much as her indifference had a moment ago.

"Nice bedside manner you've got there, Bones." Kirk pushed himself away from the door frame and moved toward them.

McCoy searched the captain's face for a moment to gauge his seriousness. "How long have you been eavesdropping, Jim?"

"Long enough." Kirk's expression was bland and controlled, giving away no secrets.

"The whole time," Janara said. McCoy looked from one to the other, suspecting a conspiracy between them.

Kirk shook his head, denying McCoy's suspicions. "She was having such a good time giving you the runaround that I didn't want to interrupt. And since she's obviously recovered enough to answer a few questions, would you please leave us?"

McCoy scowled, but left. On his way out, he palmed the door switch and it slid shut behind him. Kirk paced the confines of the small room, trying to decide how to ask his questions. Now that the moment of truth had arrived, he realized he was worried that Janara's answers might not be the ones he wanted to hear. He stopped pacing and faced her.

"Lieutenant Tenaida said he was with you in the geology lab last night. When was he there?"

Janara's right eyebrow lifted in curiosity, but her answer was as calm as if Kirk questioned her in Sickbay every other week. "He came after the diplomatic dinner was over, around 2100 or 2130. He brought me a tray of food, so you should be able to get the time from the food synthesizer logs. We worked on the density distribution equations for the Shansar system until he left to prepare for his duty shift."

"Did he check any instrument readings on the bridge last night?" Kirk turned away from her, resuming his pacing. Suddenly, he realized how much he wanted to hear her give him the right answer, the answer that would confirm his—and Spock's—opinion of Tenaida.

Janara's other eyebrow lifted in surprise at the tension in Kirk's voice and at the apparent irrelevance of the question. "To the best of my knowledge, no."

"Lieutenant Whitehorse, can you account for Tenaida's actions during the entire third shift?" Kirk stopped in the middle of the floor, waiting for her answer.

"Yes, Captain. We were working on the Shansar model the entire time."

"Thank you, Lieutenant." He turned, slapped the control to open the door, and strode from the room.

Waving a farewell to McCoy, Kirk headed for his office. The interview had left him with a vague sense of dissatisfaction that he could not immediately identify. Janara had given him the answers he wanted to hear, but he could not escape the nagging feeling that he had asked the wrong questions. He wished Spock was around to spot the flaws in his all-too-human logic.

"Is there someone you are expecting to return to this seat?"

Kristiann Norris looked up from the remains of her sandwich. "No, Speaker t'Stror," she replied. "Captain Kirk was sitting there, but he left."

"Would it be annoying to you if I were to join you?"

"Of course not. Be my guest. But aren't you a bit late in getting lunch?"

t'Stror shrugged, a gesture copied from his human colleagues. "I had to escort my ambassador to his quarters so he could spend some time with his ladies before the afternoon sessions begin. And one must observe the courtesies when one is with one's master's family."

"Master? I thought he was your employer." She hesitated for a moment to phrase her question carefully. "Speaker, would it be impolite to ask exactly what your relationship is to the ambassador?"

t'Stror stared at his lunch. His tray held a bowl of unidentifiable green mush and a glass of red juice. He toyed with his spoon, stirring his soup without tasting it. Finally he looked up at Norris. "I cannot explain well. The words I do not have. He is my employer, yes. But also he is my master, my overlord. I serve, and he has absolute power in ordering my behavior." The short Kaldorni cocked his head to one side. "But he must have responsibility, too, when he gives orders, because he has the power. If his judgment is wrong, he may lose the right to command. Especially if he repeats a mistake."

"You mean, if he makes a bad decision, he may lose his job as ambassador?"

t'Stror nodded, a curious bobbing gesture to each side of his body. "He loses his job of ambassador, his voice in the affairs of clan Stror, his honor-name Klee. The honor-name is most important to us. It is very bad if one proves to be not responsible in the job one holds. One could lose wives and land if he is judged unworthy, because how could any woman bear offspring to such a man?"

"I'm sure I wouldn't know." As soon as she said the words, Norris knew she should not have let her personal feelings register in her voice.

"Offense was not intended. It is that, for us, the

having of wives and the making of heirs are controlled by the status of a person, and by the ability to defend against the dangers of our world. If one loses one's position, he is no longer able to protect his wives. Then they would wish to be with a person who can offer them food and clothing and give their children a place in our society."

"It sounds confusing." That line, at least, seemed safe.

"No, it is simple. Everyone has his place. When all have places and fit in, everything works easily. Maybe you don't see the places where each person fits."

"I guess I don't. Could you explain it later? It would help me to advise Commissioner Montoya if I understood you better." She smiled, hoping to convince him that her interest was sincere. "And I do want to understand."

"I would be most honored to explain in any way I can. Your people, they do not understand about The-Way-of-All-Things, and my ambassador cannot decide correctly when the balance is wrong." t'Stror lowered his voice. "May I trust you with a large secret? It is also important for me that we make a good decision. My ambassador has promised he will arrange a first wife for me if I advise him suitably."

"That sounds like a great honor for you," Norris said evenly. She hoped he could not read her dislike for the way he discussed women as though they were property. Still, the Federation team needed this kind of information on Kaldorni attitudes. So far, they had volunteered little enough on their culture. She excused herself and stopped by her room to record some notes on the conversation before returning to the briefing room for the afternoon session.

Kirk entered his office and dropped into the chair behind the large oval desk. He usually preferred to conduct ship's business in the informal atmosphere of his quarters, but he felt his next chore should be performed in a more formal setting. After taking a few moments to collect his thoughts, he activated the intercom. "Uhura, locate Cecilia Simons and send her to my office immediately."

"Aye, aye, Captain." Uhura's voice carried a perplexed note.

"Thank you, Uhura. Kirk out." He thumbed the intercom off, annoyed at Uhura's curiosity. Even granted that their present assignment was not very exciting, the last thing he needed was to have the crew watching him and their passengers for any interesting gossip to lighten the tedium.

While he waited for Simons, he called up the day's reports to review. He expected she would try to demonstrate her control of the situation by taking her time to arrive, and his prediction was correct. When she entered, he waved toward a chair. "I'll be with you in a moment."

She flowed toward him, her translucent indigo gown swirling around her body and shimmering to transparency under the harsh lights. The smell of her musky perfume permeated the room. She circled the desk and wrapped her arms around his neck. Her breasts felt soft and warm where they pressed against his shoulder. Against his will, Kirk felt his body responding to the contact. "It's been such a long time, Jimmy. I can't tell you how glad I am to see you again."

Her throbbing voice evoked a flood of dangerous memories, and a surge of desire swept through his body. Slapping the computer off, he spun his chair to face her. Startled, she loosened her grip on his shoulders, and he stood before she could tighten it again. He backed away to break the contact and summoned his anger as a shield to protect himself.

"Ms. Simons," he said in as icy a tone as he could muster, "would you please refrain from such behavior? I have a serious matter to discuss with you."

"And I'd like to talk about old times, Jimmy." Her voice was low and sultry. She ran her hand down the front of her gown, smoothing it against the curves of her body. "Surely, you can't have forgotten . . . everything."

"Forgotten?" Kirk swallowed, feeling hot and tense. The brief moment of contact had reminded him of the exquisite pleasure she had once given him—and the price he had almost paid for it. "No, I remember entirely too well. So consider this a fair warning—I don't intend to put up with any of your tricks on my ship."

"But, Jimmy—" Like a viper, she struck, locking her arms around his neck before he realized her intentions. She kissed him savagely. The pheromone-laden musk of her perfume went to his head like a strong drink. He forced himself to resist the traitorous response of his body. Twisting clear of her embrace, he pushed her away.

"I said I wanted none of your tricks," he said in a voice that shook with anger and with other emotions he did not want to acknowledge. "And I meant it!"

"But, Jimmy—" She glided toward him, her arms reaching out to embrace him again. He grabbed her wrists and jerked downward. The movement pulled her off balance and she dropped into his chair.

"There will be *no*—absolutely *no*—repeats of that last performance. If you try, I'll confine you to your quarters." Kirk took a deep breath to steady his voice. The thought of how easily he could surrender to her heightened his anger. He forced his mind back to business. "Furthermore, I want you to leave your daughter alone."

"But, Jimmy, you can't believe—" She shifted position, leaning back and extending her leg to attract his attention. Her gown pulled tight across her full, rounded breasts.

Kirk gritted his teeth, resisting the flood of desire she stimulated. "Lieutenant Whitehorse told me what happened this morning. I'm ordering you to stay away from her—unless you want to spend the rest of the trip in the brig. Do I make myself clear?"

Simons lowered her head and studied Kirk through fluttering eyelashes, looking for a clue to the enigma he presented. This was a different James Kirk from the brash youth she had known, and Simons was no longer sure how to manipulate him. So far, his resistance to her tactics was nothing short of amazing. By now, he should have been begging for permission to serve her.

"After a blow on the head like that, you could hardly expect my poor Janie to tell the truth about who hit her. She's probably scared to death he'll retaliate."

"I warned you," Kirk repeated. "I do not intend to put up with *any* of your tricks. And that goes double for your anti-Deltan bigotry! Deltan males may have a reputation for violence under extreme provocation, but it's not their exclusive territory. *If* you know what I mean."

Simons raised her head and glared at Kirk. He returned her look without the slightest sign of yielding. She sighed in defeat. "I understand you, Captain Kirk."

"In that case, I won't take any more of your time." Kirk felt the tension drain from his body as the overwhelming riptide of desire ended as suddenly as it had begun.

Simons crossed the room. At the door she paused. "You haven't heard the last of this," she said in a freezing tone. Before he could answer, she swept from the room.

Kirk sank into his chair, letting its contours absorb his weariness. His chronometer told him the interview had taken only a few minutes, but he felt as though it had drained him of a day's worth of energy. He activated the computer screen and retrieved his reports, but his mind was still on Simons. The affair with her was far from settled. He just wished he could anticipate her next move.

* * *

Ambassador n'Gelen l'Stror Klee was worried. His entire career, and possibly his family and reputation, was riding on his ability to conclude an agreement favorable to his people. The ambassador had spent most of his life serving his clan and his world, and all his experience had been required to procure his position in the current negotiations. Failure on this assignment would mean the loss of the status he had used to obtain the appointment. The difficulty was that the Federation commissioner seemed unwilling, or perhaps incapable, of understanding even the most basic concepts about The-Order-of-Things.

He stretched farther out on the bed and allowed his youngest wife to massage the tense muscles in his back. In the last few days, she had softened and ripened. Soon, the family would need to discuss the best configuration for the child her body was preparing to initiate.

His third eldest wife fed Klee pieces of cheese and fruit from the plate she held. The cheese was synthetic, and he considered rejecting it with an angry comment about the discord of such constructs. However, a brief meditation showed him that more disharmony would be created by such an action, for it would disturb the serenity of his wives without creating a counterbalancing harmony. Such an action would be irresponsible.

While he nibbled his food, Klee tried to divine new ways of explaining That-Which-Is to Commissioner Montoya and those he represented. To any Kaldorni, the natural flow of the Universe was as obvious as the rising of a planet's primary at dawn. To deny either was to fly in the face of all logic, and the resulting disharmonies could destroy not only the individual but also his entire clan. Commissioner Montoya seemed incapable of understanding that the natural order of the Universe dictated the planet Yagra IV should be settled by the Harmonious Unities of the Kaldorni Way.

Perhaps the fault was his, Klee thought. Maybe he should have requested to converse with a different representative of the Federation. Montoya could know little of harmony when he claimed so discordant a female as sole wife. Hot-Fire-Woman, who burned all she touched, must surely have disturbed the commissioner's harmony, perhaps beyond the point where he could regain his balance with respect to the Universe. Her influence was spreading even further, Klee was sure, for he had noted the times and places of his mouthpiece t'Stror's language lessons, and knew that spoken communications must be only a small part of the curriculum.

When Kirk stepped onto the bridge, he knew immediately that something was wrong. The star patterns on the viewscreen had changed, and the ship was traveling at much too great a speed.

"Sulu, what's our course?"

"One-two-four mark five, at warp six. As per your orders, sir." There was a note of surprise in Sulu's voice.

"*My* orders?" A red haze washed over Kirk's vision. Someone was interfering with his ship, issuing counterfeit orders in his name. For a moment, all he could think of was getting his hands on that person and throttling him. Kirk took two long, shaky breaths, trying to control his temper. After a few seconds, his anger faded. "When did I order this course change, Mr. Sulu?" he asked in a deceptively quiet voice.

"About an hour ago, sir. Commander Brady came up here after Commander Uhura gave you Dr. McCoy's message. He said you'd ordered him to make the change."

"But I went straight to Sickbay. I haven't seen Mr. Brady since I ordered him to analyze that log extract," Kirk said, half to himself. He shivered with an unwelcome premonition. He stared at the viewscreen, feeling his anger rekindle. "Get Commander Brady up here at once."

Brady entered the bridge and automatically looked at the screen. He frowned and moved to Kirk's side. "It seems we have a serious problem, Captain."

Kirk snorted. "You have a gift for understatement. Right now, I think I'd even be glad if you told me it was one of your practical jokes. However, I suppose you're going to tell me you didn't order this course change?"

"I've been in my quarters, working on the tapes of the first course change. I haven't been on the bridge."

"And everyone here is convinced it was you?" Kirk looked around the bridge. Uhura, Sulu, and ben Josef nodded. "Uhura, play back the log recording of that. I want to see it for myself."

"Yes, sir."

Kirk watched Brady enter the bridge. He requested a status report and ordered the course change. Then Brady left the bridge.

If seeing was believing, the fourth time through the scene should have convinced both Kirk and Brady. The person giving the orders looked and sounded exactly like the first officer. But Brady kept shaking his head. "I never left my quarters. I *know* I wasn't on the bridge."

Chapter Four

BRADY SHOOK HIS HEAD, obviously still trying to break the sense of unreality that gripped him as he watched himself ordering the course change. Kirk studied his friend's face as the scene repeated on the monitor. After a few moments, he was convinced that Brady's astonishment was genuine. Therefore—to borrow Spock's favorite phrase—logic dictated that, unless Brady had become a much better actor since his days at the Academy, the course changes were not an elaborate practical joke he was playing on his old friend. "Uhura, run an identity check on that recording."

The computer took a long moment to answer the communications officer's query. Kirk was almost ready to send for Maintenance by the time Uhura looked up from her board. "Indeterminate, sir." She tapped the amber histogram on her screen. "Shall I run it again?"

"No." Kirk released a breath he had not realized he was holding. Brady's expression reflected the same shock and angry puzzlement Tenaida had shown watching the recording of "his" actions earlier.

Kirk took another look at Uhura's screen and realized what had been bothering him all morning. Having two different impersonations within twelve hours—of both the ship's first officer and of its science officer—was disturbing. Even more troublesome was the accuracy of the impersonations. When the computer tried to identify the individuals in the log extracts, it had compared the recordings with the ship's master files on Brady and Tenaida. Many things could cause the computer to report an anomalously low correlation between a single recording and a person's master file: damage to the vocal cords might distort voice patterns, physical injury or the passage of many years would alter the physical characteristics, and various other factors could distort physiological parameters.

But Kirk could think of no way an impostor could make a recording that came this close to reproducing the data stored in another person's file. Starfleet Security would want an answer to this problem, but it would take them three weeks to get an expert to the *Enterprise.* And Spock would be away on leave for another two weeks. Meanwhile, something strange was happening on his ship, and he wanted to know what. When he broke it down into those terms, Kirk's decision was obvious. His only difficulty was that the people best able to solve the mystery were the ones accused by circumstantial evidence of committing the offense.

"Give Brady and Tenaida copies of both log extracts. And get the records officer on it, too," Kirk told Uhura. "Hopefully, the three of them can figure out what's going on. Also, notify Security Chief Chekov, so he can take appropriate action." *Whatever* that *is,* Kirk added to himself.

"Right away, Captain." Uhura copied the log extracts onto a tape and gave it to Brady. The first officer crossed over to Tenaida's station. They talked for several minutes before the records officer, Marg Layton, notified them she was free to work on the problem with them.

Kirk took his place in the command chair. His mind twisted around the problem of the course changes, trying to figure out how they could have occurred. The answers that fit his meager facts displeased him. One possibility was that Brady and Tenaida had been under mental control when the course changes were made. Coercion might produce the discrepancies in the identity checks, but the captain wanted to believe Brady when he said he had been in his quarters all morning. Kirk and Brady had been friends for twenty-five years, and Kirk knew when Brady was pulling his leg. Brady's reaction had convinced Kirk that he had not made the course change, even under duress. Also, since Whitehorse had corroborated Tenaida's alibi, Kirk assumed the Deltan had not ordered any course changes, either.

The other possibility was even worse. If Brady and Tenaida were not responsible, someone else aboard the *Enterprise* was—someone who could make himself look enough like the ship's first officer and its science officer, and who could sound enough like them, to fool almost anyone. *In fact, I would have sworn it was Patrick,* Kirk thought. He shuddered at the possibilities opened up by having doubles for both Brady and Tenaida aboard the ship.

"Captain?" Brady's voice interrupted his thoughts.

"Yes?"

"Are you going to change course?"

Startled, Kirk checked the screen. He had been concentrating so hard on the problem of who had ordered the course change that he had not yet corrected the actual mischief, even though he had been staring at the viewscreen.

"By all means. Mr. Sulu, return us to our original heading and reduce speed to warp factor two. Again."

"Aye, aye, sir."

Ben Josef entered the course change into his navigation computer to calculate the coordinates. After a few moments, he passed the new heading to Sulu, and the helmsman brought the ship around to its assigned course.

Watching the stars drift across the viewscreen suggested something else to Kirk. "Mr. ben Josef, those course changes didn't put us near any habitable star systems. When you get a minute, would you correlate the headings and see where they were taking us? Give your results to Commander Brady or Lieutenant Tenaida."

"Aye, sir."

"Commander Sulu and Ensign ben Josef. One more thing." Kirk paused for emphasis so everyone would know how serious the order was. "Until we get to the bottom of this, you are to make *no* course changes unless both Commander Brady and I order it—simultaneously. Is that understood?"

"Yes, Captain."

"Aye, aye, sir."

The navigator and the helmsman exchanged relieved glances. Kirk could not blame them. Having all orders given by the two senior officers was the only precaution he could take to keep the mysterious intruder from issuing still more troublesome directives. And even that measure could be circumvented by someone with sufficient determination. Kirk grimaced. It had started out to be such a lovely day.

Cecilia Simons was frustrated and bored. Her role as Joachim Montoya's pretty playgirl wife was becoming tiresome, and, to complete her dissatisfaction, anyone she wanted to talk to was occupied and unwilling to interrupt his work to entertain her. She had even gone to Sickbay on the pretext of visiting her daughter, but McCoy had refused to let her see Jane.

Not that she had any real interest in the girl. Simons had always made an extravagant show of being a good mother, but five minutes with her half-Deltan daughter was all it ever took to drive the best intentions from her head. When Jane-Anne was a child, her silent, sober mien and precocious intelligence had been a constant irritation to her mother, and Simons could not remember ever being free of the conviction that her daughter was reading her mind. The child's hysterical protests that she would never willingly eavesdrop on another person's thoughts had failed to convince Simons that the mental voyeurism was accidental; she was certain Jane could have avoided using her powers if she had wanted to. Simons was also sure that her husband's family had encouraged Jane to spy on her mother because they thought Simons was not a suitable consort for her husband.

As an adult, Jane-Anne managed to be an even greater aggravation than she had as a child. Simons felt her daughter's use of her Deltan calling name was intended as a direct insult, and she redoubled her efforts to initiate Jane into the joys of being a human female. In response, Jane-Anne retreated even farther into the Vulcan-like discipline that most Deltan sensitives observed when constantly surrounded by humans. The campaign had resulted in several confrontations such as this morning's, and Simons blamed them on *Enterprise*'s Deltan science officer who, she was sure, was trying to seduce her daughter into returning to Delta Four.

Simons poured her family woes into t'Stror's ear when she found him finishing a late lunch. The rotund Kaldorni listened sympathetically as he shoveled down his soup.

"I don't understand it," she concluded her tale. "She's always been fascinated by Deltan mind-reading tricks and the Deltans' alleged ability to empathize with others. It's just a circus act, of course, but she must think this Tenaida can teach her something about that. I suppose it was inevitable, considering he's the first Deltan she's ever been around."

"This mind reading of the Deltans—is it something of importance to them?" t'Stror asked.

Simons dismissed the idea with a contemptuous

wave of her hand. "Who knows what's important to a Deltan? They spend a lot of time on it, but they also worry about so many other trivial matters."

"That is not to the Deltan mind an exclusive habit. Does the mind reading concern them because there are many that possess this trick?"

Simons scowled. "How should I know about Deltans? All the ones I knew could do it. I wish Janie would stay away from them. Such tricks could be dangerous."

A calculating expression crossed t'Stror's face. He scraped the last spoonful of green mush from his bowl. "The lady Simons should not worry herself so much about her daughter. It grieves this humble person to say so, but this child can have no honor left if she must disobey so lovely a mother. In our world, such an offspring is rejected from the protection of the clan."

"That's not usually the way we humans do it."

t'Stror shoved his chair back and stood. "I am expected to attend my ambassador now for the continuation of our work aboard this vessel." He bowed slightly, extending and rotating his wrist in the Kaldorni gesture of leave-taking.

Simons stared at his back as he waddled out the door. What *was* she going to do with the rest of the afternoon? Kirk had destroyed the possibility of any casual dalliance she might have initiated by filing pictures and capsule biographies of the ship's passengers on the bulletin boards and the ship's news circuit. Much to Simons' disgust, her file listed her as Montoya's wife of three months, which resulted in respectful treatment from every crewman. If there was anyone on the ship who had not seen the damaging biography, he was so buried in his work that Simons would be unable to find him.

After wandering the ship's corridors for the better part of an hour, Simons discovered the library lounge. Her boredom evaporated. Access to a computer terminal that could not be traced to her was almost as educational as spending the afternoon with a crewman. Simons entered the unoccupied room and chose the console farthest from the door. She activated it, using an access code she should not have known.

Three hours later, Simons logged off the computer and left the still-deserted lounge. By the time Montoya finished with his day's work, she was languishing in their quarters, claiming to be bored to tears with the *Enterprise*'s selection of erotic entertainment tapes.

"Captain?"

"Yes, Tenaida?"

"I have just finished checking Mr. ben Josef's results. His projections show the intruder's course changes would have taken us into an uninhabited region of space."

"Would you check those calculations again and also search for the closest planets?"

"Yes, Captain." Kirk knew the Deltan could make the computer perform as if it were an extension of himself; Spock was the only person the captain knew whose skills exceeded Tenaida's. Kirk envied the ability, knowing that his own considerable skills with the computer were eclipsed by the Deltan's, and would never approach the Vulcan's.

A yeoman appeared at the captain's side. He took the noteboard she handed him, scanned the fuel consumption report, keyed his initials onto the form, and gave the board back to her. She handed him another datapad. He glanced at it and nodded. "That will be all, Yeoman."

The second board summarized crew activities for the past week—merit notices, reprimands, project summaries, and other miscellaneous matters. Last were the requests that required Kirk's attention. The final item was a transfer application from Janara Whitehorse. Kirk scowled. The request made no sense. He bounced to his feet and strode for the door. "Mr. Sulu, you have the conn. If anyone needs me, I'll be in my quarters."

Kirk called up the complete file on his console. Whitehorse's formal request gave no more information than the summary had, but on the recording, her movements were stiff and her speech seemed unusually stilted. The recording showed no more personality than did the featureless beige background behind Whitehorse. Frowning, Kirk keyed on the intercom.

"Uhura here."

"Uhura, find Janara Whitehorse. I want to see her at once."

"Aye, aye, sir."

"Thank you. Kirk out." He turned off the intercom and sat back in his chair. After this morning, he could see why Whitehorse might want a transfer, but the first place she could leave the ship was at Starbase 15, when the *Enterprise* returned there to pick up Spock. Considering that most of Whitehorse's problems were caused by her mother, Kirk felt he should talk with Whitehorse before he approved her request.

The door buzzer interrupted his thoughts.

"Come."

The small half-Deltan woman crossed the room with an effortless stride and stopped in front of Kirk's worktable. "You asked to see me, Captain?"

"I'd like to discuss your transfer request."

She blinked in surprise. "I did not request a transfer."

"I have it right here."

"I made no such request."

"Lieutenant Whitehorse, I have here a transfer request from someone who looks and sounds like you. Do you doubt my word?"

"I merely state a fact: I have not asked for a transfer. Furthermore, it would be futile to request a transfer merely to escape my mother. I could not leave the ship before this mission is finished."

Exasperated, Kirk played the message. Whitehorse watched it with detached interest. About halfway through the recording, Kirk glanced from the screen to her impassive face. Puzzled, he looked back at the screen, then froze the image. The face on the monitor was as skinned and bruised as the woman facing Kirk, but where Whitehorse's left eye was swollen nearly shut, the image on the screen showed a blackened right eye.

"My apologies for disturbing you, Lieutenant," Kirk said when he recovered from the surprise. "That was all I wanted."

She turned and left the room. Kirk studied his screen a little longer, then dropped a tape in the slot and copied the message. Brady, Tenaida, and Layton could examine another mysterious recording while they were analyzing the extracts from the ship's log.

Janara Whitehorse stared at her computer screen, trying to make sense of the paragraph she had read five times. Her head ached abominably, in spite of the painkillers Dr. McCoy had given her—and the medication interfered with her concentration. She shuddered as a crewman, still upset from a fight with his lover, passed her door. When she tried to push away his images of anger, her mind was slow to respond, as if her brain had been packed with cotton. McCoy had said she should rest, but if she tried to sleep with her mental barriers down, she knew the random thoughts of other crew members would induce nightmares of monumental proportions.

She picked up the bottle of *boretelin* and turned it over in her hands, feeling the rough, knobby texture of the glass. The drug offered a temporary escape from unwanted telepathic intrusions, but it was not the answer to her problem. Tenaida was right; she should seek additional training—on Delta Four or, perhaps, even on Vulcan. However, the requirements of her job left few opportunities to take the extended leaves she needed to pursue her study of the Deltan mental sciences or the Vulcan disciplines for mind control. There had to be an answer to the problem, but today it seemed more elusive than usual.

Her computer screen went blank, and she realized how long she had been staring at it. She rubbed her forehead, trying to clear away the fog. Her mind was too sluggish to work on technical material, but perhaps she could review the beginner's vari-grav gymnastics routine that she had promised to teach Uhura.

Vari-grav gymnastics was a Deltan elaboration on the human sport of gymnastics. Moves from similar activities originating on a dozen Federation worlds had been synthesized into a coherent whole, with challenge added by performing in a changing gravity field. Vari-grav gymnastics was an ideal form of exercise for spaceship crews because it provided maximum physical conditioning for the space and equipment used. Beginning routines were uncomplicated, with moderate shifts in gravity and clear-cut musical cues, but advanced routines became extremely complex and forced the performer to rely on subtle clues to signal the changes.

For Uhura, Janara had chosen a simple routine called "Birds in Flight." The gymnast worked between two sets of uneven parallel bars; with the gravity drops, the performer soared upward as if she were a bird, using her momentum to carry her from one set of bars to the other. "Birds in Flight" was a good beginners' routine because it used a few basic moves to excellent advantage and gave the student an immediate sense of accomplishment. Also, it was easy to modify as the gymnast's skills increased.

After forty-five minutes, Janara decided her coding was correct and stored the program. She crossed the room and stretched out on the bed, allowing her mind to replay the routine over and over. She was still following the swoops and dives of her mental gymnast when she drifted to sleep.

Brady, Tenaida, and Layton entered the bridge and crossed to the captain's chair. Layton, a tall, angular woman in her midfifties, stopped half a step ahead of the other two. "Captain, we have finished analyzing the computer log extracts."

Kirk searched Layton's face for clues. Her expression was neutral, but behind her, both Brady and Tenaida appeared tense. "All right, Commander. What have you got?"

"I think we should discuss it in a more private location."

"Very well." Kirk bounced to his feet and headed for the door. "Mr. ben Josef, you have the conn. Layton, Brady, Tenaida, come with me."

"Aye, aye, sir." Ben Josef signaled his backup and took the command chair as the senior officers left the bridge.

Kirk controlled his impatience until they were seated around the computer console in his quarters. "All right. Let's have it."

Layton dropped a tape into the input slot and stepped back, gesturing for Tenaida to explain the analysis. Kirk moved his chair closer to the screen. The image of Brady ordering the course change appeared. Tenaida cut to another block of data; the image shrank to half-size and a group of crimson and scarlet sine curves filled the top of the screen.

"This," Tenaida pointed at the overlapping curves, "is the identity pattern the computer generated from the recording." He entered a command and the computer superimposed a group of blue sine curves over the red curves. "The blue shows the identity pattern stored in the computer's memory for Commander Patrick Brady."

Kirk studied the two templates. Large sections of pattern were identical, indicating how closely the double resembled Brady, but other parts of the composite degenerated into a random assortment of lines.

"There is an 81.7 percent correspondence between the two arrays." Tenaida's voice was flat, almost a monotone, as he recited his statistics.

Brady propped his chin on his hand and stared at the screen with a look of intense concentration, as if he could force the answers from the data by sheer force of will. "As we all know, 80 percent is too high for the resemblance to be chance or a good makeup job. But it's too low a correlation for me to have made that recording."

"That's correct. Given normal circumstances."

Kirk brushed his hair off his forehead. The temperature in the room seemed to have jumped upward. "All right, Tenaida," he said. "What does it do with your double?"

Tenaida called up similar information for the log extract that showed him recommending the course change. The random, nonoverlapping areas were more pronounced and appeared more chaotic to Kirk. "The match isn't as good," Kirk concluded after studying the orange and green curves on the screen for a moment.

"Seventy-three-point-five percent. However, we found an interesting correlation when we combine the two files." Tenaida ordered the computer to merge the two sets of composite identity patterns.

"I see what you mean." After Kirk's mind worked its way beyond his initial impression of technicolor spaghetti, he saw a chilling pattern in the data. The parts of the curves that matched neither Brady's nor Tenaida's identification patterns were nearly identical. "Could the same person be responsible for both course changes?"

Although he maintained an outward calm, Brady's fingers tapped a complex rhythm on the table. Tenaida stared at the screen, refusing to look toward the captain. Kirk realized he had just put his finger on the problem.

Lieutenant Tenaida responded, "There is a 96.4 percent correlation in the parts that don't match either Commander Brady's or my personnel records. However, the computer needs a larger data sample to determine with certainty that both recordings were made by the same person."

Insufficient data. Kirk cringed, realizing how much risk to his ship might be involved in collecting *sufficient* data. "What about Lieutenant Whitehorse's transfer request? We know she didn't record that." Under the table, Kirk clenched his hand into a fist, struggling to control his impatience. Tenaida always presented his data in a detailed, logical sequence, building an incontrovertible chain of evidence to support his conclusions. That slow approach was fine for abstract scientific results, but just now, when the safety of his ship was involved, Kirk found it difficult to endure.

Tenaida displayed the composite identity profile made from the recording and from Whitehorse's personnel file. Miniature reflections of the screen shone in the Deltan's dark eyes. "Eighty-nine-point-six percent overlap."

"How does that match up with the overall composite?" Kirk leaned closer to the screen to get a better view.

Tenaida combined the Brady/Tenaida/intruder profile with the image of Whitehorse and her double. The divergent sections merged with the composite intruder profile.

"Analysis, Tenaida?" Kirk straightened, feeling his tension wind tighter as he waited for the answer.

"Still insufficient data to reach a positive conclusion about the impostor. However, this lowers the probability to 1.7 percent that the correlations are caused by chance."

"In other words," Brady said, "the data isn't good

enough to meet your professional standards, but if the captain insisted, you'd say those recordings were made by the same person."

Tcnaida weighed the statement to make sure he would not get trapped by a hidden flaw in Brady's reasoning. "Correct."

"Would you speculate about this individual?" Kirk asked.

Tenaida stared across the room, frowning slightly as he considered the confidence limits he could place on conclusions drawn from such a small sample. "You realize, of course, that I don't have enough information to give you an unassailable answer."

When he heard that, Kirk felt himself relax. In spite of Spock's lessons on never revealing conclusions until they were proven facts, the Deltan had convinced himself to share his conjectures. "Of course, Tenaida. If we had the facts, we wouldn't need speculations."

The tension in Tenaida's shoulders eased. "Very well. Commander Layton, Commander Brady, and I discussed the possibility of the recordings being made by someone skilled in biocosmetics and image projection. Commander Layton believes this adequately explains why we can appear to be in two places simultaneously. However, I must point out the extreme difficulty in bringing the necessary biofabricator aboard undetected, and of tapping into our restricted databases to obtain the high-quality voice patterns required for the vocal enhancer.

"Given these difficulties, I believe the evidence suggests that we are dealing with someone who can control the minds of others so completely that they are not even aware of what is happening. The person behaves so close to normal that it is virtually impossible to distinguish the individual who is being controlled from that person acting on his or her own. The major weakness in the intruder's system is that the person's identity pattern while under the intruder's control corresponds in significant percentage to the intruder's identity pattern."

"Is that possible?" Kirk murmured, trying to accept the Deltan's conclusion. "And doesn't Lieutenant Whitehorse's recording contradict your idea?"

"My hypothesis does seem improbable." Tenaida frowned. "However, I see no other way to explain how these recordings can come so close to our identity patterns without achieving complete correspondence. As for Lieutenant Whitehorse's recording, I believe the image reversal occurred when the message was being transmitted. The recording was made against a neutral background, which eliminates the visual clues that would identify the error. Our analysis revealed no other way to explain the discrepancy."

Kirk nodded. He had been thinking along the same lines, but hearing Tenaida's deductions reassured him that there was no major flaw in his reasoning. "Any ideas on motive?"

"None, Captain. Inadequate information."

"There's one thing we'd better not overlook." Brady's tone was grim. "Unauthorized course changes, for whatever reason, are not friendly acts."

"Agreed." Frustrated, Tenaida shuffled his computer tapes. "However, that does not tell us what the person's motives are."

"I suppose you're right, Tenaida." Kirk drew a deep breath, feeling the weight of the negative conclusions. "So where should we look for our intruder?"

"There are several possibilities."

"Rank them by probability."

"Given that the trouble started after we left Starbase 15, it seems likely the intruder is among the Kaldorni diplomats or the Federation negotiating team."

"Admiral Chen can send us the records for Montoya's party, so in theory we could identify this person if he is with the Federation team. I'm willing to bet that the intruder is hiding among the Kaldorni, probably disguised as the person Admiral Chen's security personnel found on Starbase 15," Kirk said.

"That is a distinct possibility. We'll have Admiral Chen send us the identity files for the Federation negotiators and the Kaldorni diplomats, of course, but someone could have altered those records or transmit the wrong data. We will have no way of knowing if the information we receive has been corrupted." Brady leaned back in his chair, frowning. He drummed his fingers against his leg, a random motion that matched the skittering of his thoughts.

"Let's also examine the alternatives," Tenaida said. "If the intruder is in the commissioner's party, he might have spent many years establishing his cover. In that case, you would also need to consider members of the ship's crew as possible suspects."

"However, we do have the files for everyone assigned to the *Enterprise,* and we can be confident of the integrity of those files." Brady leaned forward and tapped the screen to emphasize his point. "The computer can search those records for anything that matches our piece of the intruder's pattern."

Kirk looked from one to the other, caught up by their rigid logic. In spite of the disparity in their backgrounds, Tenaida and Brady gave Kirk the feeling that he was listening to one person talking in stereo. As Tenaida talked, Kirk could see Brady taking the Deltan's conclusions and relating them to the ship's operations. Kirk found himself envying the lucky captain that had either Brady or Tenaida permanently assigned to his command. With that thought, he brought himself back to the problem at hand. "Check our records if you want, though I doubt it'll do any good. Call it a hunch, but I don't think the intruder is one of our people."

Kirk looked at the screen again and shrugged, deprecating his reasoning even as he presented it. "If it is, why would he wait until now to start messing with the ship's operations? . . . No, I'm betting this person—whoever he is—came aboard with our passengers, probably with the Kaldorni. But who is he? And why does he want the course changed? How are we going to catch him before he does something else? And, for that matter, where does Lieutenant Whitehorse fit into this? Requesting a transfer for her is hardly what I would call disrupting important ship's business. So why take the risk?"

Brady shook his head. "Captain, by the time you read the message, the intruder had released Lieutenant Whitehorse and was far from the terminal where the recording was made."

"True."

"And we don't know the answers for your other questions—yet."

"Somehow, I knew you were going to say that." Kirk leaned back in his chair, feeling a weariness born of frustration settle over him. If he had something concrete to go on, some solid information that would let him catch the intruder, he would have been ready for action. But the waiting, the efforts to accumulate enough information to guide his actions, really drained his energy. "Well, at least we know where to start. Tenaida, did you recheck where the course changes were taking us?"

"Yes. The projected destination is in an uninhabited region of space."

"What planets are closest to that heading?"

"I had the computer compile a list. The nearest habitable planet has a 52.7 percent probability of being the intended destination."

"Fifty-two percent? That's not very good." Kirk rubbed his forehead. Such a low probability demanded an explanation.

Tenaida shrugged. "I have too little information to answer your questions properly, Captain. I regret that I can do no better at this time."

"I understand, Tenaida. You may return to your duties."

"Thank you, Captain. I will let you know if I can extract any more information from these recordings." The Deltan collected the data cassettes and left the room.

"Well, Mr. Brady? What next?"

The acting first officer propped his chin in his fist. "I recommend we choose passwords so we can catch the intruder if he tries to masquerade as a command officer again."

Kirk nodded. They discussed what the intruder might do next and tried to cover each contingency. Finally, realizing how long they had been talking, Kirk said, "Do you want to make sure our *friend* hasn't done something else while we've been busy?"

"An excellent idea, Captain. I'll be on the bridge if you need me." Brady bounced to his feet and strode from the room.

Kirk turned to Layton. "You've been amazingly quiet through all this, Commander. What are your thoughts?"

Layton slid into the chair Brady had just vacated. "It was obvious you assigned me to watch those two. In case."

Kirk nodded. "A commanding officer has to consider every possibility."

"Agreed." Layton paused, considering. "I watched them run the analysis, and I checked the tapes. Everything there tests out fine. And both Brady and Tenaida seem like themselves, as near as I can tell. Dr. McCoy would be better able to answer that one, of course."

"Of course." Kirk gave Layton a long, penetrating look. "So what's bothering you, Marg? I can tell there's something here you don't like."

Layton shrugged. "I don't like their mind control hypothesis. Neither of them recalls any mental lapse where the incidents could have occurred. That bothers me. Someone would have needed to exert a considerable effort to implant false memories to cover his manipulations. Both Brady and Tenaida were working when the ship's log says they made these course changes. From the activity records on their computer terminals, the intruder had to have worked very, very quickly." Layton paused, breathing deeply. Kirk felt a finger of worry tickle at the back of his brain. In all the old mystery novels he had ever read, the suspects always had alibis—and the alibis were always worthless when examined carefully. Were Tenaida's and Brady's alibis equally worthless?

After a moment, Layton continued. "The hypothesis they presented *could* have happened, Captain, but I still have my doubts. I just can't make myself believe it. Unfortunately, I don't like my ideas much better.

"Tenaida mentioned his reservations about the use of sophisticated bioenhancements. However, I still think someone with good equipment and enough time could produce the biocosmetic appliances to impersonate Brady and Tenaida. I've even heard that Intelligence has developed vocal enhancers that allow for very accurate sound duplication. I'd prefer to think that is what's happening, even though I dislike the thought of the technology being in the wrong hands."

"I see." Kirk closed his eyes for a moment, trying to balance Layton's opinion against everything else he had heard. Any way he looked at it, something was wrong on his ship, and he had no solid explanation for what had occurred. All he could do now was hope he could find an answer before something serious happened. "Thank you for sharing your opinions, Commander. I'll certainly keep them in mind. And for the moment, would you keep a discreet eye on both Brady and Tenaida? Until we get some solid evidence, I can't honestly say either of them is *proven* innocent beyond a shadow of a doubt."

"Understood, Captain."

"Is there anything else I've missed?"

"Not that I can see, Captain. I'll let you know if I come up with anything."

"Thanks, Commander." After Layton left, Kirk stared at his computer screen, wishing Spock and his logic were available to help solve the mystery. Certainly, Spock was much more suited to the role of Mycroft Holmes. The thought of Holmes reminded Kirk of some questions raised by the previous discussion.

"Assistant, digest discussion of past hour. What other possibilities could explain this intruder's ability to impersonate command officers?"

"There are approximately 374 hypotheses that could, under the right circumstances, explain all the information to date. Shall I list them all?"

"No, just the most probable ones."

"The intruder could be one of the Fendarwi of Zeta Pictoris IV, who are never seen unless surrounded by a mental glamour that shows them to others exactly as they wish to be seen. The intruder could be using a holographic projector to create the image he wants you to see. The intruder may possess the ability to rearrange his body at will. The intruder may be similar to the Mellitus of Alpha Majoris I, differing in that it solidifies when it is ready for action. The intruder may be—"

"Enough. I was hoping you would suggest some viable possibilities."

"Given the information available, all hypotheses are equally viable at this time."

"What about biocosmetics? What information can you locate on that?"

"Biocosmetics is an expensive and delicate process that requires a biogen incubator with a dedicated computer. Each appliance is grown from organic materials according to a programmed template. In theory, it is possible to recreate any person for whom sufficient information exists to build a suitable template. Enhancements such as advanced speech synthesizers will allow duplication of vocal characteristics within the range of normal human hearing. Also, memory chips can be programmed to remind the person of appropriate behaviors and mannerisms. The major disadvantage to use of biocosmetics is that the disguises are not reusable; when removed from contact with human flesh, the appliances disintegrate within minutes. Also, private possession of this equipment is against Federation law."

"I see. Nowhere near impossible. Just extremely inconvenient to use."

"That is what the available information would suggest."

"Can you make a logical evaluation of Lieutenant Tenaida's and Commander Brady's alibis?"

"Logic dictates that an alibi is of no value unless an impartial witness was watching the person every minute of the period in question. If this is not the case, the alibi can only be used in general terms to assign probability of suspicion. Judged by this criterion, 95.34 percent of all alibis are of no value in exonerating the accused."

"I'm not interested in most cases. I asked for your evaluation of this *specific* case."

"There is a 95.34 percent probability that each of the alibis is valueless."

"Assistant, I want a logical assessment of the problem, not a list of statistics."

"My logical assessment of the problem is that there is a 95.34 percent probability that either or both Lieutenant Tenaida and Commander Brady omitted pertinent facts from their alibis."

Now we're getting somewhere, Kirk thought. "What might these pertinent facts be?"

After a noticeable pause, the computer responded, "I am unable to access that data at this time."

With a sigh, Kirk flipped off the switch and stood. It

was high time he made an appearance on the bridge to make sure nothing untoward had happened in his absence. And, when his duty shift ended in half an hour, he was looking forward to spending a relaxing evening showing Kris Norris around the ship. He hoped his mind would solve the mystery, if he relegated the problem to his subconscious for a few hours.

Chapter Five

Kirk's plans for his evening lasted until dinner time. He spent an extra half hour in the gym, practicing unarmed combat maneuvers under plus-normal gravity until his muscles rebelled. By the time he was ready for dinner, most of the day shift had finished eating. He glanced around the room, but saw neither Brady nor Tenaida.

As the synthesizer delivered his meal, he felt a twinge of uneasiness. He needed to mull over the day's events, and something warned him he would not get the quiet he wanted here. The premonition seemed silly, but he considered taking his dinner and eating in his quarters. Laughing at himself for the irrational impulse, he chose a table away from the main group of diners. He did not really want to eat in solitary confinement, and no one would interrupt his thinking, since his crew would not disturb him without cause.

"Do you mind if we join you?" Commissioner Montoya's voice intruded on Kirk's thoughts.

"Not at all." Kirk looked up to see Montoya and Simons standing across the table from him. He forced a smile. Polite conversation with Montoya did not fit his mood, and after this afternoon, he didn't want to talk to Cecilia Simons again for any reason. Nevertheless, the couple took the chairs opposite him.

Simons favored him with a smile calculated to blister the paint off the walls. "Where have you been keeping yourself, Jimmy? I was *so* looking forward to talking over old times with you."

Kirk felt the smile freeze on his face. Simons' words made it clear that she intended to ignore her failure that afternoon, and that she would keep after him until she got what she wanted. "A captain's duties keep him busy most of the time. There's more to running a ship this size than meets the eye."

"Surely your crew can run the ship without you watching them every minute, Jimmy."

Her voice, low and throaty, played his nerves like guitar strings. Her musky perfume evoked a torrent of long-buried memories and feelings. All of a sudden, the room felt very warm. He had to struggle to keep his response neutral. "There are certain decisions the captain must make."

"Well, I suppose you do have to watch some of your officers more carefully than others."

Knowing what she was implying, Kirk felt her words chill him like a bucket of ice water. "Ms. Simons," he said in a frigid tone, "all my officers are extremely competent, and I have absolute confidence in their abilities."

"But, Jimmy, you know—"

Hoping to sidetrack the discussion, Kirk turned to Montoya. "Commissioner, if I may change the subject, how are the negotiations coming?"

Montoya smiled. "It's too early to tell, of course, but I think we're doing quite well. There are substantial differences between the parties in this dispute, but we are making progress in outlining the areas of difficulty and establishing the protocols for the formal discussions."

"One of your aides said she was bothered because you weren't using the Universal Translator."

Montoya raised an eyebrow in surprise, as if questioning how Kirk had managed to become acquainted with his staff so soon. "Ms. Norris depends on her equipment more than necessary. Ambassador Klee doesn't speak our language fluently, but he has a fair grasp of what is said. And t'Stror is invaluable. I don't know where he learned English, but he must have had an excellent tutor."

Simons ducked her head and developed an intense interest in rearranging the food on her plate. Kirk watched her obliquely, trying to guess what she was hiding. She seemed uncharacteristically relieved when McCoy entered the room.

"Will you excuse me?" Simons asked. "I want to talk to the doctor about my dear little Janie's condition."

Kirk watched her retreat. She seemed very anxious to escape from the table.

"She's really upset about her daughter," Montoya said, his expression softening as he watched Simons cross the room. He turned back to Kirk. "Have you found out what happened? Ceci told me the girl had an argument with your science officer."

Kirk studied Montoya's face, trying to judge how he would react to the truth. The man seemed reasonable and intelligent on most issues, but from what Kirk had seen, Montoya's love for his wife blinded him to her faults. Under the circumstances, discretion seemed the wisest course. "According to Lieutenant Whitehorse, she ran into a wall."

"That sounds like she's protecting someone."

"Probably. But prying information out of stubborn Deltans isn't exactly my specialty. The only thing worse is trying to get something out of a Vulcan."

A puzzled frown crossed Montoya's face. "Deltan? I thought we were talking about Cecilia's daughter. Where do Deltans come into that?"

"Lieutenant Whitehorse's father was a Deltan."

"Deltan? Are you sure? Cecilia never mentioned

the girl's father, but I can't believe—I mean, the way she feels about Deltans—I don't mean to sound unduly skeptical, Captain, but are we talking about the same person?"

"We are." Kirk ran a hand through his hair. "I didn't realize she hadn't told you."

"She hasn't, and that possibility never occurred to me. Cecilia has always been quite irrational on the subject of Deltans."

Kirk smiled at the aptness of the description. "I gathered she found her association with Whitehorse's father somewhat—confining—and developed her dislike of Deltans from that."

"That explains a great deal. Thank you for telling me, Captain. It's been difficult trying to cope with her prejudices, but at least now I see where they come from."

"I'm glad to be of assistance."

"Captain?" Montoya took a deep breath, then plunged ahead, "May I ask you a personal question?"

"That depends on how personal it is."

"I was wondering how well you knew my wife."

Kirk took a mouthful of vegetables and chewed slowly, stalling for time. He suspected that the full truth was the last thing he should tell Montoya. "Not that well, I suppose. She calls me her 'old friend,' but I knew her for only a short time, and that was over fifteen years ago. I hope you don't think I would use the acquaintance to intrude on your marriage."

"Not at all, Captain. It's just that you appear to have made a lasting impression on her."

"She made one on me, too, Commissioner, but it's not something I want to talk about." He was almost relieved to see Simons returning from her discussion with McCoy. She dropped into her chair, a disgusted expression on her face.

"Dr. McCoy has completely forbidden me to see Janie. Me! Her mother!"

Kirk struggled to hide his amusement at Simons' feigned display. If he had not known better, she might have convinced him her feelings were real. "The doctor's orders were fairly inclusive, Ms. Simons. He let Lieutenant Whitehorse out of Sickbay on the understanding that she would spend the next few days resting. With no visitors allowed."

"But her mother isn't a visitor. She's family." Montoya straightened in his chair, ready to challenge anyone who would deny Simons what she wanted.

"The distinction is meaningless in this context, Commissioner. Dr. McCoy felt Lieutenant Whitehorse shouldn't do anything for a day or so. She had a nasty bump on the head and needs time to recuperate." As he paused, Kirk felt inspiration strike. "Think of it this way, Commissioner. If you had a bad hangover, how many people would you want to deal with?"

After a moment's thought, Montoya relaxed and a smile spread across his face. "Your point is well taken, Captain." He turned to Simons. "Cecilia, love, perhaps the doctor should have been more diplomatic, but I think you should do as he asked. It sounds like your daughter needs her rest."

Simons heaved a theatrical sigh. "If you're sure that would be best, Yonnie. It's just that I haven't seen Janie in *so* long—"

Montoya squeezed her hand. "I think you should listen to her doctor. If it's only for a couple of days, you'll still have plenty of time to visit."

"I guess you're right." Simons' voice was pitched to convey the proper degree of resignation. "It just seems so unfair."

Kirk glanced at his chronometer and was relieved to note it was almost time to meet Kris Norris. He forced his best diplomat's smile. "I hate to leave such charming company, but I have an appointment. If you'll excuse me." He rose, picking up his tray to return it to the cleaning station.

"It's been our pleasure, Captain." The smile that accompanied Montoya's words made Kirk realize that the commissioner's professional charm was beginning to grate on his nerves. "I hope we'll have a chance to talk again later."

"Perhaps." Kirk left them, trying to forget the sight of Simons' molten farewell smile. It promised many things, but he preferred not to explore any of those possibilities.

"He didn't even offer to give *us* a tour of the ship." Simons let her annoyance show in the petulant tone of her voice. She had hoped to have another chance to bring Kirk under her influence.

"I'm sure Captain Kirk's duties don't allow him to be a tour guide for every diplomat that travels on his ship." Montoya gave her hand a reassuring pat.

"Part of a captain's job is to be a good host. Besides, he and I are old friends, and he ought to be more pleased to see me." She ignored Montoya's attempt to mollify her. From her perspective, the day was going from bad to worse. Unless she found a way soon to weaken Kirk's control, her freedom to act on board the *Enterprise* would be severely limited. The thought left her in no mood for her husband's lesson in diplomatic interpersonal relations.

Montoya looked at Simons in surprise. He had not seen this sulky aspect of her personality before. A cold shiver took him as he realized he had contravened her expressed wishes more often in the past two days than in the rest of the six months he had known her. The implications of the thought disturbed him.

"Would you like to walk with me for a while?" he asked. "I'm not as familiar with the *Enterprise* as Captain Kirk, but I've been ignoring you too much this trip, and I'd like to make up for my bad manners."

She sighed and gave him a lost, helpless look. "I suppose. It's just that I feel completely useless when you're working. And Jimmy acts like I had the plague."

"People change." Montoya tried to put as much

reassurance in his voice as he could muster. "A captain's responsibilities must alter the way he looks at the universe. The old friend you remember may not exist any more." Simons' use of the diminutive "Jimmy" seemed incongruous when Montoya compared it with his own perceptions of Captain Kirk. He was beginning to wonder if the "old friend" had ever existed outside his wife's imagination.

"Do you really think he's just too busy to spend time with me?"

"I don't know. You'd have to ask him. But Captain Kirk's duties dictate many of his actions. . . ." Montoya gave her an affectionate smile. "Now, shall we take that walk, or are you going to spend the evening feeling neglected?"

"If you're sure I won't be any bother . . ."

He clasped both her hands in his. "This assignment is extremely important, and it's going to take a lot of my time. I'm sorry it has to be that way, and I know it's terribly boring for you—especially when you can't spend the time visiting with your daughter like you'd hoped." He gave her a lopsided grin. "But if I can't spend an evening with my wife, there's something very wrong with the mission."

Simons allowed his pleading to soften her mood. "All right, I accept. I shouldn't have let my frustrations get the better of me."

Relief softened the tense lines around Montoya's mouth. "That's better. And I promise, I'll make it up to you for this trip as soon as I can."

She rewarded him with a warm hug and a quick, passionate kiss. "Apologies accepted, Mister Commissioner. I promise, I'll try to be a good girl."

He rose and offered his arm to her. "Then shall we tour the ship, Madame Commissioner?"

"I haven't heard a better offer all day." She gave him a smile of rainbows and starflowers as she linked arms with him.

* * *

Kirk met Kristiann Norris in the corridor outside her quarters. She was leaning against the wall, watching the comings and goings of the crew with evident interest.

"Jim, I hope you don't mind me spying on your crew." She accompanied her words with a grin. "It's much more interesting than the walls of my cabin."

"No, I don't mind—as long as they don't." Kirk felt an answering grin spread across his own face. "But I expected you to be resting after a hard day's labors at the conference table."

She wrinkled her nose when he said the word *resting*. "My brain may have been working all day, but my body was just sitting in a chair. Do you suppose I could talk to the recreation officer about a temporary locker assignment for the gym?"

"I think we could include that on our agenda. Shall we start with the bridge?"

Although he made no effort to hurry, Kirk finished the tour in an hour. Long experience had taught him that most visitors liked to look at the engineering section from the doorway, but did not appreciate it if he took them inside and allowed Scotty to explain the intricacies of the warp drive engines or the structure of the dilithium crystals and their role in power generation. For that matter, Kirk himself was sometimes lost when his chief engineer became involved with the details of his favorite subject.

Kirk was pleased when Norris showed an above-average interest in the traditionally *boring* parts of the ship, but he did not tax her patience with a complete tour of the support services. Instead, he showed her the library lounges, the gymnasium, and the swimming pool, and they strolled through the botany section and the hydroponics lab.

"Many of the crew come here when they want to relax." He waved his hand at the plants surrounding them. "It makes them feel more like they were on a planet."

Norris looked at the vines spilling off their trellises. "It would have to be a jungle planet. I've never seen so much vegetation concentrated in one place in my life."

Kirk laughed. "I know what you mean. I was born in Iowa, and the plants there grow outward across the land, not upward on top of each other. Still, we haven't quite got enough space on the *Enterprise* for cornfields. We have to fit the plants into the smallest space we can."

"I see." They reached the end of the hydroponics section. Kirk opened the door for Norris and guided her to the turbolift. "Deck Eleven," Kirk ordered, giving Norris a warm smile. "I saved my favorite part until last."

The forward observation lounge on Deck Eleven was called the Captain's Lounge by the crew of the *Enterprise* because it was Kirk's favorite location for stargazing. It was the smallest of the ship's observation lounges, so Kirk felt less as though he were intruding on the off-duty activities of his crew than if he went to one of the bigger lounges.

They stepped out of the turbolift and Norris froze, her eyes widening at the panorama presented by the viewports. Kirk stopped beside her, enjoying her awe-struck expression as she absorbed the scene—the jewel-like stars showcased against the black of space. With the ship on warp drive, the view "through" the ports was actually a holographic projection of what the normal-space view would be. However, the computer took the information for the projection from the main sensors, and more than once, the realism of the scene had fooled Kirk into momentarily thinking the ship had dropped out of warp drive.

Kirk pointed out a half dozen major star systems, then allowed Norris to enjoy the spectacle without commentary. When her senses could absorb no more of the view, she removed her nose from the viewport and sat beside him.

"It's gorgeous." She sighed, overwhelmed by the magnificence of the scene.

Kirk felt the peacefulness of the starscape soothe away the day's worries. "Whenever I wonder why I'm in Starfleet, I come up here."

Norris gazed dreamily toward the viewports. "Mmmmm, this is enough to make me want to enlist. Where's the dotted line for my signature?"

"Talk to the recruiter at your nearest Starbase. He'll be glad to give you all the details."

She laughed. "I'll just bet. Including how many years it would take to work my way up to anything higher than yeoman."

"Well, you weren't really expecting to get command on your first ship, were you?" Kirk settled back in his chair, enjoying Norris' companionship and the feeling that he did not have to work to impress her.

"No, of course not." She was still watching the starfield. "Actually, I think I have the job I want for now. It's just that the stars are so gorgeous—"

Kirk's reply was covered by the opening of the turbolift door. Footsteps crossed the lounge, and two people approached their seats. Much to Kirk's annoyance, it was Montoya and Simons.

"Jimmy," Simons purred, "we've been looking all over for you. A crewman said you were giving a tour, and we wanted so much to join you."

Kirk rose, feeling his body stiffen as Simons' words reminded him of all the day's problems. "I didn't know you wanted to see the ship. I would have arranged for a guide."

"But the captain's tour would have been so *much* more interesting. And you couldn't *possibly* be having a private party with little Krissy Norris. She's hardly your type." Simons' tone implied that she knew exactly the kind of woman Kirk wanted.

"If you'll excuse me, Captain, I'll return to my quarters." Norris stood, shoved past Montoya, and rushed from the lounge.

"As a matter of fact, it was a private party." Icicles dripped from Kirk's words.

Simons stepped in front of Kirk, blocking his attempt to follow Norris, and hung her head in mock contrition. "Please don't be mad at me, Jimmy. I didn't mean to upset you."

Kirk heaved an exasperated sigh. He wanted nothing more than to be rid of Simons, but the available methods for removing her from the ship were likely to have unfortunate repercussions. "Permitting" her to take a space walk without a life support belt contravened both the spirit and the letter of his orders. *Oh, well,* he told himself, *it's a pleasant fantasy.* And imagining potential violence made it easier for him to hold his temper in check.

"Captain." Montoya's voice disrupted Kirk's reverie. "I have seen enough of the ship for one evening. If you wish, I'll convey your apologies to my aide for the interruption."

"I'd be most grateful, Commissioner."

Montoya turned to his wife. "Cecilia, are you coming with me?"

"If you don't mind, Yonnie, I'd like to stay and look at the stars for a few minutes."

"As you wish, my dear." Montoya gave her a quick kiss and nodded a farewell to Kirk.

The moment the turbolift doors closed behind Montoya, Simons flowed into Kirk's arms. Pressing her body against his, she covered his face with passionate kisses. "My darling," she whispered, nibbling his ear, "you don't know how hard it is for me to control myself."

What she really wanted to control, Kirk thought sourly, was him. Nevertheless, her scent and the heat of her body against his were beginning to have an effect. Before her charms could melt his resolve, he grabbed her arms and pushed her away. "This is another time and another place, *Deirdre.*" He emphasized the name to remind her of the negative side of their former relationship. "Whatever was between us in the past is dead and over. And I want no more attempts to revive it."

She returned to him, slipping her arms around his neck. "Are you sure that's what you *really* want?"

Kirk's anger flared. He pushed her away again. "If you recall, I warned you that I wouldn't tolerate any of your tricks on my ship. Especially not that one. Did I not make myself clear?"

"Oh, Jimmy." Tears gathered in her eyes. "I didn't mean to make you mad at me. I only thought—"

"*Did I make myself clear?*" he repeated.

Her shoulders slumped in resignation. "Very clear, Captain."

"That's better." Kirk straightened his uniform. "Now, before you start rehearsing a major case of wounded pride, let me remind you that you are traveling on my ship with your husband—and I can't afford to offend him."

Simons gave him a look that said she pitied his innocence. "Marriage contracts are made to be broken. Besides, Joachim doesn't know everything."

"You can think that, but I'm still not willing to be a party to your adulteries."

"Jimmy, you have such a restricted view of things." She examined his body knowingly, and a sultry smile spread over her face.

Kirk scowled. "I warned you. And I'm getting tired of repeating myself. If you don't stop this, I'll have you confined to your quarters for the rest of the trip."

"Well, if you *insist* on being boring . . ." She turned her back on him. Strolling to the wall, she leaned against the viewport and stared out at the stars. Her black hair blended into the darkness before her.

Kirk studied her, deciding her surrender would last long enough for him to ask a few questions. "Satisfy my curiosity—just between *old friends.* Why did you marry Montoya? And how long do you intend to stay with him?"

She propped her chin on her arms and stared at the starscape. Her voice sounded as cold and empty as intergalactic space. "I married him because he had money and wanted to spend it on me. And he was the most interesting man around at the time." She gave a short, tired laugh. "That wasn't saying much, I'm afraid. As for how long I stay with him . . . He insisted on a perpetual contract, but that doesn't mean anything. When I find someone I like better, I'll leave him."

"You mean, someone who has more money to spend on you?" He knew that was only a small part of the story but he did not expect she would tell him anything approaching the full truth.

Simons stepped away from the viewport. The light fell across her face, emphasizing her heavy makeup. She gave Kirk a smile that told him she was not fooled by his question. "As husbands go, Joachim is a decent enough sort. But I like excitement, and he doesn't supply very much."

Kirk recognized her performance for the work of art it was. "I'd think at your age, you might be a bit more interested in security. Your looks aren't going to last forever." In this light, her makeup did little to hide her years. Crow's-feet were beginning to web her eyes, and the lines around her mouth were deeply etched.

"My age? Just how old do you think I am?"

Kirk felt a brief flash of pity for her effort to hide behind the illusion of youth. He shook his head and said in a gentle voice, "Remember, you have a daughter on my ship. I have access to her personnel records."

"Oh." She turned away from him. "I should have known my daughter was behind all this."

"I'm not sure what you mean by 'all this,' and I don't think I want to know." Her words rekindled Kirk's anger, and he had to struggle to keep his voice level. "But your daughter has nothing to do with what we've talked about this evening."

He brushed past her, headed for the turbolift. Halfway across the room, he looked back. She was slumped against the wall, looking small and lonely. He almost relented, but knew it would be a monumental mistake. "Remember what I told you—behave yourself or I'll confine you to your quarters."

She did not move, but he heard her muffled reply anyway. "Understood, Captain."

He entered the turbolift. The solitude of his quarters promised a welcome escape from his tiresome passengers.

Kirk looked up from his reading when the door buzzer signaled. "Come."

McCoy entered. He crossed the room and set a bottle of Saurian brandy before Kirk. "If I'm not interrupting anything, Jim, I thought I'd come pay off the bet."

Kirk turned off the viewer. "I was just relaxing. Now, what's with the bottle?" He took two glasses from the cabinet and put them next to the brandy. McCoy perched on the table, opened the bottle and poured two drinks.

"You bet me a bottle of Saurian brandy that Cecilia Simons would show up in Sickbay, claiming Tenaida beat up Janara Whitehorse. Well, she did, and you predicted almost to the word what she was going to say."

Kirk sipped his drink and studied McCoy over the rim of his glass. "That seems to bother you, Bones."

McCoy frowned. "It's not that. It's just that, when she was telling it her way, she believed it so strongly that I could almost see it happening. That doesn't make any sense."

Kirk nodded in agreement. "There's a lot here that doesn't make any sense."

"Oh?"

"Actually, I had a fascinating conversation with her this evening—after I threatened to confine her to her quarters." Kirk described the encounter in the observation lounge.

"How long do you think she'll pay attention to your warning?"

"For a while." Kirk snorted. "Until she can figure out a way to circumvent the intent, anyway. I'm getting tired of her throwing herself at me every time I turn around."

"I'm disillusioned." McCoy's eyes twinkled with mischief, and his voice slipped into a Southern drawl. "I thought you liked being assaulted by beautiful women."

Kirk saluted the doctor with his glass. "Beauty is in the eye of the beholder, Bones. And my eye perceives very little beauty in that woman. What's your opinion of her?"

McCoy swirled the brandy in his glass, watching the eddy patterns in the liquid. Like his thoughts about Simons, the fluid circled back to where it had started. "She seems very disturbed. She's extremely neurotic, possibly even psychotic. Granted I haven't run any medical tests on her to back up that diagnosis—nor am I likely to get the chance to do it—but I don't know what else to call it. She sees the world exactly as she wishes it to be, and she ignores everything that contradicts her view of things. The thing is, she's so good at it that everyone around her ends up believing it her way."

"That's crazy."

"Maybe." McCoy took a swallow of his drink. "But you've seen what happens to the people around her. The men in particular. How do you explain Montoya heading back to his quarters so Simons can make an uninterrupted pass at you?"

"I was wondering about that one, myself. In the meantime, what should I do about her?"

"I'll let you know if I think of anything." McCoy drained his glass and set it on the table. "If that's all, Jim, I think I'm ready to turn in. It's getting late."

Kirk swallowed the last of his drink. "I think you're right, Bones. It has been a long day."

After McCoy left, Kirk cleaned the glasses and put the brandy away. Any other chores, he decided, could wait until morning. He went to bed, but sleep eluded him. The day's events circled through his mind, and they did not inspire relaxation.

"That didn't take long." Montoya was surprised that his wife had returned to their quarters so soon. He laid aside Norris' notes on her noontime conversation with t'Stror. He had been studying them for insights into Kaldorni psychology.

"The captain had work to do, and I didn't feel like stargazing alone." Simons sat beside him, wrapped her arms around his neck, and nibbled suggestively at his ear. "Of course, there are other things we could do."

"There are indeed." He took her in his arms, grateful for the chance to show her that he could put her needs before his work. "But why this sudden interest? Fifteen minutes ago you were intent on renewing your friendship with the captain."

"I finally realized what an awful bore he's become. He even threatened to confine me to quarters unless I behaved myself. So—" she blew softly in his ear, "—I decided to behave myself."

"I approve wholeheartedly." Desire for her flooded him, erasing all other thoughts. He cleared his work off the bed, scattering notes and computer tapes in his haste. She pulled him down beside her, and they made love. It was only much later that he remembered her words and wondered what Kirk had meant when he ordered Cecilia to "behave" herself and why Kirk would consider confining her to her quarters.

A nondescript ensign wearing an engineering uniform strolled the corridors as if looking for an acquaintance. He never spoke, but after several hours, he had covered every corridor on the *Enterprise*. He memorized the locations of major departments, ship's services, and escape routes.

Finally, he returned to the quarters assigned to his alter ego. By the time the other's visitor appeared, the nondescript crewman no longer existed.

Chapter Six

THE NEGOTIATIONS hit a snag late in the third afternoon when Ambassador Klee's youngest wife became ill. After giving lengthy instructions to t'Stror and his other aides, Klee left. Almost immediately, problems developed.

Montoya asked why Klee had not requested that a doctor examine his wife and then gone to her when the afternoon's session was over.

t'Stror's face took on an expression of blank incomprehension. He cocked his head to the side and blinked his green-gray eyes, as if asking Montoya to explain his absurd question. "But the commissioner must understand it would be the greatest insult for the ambassador not to attend upon the lady himself. To send a person of lesser rank than she—it would destroy the harmony of all of the ambassador's wives. Surely the commissioner must see this."

Montoya's brow wrinkled with the effort of trying to link the disparate concepts in t'Stror's statement. "I'll accept your word for it, Speaker t'Stror. However, I do not completely understand what you mean by 'harmony.' Could I ask you to explain it?"

t'Stror tilted his head farther to the side, studying Montoya as if he were a child who was slow to learn his lessons. The Harmony of the Universe was the cornerstone of Kaldorni philosophy, but all non-Kaldorni seemed baffled by the concept. "Explanation is not an imposition. But it is a difficult idea to explicate—your language has not the words for me to express myself."

"We understand how troublesome it is for you." Montoya gave the Kaldorni a reassuring smile. "However, it would help us if you'd try, within the limits imposed by the inadequacies of our language."

"As long as the commissioner comprehends that the terminology must be imprecise." t'Stror laid his hands on the oblong table, fingers spread to indicate speech in the declamatory mode. His dark skin blended with the simulated wood tones of the table.

"Of course. We appreciate your effort." Without taking his eyes off t'Stror, Montoya gestured to Yeoman Menon, who was operating the recording equipment in the room's far corner. He wanted to be sure she got multiple recordings of this speech.

t'Stror launched into an involuted explanation of the Kaldorni ideals of Harmony, Duty, Respect, and Honor. As he listened, Montoya realized the problem lay not in understanding the individual concepts, but in untangling the interrelationships and in defining the degree to which they permeated the Kaldorni world view and determined individual actions. Halfway through the discussion, the commissioner glanced at Kristiann Norris. Her expression—lips compressed in a straight line and one eyebrow slightly raised—told Montoya she thought t'Stror was omitting something from his explanation. Montoya made a note to ask her later; Norris' instincts on such matters were generally accurate.

t'Stror finished his lecture. In turn, he looked at each of the Federation team, daring them to question his explanation. When no one accepted his challenge, he brought up a new subject. "My ambassador has requested me to ask why the commissioner insists the rules we discuss for the meetings with the Beystohnai must be so discordant. Surely it must be seen that the harmony of the attendants is dissolved when equal association for all negotiators is demanded."

Montoya straightened in his chair, sensing this was the key issue in the discussions. "We of the Federation feel that the—harmony—is destroyed if all parties in a dispute do not have equal say in resolving their differences."

A beatific smile spread across t'Stror's features. "Then my instructions make it clear to me that I should terminate this session. There can be no accordant determination from a deliberation where the Harmonies of the Universe are disrupted by the discordant fraternization with greatly inferior persons." He stood, enjoying his moment of power as the rest of the Kaldorni delegation massed behind him. In a group, they walked out of the room.

Montoya watched the Kaldorni exit in stunned silence. Vreblin and Zayle stared at the far wall to avoid meeting the commissioner's eyes. As the door closed, Norris murmured, "Manifest Destiny."

"What?" Montoya was caught off-guard by the seeming irrelevance of her comment.

"Their concept of *Harmony*. t'Stror didn't put it in quite those words, but it resembles a human concept called *Manifest Destiny*. It gives the Kaldorni the perfect out. If our suggestions prevent them from moving into the Yagran system or obligate them to serious negotiations to limit their expansion—they claim the proposal disrupts their *Harmony*, and they can't discuss it any further."

Montoya chewed on his lower lip. "Are you sure about this?"

Norris doodled a few lines on her noteboard. "No. I don't have anything to back it up except a feeling. But it fits the facts we have so far."

"Pretty skimpy facts," muttered Vreblin.

"I agree. But they haven't been especially generous in giving us useful information, either." Norris held up her hand to silence Vreblin's protest. "Yes, I know they've talked a lot. But they haven't included much solid data in what they've said. I keep wondering if something is being lost in the translation. I wish I had my Universal Translator in here!"

"You always want your gadgets around," Zayle said.

Norris shrugged off the comment. Zayle disliked the Universal Translator because he was unable to master the complexities of its control language. "Machines have their problems, of course, but they don't deliberately misconstrue what is said."

Montoya gestured for silence. "Kris, do you think t'Stror is intentionally mistranslating what the ambassador says?"

"I don't know. t'Stror translates when the ambassador can't express the concepts he wants to discuss, and Ambassador Klee's English is better in some areas than in others." She paused, looking for a way to summarize her concern. "It feels as though the emphasis is changed in the translation—that maybe Ambassador Klee is stressing one thing and t'Stror tells us he's more worried about something else."

Montoya thought for a moment, remembering a frustrating hour the previous morning when neither side had been able to understand what the other was trying to say. "Your instincts are often right, Kris. While the negotiations are suspended, why don't you analyze the transcripts for evidence to back up your theory?" He turned to Yeoman Menon, who was still behind the portable recording station. "Could Ms. Norris get a copy of the sessions to date?"

Menon tapped her fingers against the side of the console. "I'll need authorizations from both you and Captain Kirk to release the transcripts. Once I have those, I can get you a copy within half an hour."

"Good enough. I'll sign the authorization form now."

Menon entered a code into her console. The workstation beeped twice and she handed Montoya a datapad. Montoya scrawled his signature across the pad while still talking to his aides. "Kris has her assignment. The rest of us will get some coffee and look for other ideas."

The three men left while Menon was shutting down the recording equipment. Norris picked up her noteboard. "If you don't mind, I'll tag along so I can get those transcripts as soon as they're ready."

"That will be fine." Menon picked up the signed authorization form and led the way out of the briefing room.

Kristiann Norris and Sushila Menon met Captain Kirk in his quarters fifteen minutes later. After listening to Norris' explanation, Kirk signed the authorization without comment. He sent Menon to copy the transcripts, but asked Norris to stay.

"Planning to use the Universal Translator on the recordings?" he asked, afraid she would not talk to him after the way Simons had interrupted them in the observation lounge.

"Not at the moment." A rueful smile played across her face. "Commissioner Montoya told the Kaldorni we wouldn't use the translator on the recordings. However, there are other ways to determine whether the translations we're getting are accurate. It's slow, but I'll probably start with a word frequency analysis. If analogous words don't match up in different parts of the discussion, I'll know something funny is going on." She nibbled on the end of her stylus. "I'll probably try analyzing facial expressions, too, but that's trickier because everybody's hiding something there."

Kirk chuckled. "Poker face."

Norris frowned, trying to place the reference. "Oh. Yes." Her expression cleared. "And gestures and facial expressions vary so much from culture to culture . . ."

"Well, good luck. If you need help with the ship's

computer, ask Lieutenant Tenaida. If my science officer has some specialized programs tucked away somewhere, Tenaida will know where they are."

"Thank you, Captain. I'll keep that in mind." She turned to leave, but Kirk's voice stopped her.

"Kris, I'd like to apologize for what happened the other night. I hadn't intended to meet those particular people."

She faced him again. "It's all right, Jim. I assumed you wanted to renew your old friendship."

Kirk gave a short, humorless laugh. "No, that's one *old friendship* I'd just as soon forget. However, she's here, and I can't do anything about it—but I should have apologized sooner for allowing the interruption."

"Actually, the apology should have come from her. She's the one who was rude." Norris' eyes flashed with anger and, in spite of herself, she let it show in her voice.

"You don't like her very much." Kirk realized how much of an understatement that was as soon as he'd said the words. He decided that Norris' dislike for Simons increased his respect for her.

"Why should I? She makes a complete fool of Joachim, and he's the only one who doesn't see it."

"She's made fools of a lot of men. Most get their eyes opened eventually."

Norris frowned. "*Eventually* is pretty indefinite. And usually too late."

"I suppose," Kirk responded evenly and then grinned. "Not to change the subject, but would you like to wander through the recreation deck for a while this evening? To make up for my slow apology?"

"I should spend most of the evening working on the transcripts, but I'll need a break sometime." Norris ruffled her hand through her short hair. "Yes, a walk would be delightful. Will you promise there won't be any interruptions?"

Kirk gave a chuckle. "That's a promise a captain

can rarely keep. But I'll do everything that's humanly possible."

"Fair enough."

The door buzzer sounded. "Come," Kirk said.

Menon entered with the copy of the negotiation transcripts. Norris took the tape. "I think it's time for me to go to work. I'll see you later, then." The door closed behind her.

It was black, an immense catlike being with fifteen-centimeter, saber-shaped canines thrusting down from its upper jaw. Its topaz eyes glowed with a savage hunger, a ferocious joy of killing. It was hunting, searching its murky jungle habitat for a particular quarry.

She clung to the tree branch high above the jungle floor, terrified the giant cat would scent her. Its huge, ravenous form glided between the tree trunks. Directly below her, it paused and sniffed the air. Looking up, it stared at the tree limb where she clung.

The cat sprang, an impossible leap that brought it nearer, and nearer, and . . .

Janara cried out and woke. She was drenched in sweat, and her heart was racing. Pulling the blanket around her shoulders, she sat up. The familiar furnishings of her quarters coalesced from the shadows, but the image of the attacking cat still remained, as sharp as if it were in the room. She slowed her breathing and struggled to empty her mind of all thought. The cat wavered, unable to focus on the nothingness. With a final yowl of frustration, it vanished.

Janara reached for the pill bottle. Her hands shook as she removed the top, dumped out a couple of brown tablets, and gulped them down. Her attacker was still searching for her, trying to reestablish contact. She concentrated on her breathing, keeping it slow and even, and on blanking her mind to the telepathic intrusion. Slowly, as the *boretelin* took effect, the image of the sable cat faded from her awareness.

Half an hour later, she recalled her consciousness and took stock of herself. She felt tired and shaky, emotionally drained from combating the psychic assault, and physically run down from her previous injuries.

Fingering her bruised cheek, she felt that it was sore and swollen, and the scraped skin was heavily scabbed. Janara had considered using a healer's trance to mend the damage, but, in the end, had confined her efforts to the most serious injury—the part of her skull that had struck the console. The superficial cuts and bruises were healing nicely, even without the accelerated cell growth that the trance produced. However, it would be several more days before her face returned to normal. Thinking of her mother, she was grateful to McCoy's *no visitors* orders, which had delayed the inevitable confrontation with her.

The walls of the room closed in on her, mocking her with her mother's voice. Janara gritted her teeth, fighting the illusion. If she stayed in her quarters much longer, the confinement and the worry over Simons' next move would be as taxing as the activities McCoy had ordered her to avoid. She looked at her chronometer and was surprised to see it was an hour into the evening shift. Uhura would be working out in the gym now.

Janara rolled from the bed and padded to the wardrobe. After pawing through the jumble of clothes, she found a chocolate wraparound skirt and a light brown leotard that matched her skin. She squirmed into the clothes and smoothed her hair into place. McCoy would object to her doing any gymnastics so soon after her injury, but supervising Uhura's lesson would get her out of her quarters for an hour.

She dropped a tape into the computer and recorded Uhura's routine. Before turning off the machine, she checked her message file. A brief note from Tenaida suggested modifications on the Shansar equations. Uhura said she would be in the gym at the scheduled time for a workout, and she invited Janara to come for a visit.

The rest of the messages were from her mother. Their tone ranged from apologetic to threatening, from conciliatory to enraged. Taken as a whole, they reflected poorly on Simons' mental stability. Janara knew her mother should be committed for intensive therapy, but she had few illusions about Simons' willingness to undergo treatment.

Janara transferred Tenaida's message to the bottom of her Shansar calculations and erased the rest of the file. Turning off the computer, she put the tape in her pocket and headed for the gymnasium.

Kirk took the long route to Engineering, his personal method of inspecting his ship. The captain's meandering course through the upper decks took an extra fifteen minutes, but gave him a more accurate feel for what was happening on the ship than a week's worth of status reports. He was approaching the end of his inspection, on the port side of Deck Seven, when he saw a man leaving the briefing room. He froze, startled to see someone wearing a captain's uniform. The spy!

Kirk broke into a run, but the noise alerted the impostor, and he raced for the turbolift. Kirk increased his speed, but was easily outdistanced. The intruder seemed to move as if accustomed to a much higher gravity.

Kirk skidded to a stop at an intercom panel. He called Security, but even as he spoke, Kirk realized the effort was futile. By the time the *Enterprise*'s security people could respond, the intruder would have more than enough time to remove his disguise and dispose of the incriminating uniform.

Still breathing heavily from the run, a very frustrated Captain Kirk continued toward Engineering. It was bad enough having a spy on the ship, but when the intruder escaped him so easily, it added grave insult to the injury.

"Damn!!" Kirk balled one hand into a fist and smashed it into the other. "Damn this entire mission to Teller's deepest Hell!!" Neither the gesture nor the swearing helped his mood.

Cecilia Simons picked at her dinner, trying to hide her frustration and her boredom. Montoya was working, and she was wondering how to spend her evening when t'Stror entered the room. He got his food from the dispenser and brought his tray to her table.

"Is it permitted that I join the madame commissioner?" he asked.

"Of course! I was trying to figure out what to do with myself. Joachim is off somewhere talking with his aides, and no one seems to care about me."

"The lady should not be so unhappy because her foolish husband ignores his duties to her. But should I ask if it is permitted that I speak with you? The Commissioner Montoya may be most unhappy because of my actions of this afternoon."

"He didn't say. He doesn't control me, anyhow, but he'd probably like me to spy on you for him." Simons gave him a wicked smile. "And, of course, you'll tell me all your secret plans."

"I have no hidden schemes. My ambassador commanded that I was to promote understanding. But the Commissioner Montoya wished not to understand, so I had no choice but to order our leaving." Between sentences, t'Stror gulped large bites of his food.

Simons waved away his explanation. "That's all right. I'm not interested in my husband's cloak-and-dagger games. I'm much more concerned about my daughter telling me that she's been going off to Delta Four to learn their mental spying tricks. I can't imagine who could have gotten her interested in that superstition again."

"I do not think I understand."

"Me, either. But I'm told she's been going to Delta when she has time off instead of visiting me. What else could she want there?" Simons took a mouthful of her dinner while she calculated the effect of her words on t'Stror. Would he extrapolate the Deltan *danger* to mean Tenaida and convince his ambassador to insist that Kirk banish the scientist from the ship?

After a moment, she shifted her expression to one of concerned sympathy. "Why should Yonnie be unhappy with you for following orders?"

"One doesn't know. But I have been told there is an ancient human myth about a king who beheaded the carrier of unliked news. It might be that the commissioner would express similar displeasure if he did not concur with the instructions of my ambassador."

"Maybe." Simons had trouble visualizing Montoya becoming angry under such circumstances. "If so, he didn't tell me. He was more worried about the reasons behind your orders. Also, he didn't understand why the ambassador left in the middle of the afternoon."

"The youngest wife of my ambassador was feeling unwell, and it is proper that he should be with her. He is most worried because another is now sick. May I tell you a thing that you should not tell around the ship?"

"Your secret is safe with me."

"I think my ambassador's wives ate something that is causing this illness. I do not know this to be a certain fact, but I think the one who prescribed the making of our foods may have written a wrong ingredient into the directions."

"Is it serious? Who programmed the synthesizers?"

"One cannot know yet if it is serious. One wonders, since it is this person's belief that the Deltan scientist programmed the machines."

Simons suppressed a grin. t'Stror had taken the bait. Now, if only he could convince Ambassador Klee that Tenaida had willfully misprogrammed the food synthesizers! At the ambassador's insistence,

Kirk would have to confine Tenaida to the brig, and she would be free of the Deltan's unwelcome presence.

t'Stror swallowed the last of his dinner. "But I must attend my ambassador to see if he has need for me to do anything. I hope that we may arrange a language lesson for the usual time."

Simons gave him a brilliant smile. "A language lesson is a fabulous idea. I'll certainly be there."

"Until when I expect you." The short Kaldorni stood and bowed. As he left the room, he was calculating how much longer he could use Simons. Soon, he knew, the dangers of associating with her would outweigh the benefits of the information she provided.

Uhura was doing warm-up exercises when Janara got to the gym. She looked up from her leg stretches. "I was afraid you weren't coming."

Janara started checking the control unit for the gravity generators. "Dr. McCoy won't let me do any work until tomorrow, so I've been climbing the walls from sheer boredom. But he forgot to put teaching gymnastics on the list of forbidden activities, so I figured my sanity required that I help you with your routine."

Uhura laughed. "I don't think the doctor will agree with your logic, but what he doesn't know can't upset him."

"It's an easy routine. I can sit by the control console and tell you everything you need to know."

"Good! Those exercises you gave me are tricky enough. I don't want to grab onto something I can't handle."

"Actually, the routines are easier than the exercises because they're more structured."

"Does that mean more like dancing?"

"That's what most people say. The routines are choreographed to fit the music, so dancing is probably the best comparison." Janara dropped the tape into the machine and activated the animation display. "Come watch what you'll be doing."

The screen showed two sets of uneven parallel bars. The outline of a female figure was shown in the third position. When the music started, the animated gymnast swung herself into a handstand on the lower bar. From there, she worked a series of spins and transfers between the lower and upper bars. Numbers in the screen's lower corner counted the elapsed time and displayed the timing and magnitude of the gravity shifts. Most were small, but they were timed to add to the momentum of the gymnast's spins.

The routine became more complex, adding twists and handstands to the basic pattern. As the music swelled to a crescendo, the figure whirled through a triplet of rapid spins and released the upper bar. The gravity dropped to half its previous intensity. She executed a double somersault while her body arced toward the second set of bars. The animated gymnast caught the bar and swung around it. Carefully timed increases in the gravity subtracted from her body's momentum. After another series of twists and handstands, the music returned to its main theme, and the gymnast started the routine over.

Janara stopped the computer. "That's it. There are some variations later so you won't get bored, but once you master the first section, you've got it."

Uhura slipped a net over her dark hair. "Some of those moves look familiar."

"Suspiciously like the exercises you've been working on, I'll bet." Janara shifted the tape from the animator to the control unit.

"That wouldn't have anything to do with the fact that you taught me the exercises, would it?"

"Trade secret." Janara gave the equipment a final check. "You teach a few exercises, then put them in a routine. It makes the student think learning is easy."

"I should have guessed. Just like music lessons. Or studying a new language."

"Same principle. If you're ready, we can start. I'll prompt you, and we'll drill the first half minute of the routine until you get it."

"Sounds good." Uhura took the center position near the lower bar of the left-hand set. She flexed her knees, ready for the first move, and Janara started the music.

Uhura was a quick learner. Twenty minutes later, Janara added to what Uhura was practicing.

Her second time through the initial minute, the gravity generators on the far wall cut on sharply for two seconds. The unexpected lateral acceleration jerked Uhura's body out of position on the upper bar. Before she could recover, a 250 percent increase from the floor generators slammed her across the lower bar. Stunned, Uhura slipped toward the floor. Janara slapped the override panel, lowering the gravity in the workout area to one-tenth of ship's normal. Even so, Uhura cried out as she hit the floor.

Janara punched the emergency button to summon a medical team. The response indicator lit. Janara locked in the override signal and went to Uhura.

"What happened?" Uhura whispered. Her face had an ugly grayish tinge from shock.

"Don't talk now." Janara passed her hand over Uhura's torso, about six centimeters above the skin. "You've got five broken ribs. I don't know what's wrong with the machine. But I will find out, if I have to take it apart circuit by circuit."

Uhura closed her eyes. Her breathing was rapid and shallow. Janara frowned, worry gnawing at her as she watched the other woman. Every breath pushed against the broken ribs, and only luck had saved Uhura from a punctured lung. Janara probed the injury again, trying to evaluate the danger. Her training in the healer's art was limited, and she hesitated to practice her erratic skills where her senses could not evaluate her work. Much to her relief, the medical team arrived before she was forced to a decision.

McCoy entered at a run. He passed his already activated tricorder over Uhura's body. "Broken ribs and shock. Immobilize her, and get her to Sickbay immediately." Lowering the tricorder, he turned to Janara. "What happened?"

"The controller jumped the gravity. She hit the bar at about two-and-a-half g's."

McCoy glanced at the bars. "She's lucky it wasn't her head."

"Yes."

With a force bar immobilizing her torso, the medics moved Uhura to the stretcher. McCoy started to say something to Janara, but changed his mind and followed the stretcher from the room. Janara pulled the access cover from the gravity control unit and began running the diagnostic programs.

Captain Kirk and Kristiann Norris strolled casually through the hydroponics lab. The exuberant foliage and the dim lights that signaled nighttime for the plants made it seem as though they had been transported to a jungle planet. The air was scented with the sweet fragrance of miraberry blossoms. Norris took a deep breath, letting the romantic illusion dispel some of the day's tension. She had been telling Kirk about her attempts to unravel the Kaldorni linguistics without using the Universal Translator.

The intercom whistled for the captain. Kirk, irritated at having the peaceful interlude interrupted, pushed his way through the tangled vines to reach the intercom panel. An impatient scowl darkened his face as he listened to the message, but puzzlement had replaced annoyance by the time he rejoined Norris.

He gave her a rueful grin. "I seem to remember saying that a captain can never promise an evening without interruptions. I'm sorry, but duty calls."

Norris glanced at her chronometer. "I should be getting back to work, anyway. Is anything wrong with the ship?"

"No. Someone was injured in the gym an hour ago, and her coach wants to discuss the accident with me." His mouth twisted into a perplexed frown. "I don't know what I can do about it, but she insisted on speaking with me."

"Well, I enjoyed the walk and the break in my work. I'm sorry you have to go so soon."

"A commanding officer's work is never done." Kirk smiled an apology. "Maybe we can finish our walk some other time." He left Norris at the door and hurried to the gym.

When Kirk entered the room, Janara's head and upper torso were buried in the control console for the gymnastics gravity generators. She wriggled out when she heard his footsteps. Kirk wondered how her normally impassive face could appear so grim. She straightened, waiting for him to reach her.

"All right. What's this all about?"

She gave him a terse account of the accident and of her attempts to locate the problem. She had found no program errors on the tape and no mechanical failures in the control unit.

"All right. You've told me what *didn't* cause the accident. Now would you mind telling me what *did?*" A small voice in the back of Kirk's head warned, *You're not going to like it, James T. Kirk.*

Janara displayed a block of program code on the screen. Kirk studied the lines. He rarely worked with the programming system used by vari-grav controllers, but he recognized a timer series and a subroutine call keyed to the timer reading.

"Does that do what I think it does?"

Janara nodded. "After fifteen minutes of running time, it searches for a handstand sequence in the routine. That triggers the override program, which throws out some large and unexpected changes in the gravity values. It's an extremely dangerous piece of work."

"Who's responsible for this?"

She scrolled to the beginning of the file. Kirk turned cold as he read the passcode. Shaking, he reached for a chair and dropped into it. "That's impossible," he said, staring at the cipher he knew almost as well as his own. The spy had switched tactics; from unscheduled course changes, he had graduated to attempted murder using Tenaida's identification code.

Janara recorded the program and gave the tape to Kirk. She put a second copy into her pocket along with the cassette of Uhura's routine.

Kirk turned the tape over in his hands, staring at it as if it were about to metamorphose into a poisonous snake. He would have been less upset if the spy had used Kirk's own cipher. At least, then, he would have known the programming he was looking at was impossible. Finally, he forced himself from the chair. Halfway to the intercom, it whistled, paging him.

"Kirk here."

"Captain, our course headings are being overridden by someone in Auxiliary Control. We can't change them back from here."

"Have Scott, Brady, and a Security team meet me there on the double. Kirk out." He left the gym at a dead run.

Kirk slammed into the door of Auxiliary Control. The recoil threw him into Security Chief Pavel Chekov, and the collision knocked both men off their feet. By the time they had recovered, the rest of the Security team had arrived. Scotty pushed his way forward to the door's control panel. He triggered the scanner that should have opened the door for the captain, but nothing happened. The override sequence for the lock also did not work. Scott shook his head. "It's controlled from the inside. I can't open it from here."

Chekov pointed to two of his men. "Pfeiffer, Johnstone, please escort Mr. Scott through the air ducts. And keep watch for the intruder. He may try to escape by going out that way."

"Aye, aye, sir."

Scott beckoned to the guards, and they headed for the maintenance hatch. The ventilation system would give the three men a back door into Auxiliary Control. Kirk hoped they would catch the intruder before he escaped.

After what felt like five hours to Kirk—but was only that many minutes—Scott opened the door. "He was gone before we got here," the chief engineer said.

Kirk stepped inside. Johnstone was scanning the room with his tricorder, searching for clues. He paused when the captain joined him. "Pfeiffer is checking the air ducts. The intruder might still be in there."

"Good thought." Privately, Kirk figured the intruder would have no more trouble escaping than he had had getting in undetected. The spy's timing and his knowledge of the ship's schedule were too good for the captain's peace of mind. Kirk turned to Chekov. "Get some extra men and check the surrounding corridors.

"Brady, will you help me deactivate our friend's overrides?"

"Right away, Captain," said both officers in unison.

Kirk went to the control console. A few moments' work recovered the intruder's program from the navigation bank. He read the altered course information in amazement. "Warp factor six, at bearing 124 mark 5. Our friend is certainly persistent."

"I'm not sure if that's good or bad," Brady said, reading the screen over the captain's shoulder.

Kirk frowned. "How much trouble will it be to bypass this until we can trace all the subroutines?"

Brady called up the specifications for the affected systems on the adjoining console. Scott leaned over his shoulder, following the schematics as Brady accessed them. The spy's program had overridden the primary control functions, but it had ignored all the backup provisions. "It won't be too difficult, Captain," Scott said. "The intruder isn't familiar with the design of the system."

"At least that's one thing he's not an expert on. Mr. Scott, would you and Mr. Brady isolate what he's taken over and make sure he hasn't planted any booby traps in the system? Notify me when we can correct our heading."

"Aye, Captain."

Kirk went to the intercom. "Bridge, Kirk here. Would you find Lieutenant Tenaida and have him report to my quarters at once?"

"Yes, Captain."

Halfway through the door, Kirk stopped and turned toward his security chief. "Mr. Chekov, until we catch the saboteur, I want a guard posted here at all times."

"Yes, sir."

Tenaida was waiting when Kirk reached his quarters. They entered, and Kirk handed Tenaida the copy of the program from the vari-grav control unit. "I want your reaction to that." He dropped into his chair, watching Tenaida through narrowed eyes.

The slender Deltan slipped the tape into the computer. As he read, Tenaida's face flushed with agitation. He ran through the program a second time. "It's crude, but effective. Very effective."

"Would you mind explaining?"

"This program is compiled from pieces of other programs. Whoever assembled it didn't need to know how to program the vari-grav computer. He just spliced together assorted parts of vari-grav routines already stored in the ship's computer."

"Why is your identification code on the program?"

"It must have been removed from one of my files and linked to the program."

"That doesn't answer my question. How did someone get your code?"

"My cipher is on many files in the computer's memory. The intruder might have randomly selected a file with my code on it, or he could have searched for a common identifier. There are illegal programs that can retrieve both the public and the private portions of a passcode. The alternative is that someone has penetrated the computer's master file of code listings."

"I don't like that last option. Would you get together with Commander Layton and make sure it can't happen—just in case?"

"Of course."

Kirk straightened, feeling the knots of worry-induced tension dissolve. Relief washed through him. Kirk, the person, had never doubted Tenaida's innocence; beyond his own judgment of the young Deltan was Spock's high rating of Tenaida's character and abilities. In addition, Kirk could not believe anyone would be stupid enough to put his own passcode on a program intended as a murder weapon.

However, Kirk, the commanding officer, could not afford to assume anyone was innocent, and he had needed to watch Tenaida's reactions to know that the Deltan was not withholding information. Even so, he decided to have Layton keep a closer watch on Tenaida. There was still a chance the intruder was using some form of mind control on Tenaida. If that was the case, Kirk hoped that Layton would find evidence soon to support the theory.

"This must be more of our visitor's handiwork. And we had another example a few minutes ago." He told Tenaida about the latest course change.

"Mr. Brady and Mr. Scott are working on the problem now. I'd like you to help, in case there are any booby traps waiting for us when we change our course."

"Of course, Captain." Tenaida started for the door.

"And, Tenaida, let me know what you find as soon as possible."

"I will, sir."

After Tenaida left, Kirk got himself a cup of coffee and sat quietly, thinking. He was sure there was a clue somewhere that he had missed.

Three hours later, Tenaida finished checking the computer system. After recording the intruder's program for further analysis, he erased it from the computer's memory. With the system cleared, Scott reactivated the bypassed circuits. Brady ran the diagnostics program on the navigation units a last time, then left to complete the ship's course corrections from the bridge.

Tenaida called Kirk's quarters. Several seconds passed before a sleepy voice answered.

"I am sorry to disturb you at this hour, Captain, but I have the report on the intruder's course-changing program."

"Come up immediately."

By the time Tenaida reached the captain's quarters, Kirk had struggled into a rumpled uniform and combed his hair into a semblance of neatness. Nevertheless, he still looked half asleep.

"What have you got?"

Tenaida gave him the program to read. Kirk dropped the tape into the computer and scanned through the file. "Just like the other one?" he asked finally.

"Similar. The program was assembled from pieces of the ship's standard operating routines. The person had to interpret what each program module did, but he did not have to be able to write the code. Once I determined that, I had no trouble deactivating the program without setting off the booby traps. However, it took some time to be sure I had not missed any subroutines before I purged the program."

"You got it all?"

"Yes."

"Good. Our next step is to catch the intruder. Do you have any ideas for doing that?"

Tenaida frowned, his eyebrows forming a dark line across his face. As yet, he had seen no clear pattern to the spy's behavior. "I have no practical suggestions at the moment."

"I keep thinking I'm missing something terribly obvious." Kirk sighed, feeling a weariness that had nothing to do with the late hour. He had never been good at waiting, had always preferred action. This inactivity—this vigil for a hostile intruder to become overconfident and make a careless mistake—was testing his patience to the limit. "If you come up with any ideas, let me know."

"Of course, Captain." Tenaida pulled the tape from the computer. He wanted to study the program for any clues that might help identify the spy.

Kristiann Norris looked away from her computer screen. It was almost two in the morning. Her stomach growled. She stood, stretching her cramped back muscles. *That much hard work deserves a reward,* she thought. She put the computer on standby and left the room.

The corridor was dimly lit, simulating a planet's night. The reduced illumination cast intriguing light and shadow patterns on the walls and left many of the doors in patches of darkness.

In the recreation lounge, she paused before the selector panel, debating with herself. Finally, she entered the override code Captain Kirk had shown her and ordered a large fudge sundae with all the trimmings. When the panel opened, Norris stared at the result—the sundae was positively huge! A couple of such concoctions a month would add padding to anyone's waistline.

Grinning to herself, Norris picked up the tray. Several people were on the other side of the room, and

Norris felt a twinge of guilt over such an extravagant indulgence. She would feel less self-conscious eating in a more private location.

She was halfway to her cabin when she heard a door open. A familiar figure slipped out of a room ahead of her. Norris stepped into the shadows, hoping Simons would not see her. The other woman seemed more concerned with acting like she belonged outside the Kaldorni's quarters at two in the morning than she was with looking for observers.

Norris did not move until Simons was out of sight. She checked which cabin Simons had come from, then hurried to her own quarters. While she was eating her sundae, her mind was trying to answer the question: what was Simons doing in t'Stror's cabin at two in the morning?

Chapter Seven

KIRK'S MIND DRIFTED as Tenaida explained to Brady and Security Chief Chekov how he had analyzed the spy's computer programs. Kirk still felt he was missing an obvious clue, but he could not isolate it. A change in Tenaida's voice brought Kirk's attention back to the discussion.

"After comparing the two programs I was given last night, I have concluded that they were assembled by different people."

Kirk had not expected that. "Explain," he ordered.

"The programming styles differ considerably. Whoever constructed the course change program was much less familiar with the workings of our computer system."

"Does this mean we have a second spy aboard?"

"I don't know. The spy could have brought both programs aboard with him. Most of those code blocks are standard throughout the Federation. The programs themselves need not have been assembled on the *Enterprise*—only the passcodes are unique to this ship."

"That figures. Have you determined where those course changes would take us yet?"

"No. The vectors are still too random. The probability is only 62.9 percent that the closest planet to the projected intersection point is the intended destination. However, I found something disturbing, given the ship's present assignment."

"Which is—?"

"When I added the vector from last night's course change, the planet Yagra IV was fifth on the list of probable destinations."

"It was?" Kirk asked, not liking the cold premonition Tenaida's words invoked. When he looked at Brady and Chekov, he realized they were sharing the bad feeling. *Disturbing* is an understatement."

The intercom sounded and the captain reached for the control switch. "Kirk here."

"Dr. McCoy wants to see you in Sickbay when you're free. He also asked for Lieutenant Tenaida, if he's available," Communications Specialist Palmer's voice said.

"Did he say why?"

"No, sir, he didn't."

"All right, Ensign. Tell him we'll be there shortly. Kirk out."

Kirk turned to his security chief. "What's your report on protecting the ship's vital areas, Mr. Chekov?"

"I have people stationed at all the key stations—Engineering, Auxiliary Control, the central computer area, and Environmental Services—everything. Also, I have men roving all the corridors. Everyone in Security has been warned to expect double shifts until we settle this." The sound of Chekov's voice, more heavily accented than usual, seemed to hang in the air even after he had finished speaking.

"That sounds good to me. Mr. Brady, is there anything else we should do?"

Brady shook his head. "As much as it pains me to say it, Captain, I can't think of anything more. I'll let you know if I do."

"In that case, I'll see what McCoy wants." Kirk stood and led the other three men from the room.

Joachim Montoya paged through Kris Norris' report a second time. "Those numbers pretty well prove someone's been lying to us. What does the translation say?"

Norris ruffled her short brown hair, wondering if she should admit she had already translated the recordings. Montoya's question implied that he assumed she had. "I got some pretty interesting results from the transcripts. Unfortunately, my equipment seems to be going sour, but the sense of the discussions is clear."

"Let's have it."

Norris slid another tape into her computer. Although she could have used the *Enterprise*'s system, Norris preferred her own equipment, since it already had the software she needed for her work. "I copied the most interesting parts, but we can go over everything, if you wish."

Montoya shook his head. "I'd like to see what Ambassador Klee told Speaker t'Stror before he left the other afternoon."

"I figured that." The screen filled with the images of the Kaldorni ambassador and his assistant. Norris switched the audio output through the Universal Translator. An apparent malfunction was giving t'Stror a low, guttural, but definitely feminine, voice. Ambassador Klee's voice was unaffected. Montoya concentrated on the computer's translation of their words.

"Can they not be made to understand the importance of preserving the Harmony of the Universe?" Klee asked. "In so many ways, I have difficulty in comprehending how they can act when they seem so far from the Center of Balance. Tell me, my Speaker, should we have asked to converse with a different representative, one who is not so contaminated by the Hot-Fire-Woman? I do not know how to communicate my thoughts to this Black-Silver-Man."

Montoya pushed the *Stop* button. "Hot-Fire-Woman? Black-Silver-Man?"

"Proper names, I think. The translator had fits over them. My guess is 'Black-Silver-Man' is you, because of your clothes. But I don't know what the other name means."

Montoya reactivated the computer.

"My ambassador has great patience," t'Stror said. "The Federation commissioner is like a child who must be shown the Ways of Harmony. But like a child, often he does not want what is right and so must be punished in order that he will learn."

The ambassador raised his right shoulder in negation. "One may punish one's own children to guide them in the paths of Correctness. But it is not permitted to discipline the dependents of another being. This creates more Disharmony than the original actions of the child."

"My ambassador is wise in all things. I request that I may be punished for my discordant suggestions."

"If one learns from a mistake, discipline is not necessary. Correction is needful only when the offense is repeated."

"Your forbearance does you honor, my ambassador."

A Kaldorni entered the room. Klee listened to his message, then turned back to t'Stror. "There is illness among my wives. They request that I attend the youngest and lend her strength to combat the disunity. It is necessary for me to perform the purification rituals so that she may be receptive to the medicines. I desire that you remain here and instruct the Federation commissioner in the ways of That-Which-Is. We cannot continue with these discussions until understanding exists between our two peoples."

"I hear your wishes, my ambassador, and will

126

comply." t'Stror bowed his head and extended his wrist. The farewell gesture was made to Klee's back as the ambassador hurried from the room, flanked by his honor guard.

Montoya stared at the screen, chewing on his lower lip. "There's a significant difference between that conversation and what t'Stror claimed his instructions were. Are you sure the malfunction didn't change the translation?"

"I don't think so. The problem appears to affect only the voice assignment circuits. However, when I was getting the transcripts, Captain Kirk said his science officer might have some specialized analysis programs. I thought I'd check that out."

"The Deltan? I don't know. Most of Starfleet's high-level analysis programs are Vulcan. But if he has something useful, see if it will help."

"I'll check it out right away."

"All right, Christine. What's the emergency?" McCoy was still tugging his blue tunic into place as he entered Sickbay.

Dr. Christine Chapel pointed toward McCoy's office. "I'm not sure, but I didn't think you should keep him waiting."

A short, wide figure in nondescript brown robes sat with his back to the door. The Kaldorni turned when McCoy entered the room.

"Ambassador Klee," he said with surprise. "This is an honor. How may I help you?"

Klee inclined his head in an off-center nod. "The doctor McCoy is too kind to one who is humbled to beg as the lowest no-caste. There is illness among my wives, and I have not the skills to perform the rituals correctly and remove the disharmony so that they may be healed. It is felt by my wives that the discord would be less for me to beg you to attempt your methods of healing than that my failure should cause the death of my mates."

McCoy tried to interpret Klee's actions in terms of his culture. By abandoning his jewelry and talking to McCoy and Chapel, Klee demonstrated the status he had lost when he failed to cure his wives by traditional Kaldorni methods. McCoy reached for his tricorder. "Mr. Ambassador, is it all right to examine your wives now?"

"If there were any objection, I would not be here, honored doctor."

"My mistake. Would you escort me to your quarters?"

The Kaldorni were one deck up from Sickbay. Klee was silent while he led McCoy to the quarters. They entered the rooms, and for a moment McCoy thought the environmental controls had malfunctioned. The temperature was almost as hot as the ship's sauna. "That pointy-eared Vulcan would enjoy this," he muttered to himself.

Five women were in the sleeping area, with three of them trying to assist the two on the beds. McCoy heard someone vomiting in the bathroom.

McCoy activated the tricorder. When the women moved away from the beds, the shimmering of their colorful, full gowns resembled the rainbow flash of butterfly wings. Even in their quarters, the women wore veils.

The woman on the nearest bed was curled into a tight ball around the cramping pains in her stomach. Her forehead was filmed with perspiration, but her body shivered violently under the blankets that covered her.

McCoy passed his tricorder over the woman and frowned at the readings. He repeated the scan and then tried a different woman. His frown deepened when he got similar readings on the second patient. "Mr. Ambassador, I need to move your wives to Sickbay so I can treat them properly."

The Kaldorni argued briefly in their own language.

When Klee turned back to McCoy, he had shrunk several inches into himself. "It is the wish of my wives that we do whatever you believe is necessary. The one among them who is most skilled in the medical arts was the first to become ill."

McCoy went to the intercom and called for help to move the patients. As their co-wives helped them onto the stretchers, Klee asked McCoy, "What is it you fear may be the cause of this discordant event?"

"I need to run some tests, but I think they ate some contaminated food. It would be best if your people don't eat anything until I check it out."

"All our food since we arrived has come from the preparation facilities of this ship. We have not noticed anything discordant."

"I'll have the dietitian check the synthesizer program again. Perhaps one of our standard food bases contains a trace element your race is unusually sensitive to." McCoy tried to put more reassurance in his tone than he felt. It was not likely that Jenavi Leftwell had made such a mistake.

"One of my aides is skilled in the nutritional requirements of our people. I will require that he advise you on the appropriateness of the ingredients for your synthesizer."

"Thank you, Mr. Ambassador. That would be a great help. If you'll excuse me, I'll go treat your wives." When Klee nodded, McCoy followed the stretchers from the room.

The diagnostic equipment in Sickbay confirmed McCoy's fears. Several trace minerals highly toxic to Kaldorni metabolism were present in the women's bodies. Even worse, most of the standard antidotes were almost as deadly. McCoy finally found a scavenger to remove the toxins from the Kaldorni's systems, but it worked much slower than he liked. He ordered the lab to prepare the counteragent, sent for Captain Kirk, and then bounced between his patients, checking their monitors and life support equipment, until the medicine was delivered. He was injecting the third woman when Kirk and Tenaida arrived. McCoy pointed to his office, followed the others inside, and threw himself into his chair.

"What is it, Bones?"

"I've got three of the Kaldorni ambassador's wives in intensive care. Food contamination."

"Poison?" Kirk asked. "How?"

"The ambassador said everything they've eaten came from the ship's synthesizers."

Tenaida's forehead wrinkled. "I assisted Lieutenant Leftwell with the Kaldorni's diet program. We checked it several times to exclude all deleterious materials from the ingredients list."

"One of the ambassador's aides is helping Jenavi look for anything that might have been missed," McCoy said.

Kirk shot a worried look at the Deltan. "Tenaida, would you help them? If anyone on this ship can translate glitchy computer code, it's you."

Tenaida rose. "Will you excuse me, Doctor?"

"Good luck, Tenaida." McCoy looked over at Kirk, seeing the grim set of his mouth. "You don't think this is accidental, Jim."

"Do you?"

McCoy hesitated. "It could be. The program might have called for the wrong base."

"But you don't think so, either."

The captain's uneasiness solidified the ugly suspicions McCoy had been suppressing since he had seen the first readings on the Kaldorni women. Finally, he acknowledged his concern. "No. I don't think it's an accident."

"Unless Tenaida can prove otherwise, I'd say our friend has struck again. You'd better examine all the Kaldorni to make sure they're not affected."

"Right away, Captain."

While McCoy checked his patients in Intensive Care, Kirk was planning what to say to Ambassador Klee. He needed to convince him he would suffer no further loss of status if he allowed McCoy to examine the entire Kaldorni delegation.

"Well, Tenaida, what's the story?" Kirk, leaning over the Deltan's shoulder, watched the lines of code march across the monitor. Tenaida and Leftwell had been working on the Kaldorni's nutrition schedule for over an hour.

"The food synthesizers were reprogrammed. Someone inserted subroutines that add trace amounts of toxins to the formulas for certain foods. When those foods are chosen, the subroutines are activated."

"I see. How did this happen?"

Tenaida called up a block of code. His cipher headed the listing.

Kirk scowled, even though the spy's choice had a feeling of inevitability about it. "I expected that. What else can you say about the thing?"

Tenaida leaned back in his chair and steepled his fingers to cover the lower half of his face. "I believe the person who did this also wrote the program for the vari-grav control unit. There are similarities in the coding style, and both programs indicate a disregard for the lives of other sentient beings."

"What about the course change program? Was it written by the same person?"

"I would say not. Of course, three programs are not a large enough sample to support a definitive judgment."

"I hope you *don't* get a large enough sample. Can you do something to keep our friend—or friends— out of the computer?"

"I'll work on it. The problem is to restrict unauthorized access to the computer without interfering with the ship's operations. Also, we don't know where these ciphers were obtained. The spy could have cracked the ship's data banks, but other possibilities exist."

"It would take a sophisticated codekey-breaking program to get that information from our computer."

Tenaida added nothing, waiting for Kirk to make the obvious inferences about the situation.

"The other possibility is even worse. Anyone with Starfleet's overrides to our computer system has access to a lot of privileged material."

"Agreed." Tenaida turned off the console and rose. "With your permission, I'll be in my quarters working on a way to prevent further unauthorized computer use."

"Of course, Lieutenant. Get Commander Layton to run your clearances for the command areas."

They stepped into the corridor and almost collided with Kristiann Norris. "There you are, Jim. I've been looking all over for you." She looked from Kirk to Tenaida, trying to decide to whom she should make her request. "I wanted to see if I could ask *Shan* Tenaida to borrow his analysis programs. My computer system has developed a glitch and I need to double-check its translations."

"Tenaida is busy right now." Kirk glanced at the Deltan and received a confirming nod. It was symbolic of his day so far that Norris would come to collect on his offer just after he had given the Deltan a critical assignment. "I'm afraid he has a project that can't wait."

Tenaida took a step forward and faced Kirk. "If it's acceptable, there is another person who could assist. Lieutenant Janara Whitehorse has considerable training with the Vulcan analysis programs that Ms. Norris will need, and she is more familiar with the linguistic applications of the programs than I am."

"Could she do it?" Kirk tried to remember what project Janara was working on, and whether McCoy had certified her fit for duty yet. If Janara could work on the translation problem, he would be able to keep his promise to Norris.

"You will have to ask her," Tenaida said. "I do not know the outcome of her last talk with Dr. McCoy."

"I'll see if she feels like tackling the problem," Kirk said. "That is, if it's all right with you, Kris."

"I don't know." Norris ruffled the back of her short brown hair. "What are her qualifications?"

Kirk smiled. "She knows as much about Vulcan programming methods as Tenaida."

Tenaida lifted his eyebrow in imitation of Spock's favorite gesture. "Indeed, she may know more. She studied at the Vulcan Academy of Sciences for three semesters."

Kirk gave Norris a how-can-we-argue-with-that look. "Lieutenant Whitehorse also speaks twenty or thirty languages. And she's good at keeping her mouth shut."

"She sounds ideal. If she'll do the job, I have no objections."

Kirk went to the intercom to locate Janara.

Cecilia Simons waited for the communications officer to appear in the recreation room for lunch. Palmer's noon relief was young and impressionable; Simons knew she would have no trouble holding his attention while Montoya's dispatches were being transmitted. When Palmer sat down, Simons headed for the bridge.

She checked the duty personnel when she entered. Neither Kirk nor his first officer were present, but she recognized the navigator and the communications trainee. She went up to the officer in the command chair and gave her a small, bewildered smile. "Excuse me. My husband, Commissioner Montoya, asked me to bring his dispatches up here and see that they were sent out. Whom should I talk to about that?"

"Ensign Peretz will help you." The short, stocky woman pointed to the Communications station. Her expression said, as clearly as if she had spoken, what she thought of unescorted civilians on the bridge.

"Thank you very much," Simons said in a small, meek voice. She glided across the room and gave the young trainee a smile calculated to melt three-meter armor plate. "Are you the communications officer?"

"Uh, yes, uh, I mean, no, I mean, uh, yes, I'm the officer on duty," he stammered, flustered at being the focus of her interest.

"Could you send my husband's dispatches for me?" She held out a data cassette. "I promised to do it first thing this morning, and he's going to be *so* upset that I didn't get it done until now."

Peretz glanced at his activity board. "I can send it right away." He dropped the tape into a slot, scanned the authorization codes, and pushed the transmit switch.

"You must have such an exciting job." Simons' voice was low and breathy.

Peretz twisted in his chair to see her better. "It's not really, when you do it all the time. But it's an important job, because every message to or from the ship passes through this station." He gave her a shy smile. "I think communications is the most important job on the *Enterprise,* because we keep people in touch with each other."

"You must know everything that happens on the entire ship. That makes you the most important person on it, and that has to be exciting." Over his shoulder, Simons watched the codes flicker across the readout panel.

"I guess it does seem exciting—if you look at it that way." The computer beeped to signal the transmission was complete. Peretz removed the tape and handed it to Simons with a diffident smile. "I hope your husband isn't too upset. In the future, I'd be honored to send more dispatches for him."

Simons rewarded him with another sultry smile. "If I tell him how efficient you were, *Lieutenant,* perhaps he'll forgive my carelessness." She glided out the door before Peretz could stammer a response to his sudden, unofficial promotion.

Kris Norris was not sure what she expected when Kirk told her another person on the *Enterprise* knew as much as Tenaida about Vulcan programming, but the small, silent woman Kirk introduced was not it. Janara listened to Norris' description of her problem, asked a few probing questions, and began calling programs from the main computer banks.

Norris watched with something approaching awe as Janara alternated between running specialized diagnostic routines through the portable unit and extracting data for the ship's computer to analyze. Although she knew the reputations of some of the Federation's best computer people, Norris had never watched a first-class operator at work.

After an hour, Janara recorded her results and switched off the computer. She gave the tape to Norris. "The *Enterprise*'s computer pulled some additional information from the transcripts that confirms your translation to 95 percent. There's nothing wrong with your machine."

"What? It gave one of Ambassador Klee's aides a female voice. That can't be right."

"The diagnostic programs show your equipment is within specifications. I couldn't find any programming errors."

"Then why does it give Speaker t'Stror a female voice?"

"I would suggest you ask Speaker t'Stror."

"Ask—?" Norris' voice rose in shock. Given the Kaldorni reticence about discussing most aspects of their culture and physiology, Norris could imagine t'Stror's reaction if she asked for a direct explanation of the anomaly. "Are you serious? Do you know how touchy the Kaldorni are when we ask about their private lives?"

Janara shrugged. "The problem is not in your equipment. Therefore, I cannot explain the female voice. If you wish to know about Speaker t'Stror, the logical course of action is to ask the object of your curiosity.

"However, if you do not believe he will respond favorably to your queries, then I must assume the riddle will remain unsolved." Janara swept a loose strand of hair off her forehead and tucked it behind her ear. For a moment, the sharp, pale lines of the implant scars were uncovered.

Norris stared at the lock of dark hair that covered the telltale scars. Suddenly, her mind identified the almost subliminal musky scent that had been bothering her for the last hour. "You're Deltan," she said in surprise, forgetting her previous train of thought.

Janara's mouth twisted into a humorless smile. "That's hardly a secret."

"But your name is of Earth origin."

"Many people have names that originated on Earth," Janara said evenly.

"But Deltans don't adopt human names. I mean, do they?" Most Deltans used one-word names that, Norris had been told, were equivalent to human nicknames. Deltan calling names were often taken from common plants or animals, since their formal names were too long and complex for most outsiders to remember or pronounce. Norris noticed the tension in Janara's posture. "I'm sorry. I didn't mean to pry. Please, forget I mentioned it."

Janara took two deep, slow breaths. "If I said my family history was somewhat varied, would you leave it at that?"

"Of course. I didn't mean to move in where I don't belong," Kris added quickly. "You said your analysis programs found additional information in the transcripts. Do you suppose I could add those programs to my system?"

The tension left Janara's posture. She doodled a pattern on the table top with her finger, using the lines to tally her programs. Finally, she shook her head. "I could copy a couple of them for you. However, most of them are coded in Vulcan symbology, and your unit doesn't have the capacity to run them with the conversion program. I might be able to design a program package for a larger machine, but I'd need authorization—"

She stiffened suddenly and screamed in agony, clamping her hands around her skull. As Norris watched in bewilderment, Janara stumbled to the intercom and groped for the control pad.

"Bridge. Palmer here."

"Red alert, code Alpha-One. Emergency—in Auxiliary Control," Janara gasped. "Armed security team. And medics."

Then she fainted.

"Well, Marg, what do you think now?" Kirk leaned back in his chair and studied the face of his longtime friend. Layton had never been pretty, but her strength of character attracted attention in situations where physical beauty would have been overlooked. Now, in the privacy of Kirk's quarters, the records officer's face showed the strain of the last few days.

She must be pulling double shifts trying to keep her eye on everything, Kirk thought with a surge of gratitude. A commanding officer could not ask for a more loyal or dedicated officer than Marg Layton. "Have you seen anything that would rule out any of our suspects?"

Layton toyed with her coffee cup, watching the bitter liquid swirl around the sides. "Nothing, Captain. Less than nothing. What I have seen makes things even more confusing." She gulped down her coffee and refilled the cup from the carafe on the worktable. "All those programs with Tenaida's code on them. Every time I look at one of them, I *know* he's guilty. Then I look again, and it's obvious that's exactly what I'm supposed to think.

"No person in his right mind would cobble up such a program, and then sign his name to it. So if Tenaida did do it, then the mind control theory is the only possible explanation. But watching him, I haven't seen any evidence for that, either. I'd think he'd at least show occasional mental lapses or momentary confusion. But I've seen nothing like that. And the same thing with Brady—I can't find anything that would suggest the intruder has had any mental contact whatsoever with him."

Kirk nodded. "I've tried to keep them working with other people as much as possible since—well, since this started happening. And nobody else has reported anything unusual, either."

"I've been checking the computer's work logs as you suggested, to see if someone is stealing data from our system to run a biofabricator. None of the crew has suddenly increased computer usage, but some of our guests have been fairly busy, for whatever that's worth." Layton shrugged. "I don't have anything for comparisons, so I don't know what is appropriate for them. It could just mean they need the computer time to do their jobs properly."

"Has the commissioner's wife done much with the computer?" Kirk had to fight to keep his tone casual.

Layton thought for a moment. "Actually, no. The only files she appears to have accessed were some entertainment tapes."

"Damn! I was hoping she'd do something I could trace back to her."

"Then you still consider her a suspect?"

The intercom whistled, interrupting Kirk's reply. He thumbed on the viewer. "Captain, Alpha-One priority emergency in Auxiliary Control."

"On my way." Kirk raced from the room.

* * *

Kirk arrived at Auxiliary Control just behind the security reinforcements that Chekov had ordered. When he saw the phaser rifles the men carried, a touch of fear crawled down his back. He entered the room and immediately wished he had stayed outside.

The remains of the guard who had been posted in the room were spread across the control consoles, and blood splattered the surrounding floor for a ten-meter radius. Ensign Yendes's torso had been slashed—as if by long, sharp knives—and his throat ripped out. Kirk had dealt with death many times in the past, but this was far more gruesome than he was accustomed to seeing. He left quickly, and bumped into McCoy as the doctor arrived.

"Bones, can you tell me when he died?" Kirk jerked his thumb toward the corpse. "And also anything about the—weapon—that did it?"

McCoy looked over Kirk's shoulder and his expression turned grim. He gulped, nodded, and made his way to the body. Kirk walked down the corridor a few steps and leaned against the wall, trying to keep out of the way. Opposite him, two crewmen were examining the floor with tricorders, looking for any traces of blood that the murderer might have tracked from the room.

After several minutes, McCoy joined Kirk. "He's been dead only a few minutes, Jim. I'm surprised Security didn't catch the killer in the act."

"That short a time?"

"Yes. How did Chekov get here so fast?"

"Someone called in an Alpha-One, but the intercom was dead when Palmer switched back for details. She's looking for the caller now. What can you tell me about the killer?"

"I'll do a complete autopsy when Security gets through recording the mess, but as a first guess, I haven't a clue. I'm just an old country doctor, Jim." McCoy shook his head in bewilderment. "Those cuts are deep and clean, almost like they'd been made with an old-time surgeon's scalpel. But at the same time, they're all parallel, like claw marks from a giant cat. Though anything with claws long enough to do that much damage would have to be one hellaciously big monster."

"I'll buy the *hellacious,* Bones, but if that kind of a beast was on this ship, we'd know it. You're going to have to tell us what the killer *really* used."

"Yes, Captain." McCoy leaned against the wall, looking grim and, for a moment, old. It had been a long time since he had seen a man so spread out by a murderer.

Tenaida's voice, low and questioning, came from down the corridor. Janara Whitehorse answered him at length and in Deltan. Kirk looked toward them. Janara's movements were unsteady, and at first Kirk thought Tenaida had an arm around her waist. The captain blinked, and when he reopened his eyes, he decided the illusion had been created by his angle of view. Given the standard Deltan oath of celibacy, he did not think Tenaida would have allowed himself to become involved with Janara in the short time they had known each other. And given Janara's background, he thought she'd be reluctant to trust anyone.

Janara saw the crowd in the corridor. Her knees buckled and she slid to the floor. "They weren't in time, were they?"

Tenaida met Kirk's questioning look. "*Shan* Janara received mental images of a predatory animal attacking the crewman in Auxiliary Control. She insisted on reporting to you."

"You put in the Alpha-One?" Kirk asked.

Janara nodded. She slumped against the wall, pressing her hands against her forehead. Alarmed, McCoy passed his tricorder over the small half-Deltan.

"Blasted machine," the doctor muttered. "Readings don't show anything wrong. Lieutenant Whitehorse—Janara, can you hear me?"

Janara nodded again.

"What's wrong?"

"The—the body." Her whisper was hoarse. After several seconds, she added something in a Deltan dialect that had an unusual rhythm to its sentences.

Tenaida translated. "She says she feels the reactions of everyone who has seen the body. That they are too strong to block out."

Kirk looked from Janara to McCoy. "Get her out of here, Bones. You can't do anything in there, anyway."

McCoy helped Janara to her feet. Janara swayed, too disoriented to keep her balance. McCoy had to support her as they started for the turbolift.

"She's a strong telepath?" Kirk asked. A glimmer of an idea was forming in the back of his mind.

"Her talents are formidable, but she is largely self-trained. Her gifts are more of a liability than an asset."

Kirk stared at the Deltan, wondering if Tenaida had guessed his thoughts. Before he could pursue the matter, the intercom whistled. He reached for the pad.

"Kirk here."

"Captain, the ship has just altered course to 124 mark 5. And our speed is increasing to warp eight."

"Source of change?"

"The ship's navigational controls are being overridden from Auxiliary Control."

"All right. I'll handle it from here. Kirk out." Angrily, he slammed his fist against the switch in frustration.

The security team was still recording the scene in Auxiliary Control and examining the surrounding area for clues. Even if he had wanted to face the mess, Kirk knew he could not risk disturbing the evidence. Canceling the intruder's course change would have to wait until Security finished their work.

"How soon will you be through?" Kirk asked Chekov.

"It will take us about fifteen minutes to finish our work, Captain."

"Make it less. The spy reprogrammed the ship's course again, and I need Brady and Tenaida in there to undo his handiwork."

Chekov checked with his men. "They can get in here in five minutes, if they don't mind working here before we finish our investigation and clean all the blood off the equipment."

Tenaida glanced inside the room, but his face showed no reaction to the body. "I'll do my best not to interfere with your work, Lieutenant."

Chekov went back inside Auxiliary Control. Relieved to turn his back on the gruesome scene, Kirk went to the intercom to call Brady to help Tenaida remove the intruder's latest program from the computer system.

As the turbolift door opened on Deck Seven and the doctor stepped out, Janara pulled away from McCoy's supporting arm. "I don't need to go with you to Sickbay, Doctor. I'll go to my quarters now."

"You're coming to Sickbay for an examination. You almost collapsed back there, and I want to know why."

"I told you *why,* Doctor. Now if you don't mind—" She stepped backward into the car, but McCoy, anticipating her escape attempt, stood in the door to keep it from closing.

"I most certainly do mind. *I* am the doctor here, and I'll decide what you are fit to do."

Janara squared her shoulders in rigid defiance. Before she could reply, Christine Chapel came out of the research lab. McCoy beckoned to her. "Lieutenant Whitehorse won't let me examine her. How do you convince Deltans to follow their doctor's orders?"

"Generally, Deltans don't ignore their doctors unless they have a very keen internal awareness." Chapel gave Janara a questioning look. "Are you sure you're not physically injured?"

Janara gathered her strength for a reply. "I am

suffering from what is called *lyr'yial*. It's a form of psychic overload, most often found among healers who have overworked their mental powers. The standard cure is rest and meditation."

McCoy looked unconvinced. "You're not a doctor and you can't be certain of your diagnosis. I had to practically carry you into the elevator, and I want to know that you aren't seriously ill. I've never seen anything like this in all the time I've been practicing medicine."

Chapel looked from the doctor to the small, stubborn Deltan in the turbolift. "Well, Doctor, if you insist, I'll sedate her, and we can drag her into Sickbay. But I'm not sure it will give you the answers you want. Why don't you just require a checkup before her next duty shift?"

McCoy scowled at Janara. The small Deltan returned the look with the patience of someone who knew she could outwait her opponent. Finally McCoy stepped clear of the door. "Until you get a thorough physical, I'm logging you as medically unfit for duty."

"Understood." Janara's voice carried an unmistakable note of triumph. The elevator door closed before McCoy could say anything more.

"Did you have to contradict me in front of her?" McCoy made no effort to keep the anger out of his voice.

"I'm sorry, Doctor." Chapel looked neither apologetic nor particularly worried about McCoy's temper. "You asked for my help."

Chapel's calmness was not improving his mood any. Sometimes he wondered if he should quit Starfleet permanently and go into veterinary medicine. At least his patients wouldn't be able to argue with him about proper treatment.

Chapel continued in a mild tone. "Would you like the latest report on the Kaldorni's condition?"

"Let's have it," he said, glad for the change of subject.

"The women in Intensive Care are stable. The scavengers are working against the toxins, but haven't produced major improvements yet. The lab says they'll have a true antidote ready in another hour.

"One of the ambassador's aides just came in with a mild case, and the lab tests show small amounts of toxic metal complexes in all the Kaldorni's bodies. We've started them on the scavengers to neutralize the poisons."

"I leave you here while I handle an emergency, and when I come back, all my problems are solved." McCoy gave Chapel an affectionate smile. He was lucky to have her. Her experience was greater than many planet-bound physicians McCoy knew, and he wondered how long it would be before she would accept a transfer to head up her own medical department. He glanced at his chronometer. "The medical emergency is over, and you're not supposed to be on duty until later. If you have something you'd like to do . . ."

Chapel shook her head. "I'd rather try to help the lab finish the antidote. I haven't had a chance to work on this type of problem since I left Nylara."

"As you wish." McCoy scowled. "I'd prefer that to preparing for this autopsy. That killer, whatever it was, left a gruesome mess." With that protest made, the doctor headed for the operating room-turned-morgue to check his equipment. He wanted to finish this particular autopsy as fast as he could.

Kirk dropped into his chair and waited for the rest of the somber group to find places around his cabin. Brady and Tenaida took the chairs by the worktable, while McCoy sat on the bed next to Layton. Chekov stood by the door, poised as if to respond to any threat. Kirk studied their faces while they settled in. Both Brady and Tenaida looked the way Kirk felt: mentally exhausted from trying to outthink the spy,

144

nervous from wondering where the intruder would strike next, and weighted by revulsion at the gruesome murder of the security guard.

Anger was McCoy's dominant reaction. His job was to fight death, and the killer had given him no chance. Chekov appeared unaffected, but Kirk knew only strict discipline and the desire to live up to the responsibilities of his new position kept the security chief from looking as disturbed as the rest of the group.

"All right, people. We need answers. Chekov, what's your report?"

"We have found almost nothing so far, Captain. The intruder walked through the door as if it were standing open, attacked Ensign Yendes, reprogrammed the computer, and then walked out again. Yendes did not fire his phaser or call for assistance. It is as if he did not think he was in any danger.

"We have followed the killer's trail as far as the turbolift on that level. He took the turbolift to Deck Six, where he got out near the recreation lounge. No one there saw anything unusual, and we have not been able to trace him after that."

"A pretty cool customer," Brady said.

Kirk nodded. "He isn't worried about being noticed."

"May I suggest something, Captain?"

"What, Tenaida?"

"I could program the intercoms in the turbolift to record the voice patterns of everyone who uses them. Also, we could tie scanners into the intercoms to monitor personnel movements."

Kirk scowled. Spying on his crew went against the grain, but until they identified the intruder, recording every movement and searching the records for anomalies seemed their best hope of catching the spy. "All right, Tenaida. I don't like the idea, but I don't have a better one. When this briefing is over, get together with Commander Scott and tell him what you've got in mind. But monitor only the heavy traffic areas.

"By the way, why did the scanner in Auxiliary Control let the spy get past it?"

"You're not going to like it, Captain," Brady said.

"I already don't like it. Why don't you tell me what it is that I don't like?"

Brady and Tenaida looked at each other, trying to decide who should answer the question. Finally Brady spoke. "When he entered and when he left, the scanner identified the person as Captain James T. Kirk."

"Oh." For a moment, Kirk saw the room through a red haze. He took two deep, slow breaths to calm himself. When he could speak without swearing, he said, "While you're fixing scanners, Tenaida, fix that one, too! Mind-control theory or not, I wasn't in Auxiliary Control. And no impostor should be able to create a disguise that will pass a maximum security check. So find out how the intruder managed to trick that scanner!"

"Yes, Captain."

Layton straightened abruptly. "That's it! The spy has finally made a mistake!" A brief grin of triumph crossed her face. "This time, when the intruder used the captain's identity, we know exactly where Captain Kirk was. He was with me, in this room, discussing our problem. This eliminates the mind-control hypothesis because Captain Kirk couldn't have been in Auxiliary Control at the same time."

Brady heaved a sigh of relief. "That means none of us is a suspect anymore."

"Or at least it substantially reduces the probability that any of us is guilty." Tenaida also sounded relieved.

"How good was the intruder's disguise?" Kirk asked. "Have you run an identity check on the scanner images?"

Brady nodded. "About 80 percent. Similar to the original recordings. The intruder must have a pretty sophisticated setup to be able to produce disguises that consistently score that high a correspondence. I don't know how he's managing to hide his power and materials consumption from our computer searches."

"Keep after it. Something has to break soon." Kirk turned to McCoy. "Doctor, what did your autopsy show?"

"Not a lot we didn't already know." McCoy scowled and tried to avoid meeting the captain's look.

"Yes?" Kirk prompted.

"The body appeared to have been mauled by a large animal—a saber-toothed cat or something similar. But I examined those slash marks very closely. They were too clean to have been made by any animal I've ever heard of. Also, the lab found traces of a strong, fast-acting neurotoxin in the body. Apparently, it was injected with the first attack. It would have paralyzed Yendes before he could respond to the murderer."

"Dr. McCoy, are you saying the killer was or was not a predatory animal?" Brady asked.

"I don't know what the killer was, Mr. Brady. But those 'claws' were too sharp for any animal recorded in our library banks. The cuts were clean enough to have been made with a scalpel."

"Doctor, is that all your autopsy turned up?" Kirk struggled to keep the disappointment out of his voice. He had hoped McCoy would find something definite.

"'Fraid so, Captain. There wasn't a lot left to look at."

Kirk grimaced, remembering what the body had looked like. Pushing that thought away, he turned to his science officer. "Tenaida, what about the latest course-changing program?"

"The content and programming method resemble the other course-change program. Also, the coordinates put us in the same region as the previous changes. I had the computer extrapolate the most likely destinations, but there wasn't any significant change over the last projection."

"That in itself is significant, isn't it?"

"Probably. But that doesn't give us any useful information."

"No useful information!" McCoy's pale eyes flashed with anger. "The science officer's job is to come up with *useful* information. Dammit, that thing's killing our people, and you take as long as that pointy-eared Vulcan to reach a conclusion!"

"Enough, Bones. Tenaida is working as hard as anyone to settle this. Does anyone else have a suggestion?" Kirk looked around, but no one said anything. "Tenaida, what's your progress on keeping the intruder out of our computers?"

"I was working on a double-code entry to restrict access to the system when the spy broke into Auxiliary Control. After seeing that, I would recommend more stringent controls than we originally discussed."

"What do you have in mind?"

"That you block all access to the ship's computers. Clear each person for only those programs needed for the work."

Kirk nodded. "That might do it. But how do we sell it?"

"Could we say there's a malfunction in the computer's junction processor? That we've lost primary connections to the working memory until repairs are completed?" Brady's voice, uncertain at first, lost its tentative tone as the idea solidified. "We could say we're relocating programs into storage sectors that aren't affected by the problem and rerouting the access linkages to accommodate the difficulty."

Kirk turned the idea over in his mind, looking for objections. "It's plausible. I don't think the majority of the crew will argue with it. And we can still use the double-code system to control access to the programs we release."

"We can say the codes are to keep people from overrunning their allotted memory blocks. Then if the intruder *still* gets into the computer, we'll know a lot more about how he's doing it." Brady's voice carried a note of grim satisfaction.

"I'll incorporate a tracer into the double-code program so we can detect anyone trying to break into the system," Tenaida added.

"Do it," Kirk ordered. "I'll make the announcement immediately: restricted computer access until further notice. The crew can report to you to get their programs cleared. Can you get the double-code system operating in an hour?"

"Yes."

Kirk looked around to see if anyone had anything more to say. "Unless there's something else, this briefing is over." He paused, looking at Chekov. "By the way, Mr. Chekov, you'd better double the guards on all posts."

"I have already done so, Captain. I will also have my people work in pairs or groups until we capture the thing that murdered Ensign Yendes."

"Good thinking. We don't want to lose anyone else."

"No, sir. And my people want very much to capture this killer."

"Good. Let's hope they find him soon, Mr. Chekov." Kirk turned to his science officer. "Lieutenant Tenaida, could I talk to you for a minute? The rest of you may return to your posts."

McCoy, Brady, Layton, and Chekov left the room as Tenaida waited patiently for the captain's question.

"Tenaida, I want your reaction to a wild suggestion."

"Yes, Captain?"

"You said Janara Whitehorse was an exceptionally strong telepath. Could she identify the spy if she were in the same room with him?"

"I don't know. She has received images of a preda-

149

tor stalking the ship's corridors since the first night our passengers were aboard. However, her talents are erratic and not always subject to her control."

"Would she try to locate the intruder if I asked her to?"

"Captain, I cannot speak for *Shan* Janara on so personal a matter." His face went expressionless with tension, his dark eyebrows forming harsh lines across his smooth olive skin.

"Speculate," Kirk countered.

"Most telepaths prefer *not* to sense other minds. A deliberate search for the spy would mean intruding on every other mind in the area."

Kirk frowned, puzzled. Like most nontelepaths, he had little understanding of how mind-to-mind communication worked. His only direct exposure to such things was the few times Spock had mind-melded with him. Other forms of telepathy, such as the Deltans' ability to exchange images or the wild-card human abilities such as those possessed by Dr. Miranda Jones, were outside his personal experience. "Explain?"

"We've assumed the spy is either on Commissioner Montoya's negotiating team or in Ambassador Klee's party. To find one guilty individual in either of those groups means there is a large probability of invading the privacy of a number of innocent people."

"Then you think Lieutenant Whitehorse would resist a request to help us find the spy?"

"I cannot say. She has been greatly disturbed by the images she has received. She might agree to assist you because of Ensign Yendes' murder. However, I can't predict her answer."

Kirk allowed himself a frustrated sigh. "Thanks, Tenaida. You'd better get to work on the double-code program." He pushed himself up out of his chair. Then, "But wait, Tenaida . . ." as a sudden thought sent him back to the intercom.

"Palmer, have Lieutenant Chekov send a pair of armed security guards to my quarters."

"Aye, aye, sir." Palmer's voice sounded frazzled. Kirk could almost hear her thought: *Where are we going to find two* more *security people who haven't already pulled double shifts?*

"I don't want our friend attacking you while you're working to keep him out of the computer," Kirk told Tenaida as they waited for the guards to arrive. "So far, the only thing he's been consistent about is catching someone who's alone."

The Deltan nodded. "A wise precaution, since he will know where to find me for some time."

"Unavoidable, I'm afraid. Our people have to use the computer, and the intruder will want in just as badly. The guards should prevent him from trying anything drastic."

"Agreed, Captain."

Kirk instructed the guards that they were not to let Tenaida out of their sight for *any* reason. He had no desire to see the Deltan meet the same fate as the guard in Auxiliary Control.

After Tenaida had left, Kirk activated his computer. "Assistant. Evaluate the probability that a telepathic search would be able to locate the intruder aboard this ship."

"Insufficient information."

"What information do you require to answer the question?"

"Nature of intruder, including race, psychic abilities, mental training, physical condition, and motivation."

"If I knew all that, I wouldn't need a telepath to find him."

"Also require parameters describing nature of search, including safeguards required by Federation law to protect the innocent."

"Safeguards?"

"Federation Code, Section 175, Subsection B (Mental Privacy): The right to mental privacy is an inalienable right of all Federation citizens and shall not be abrogated without due process of law.

"Section 183, Subsection A (Searches and Seizures), Paragraph 5: No law enforcement agent or other person acting in the capacity of a law enforcement agent shall invade or cause to be invaded the mental privacy of any Federation citizen or any other sentient being without first having proved reasonable suspicion before a Federation Justice of the Courts or planetary official serving in a similar capacity."

Kirk drummed his fingers on the desktop, wondering how long it would take the computer to get to the point. Obviously, a Vulcan had written this part of the Federation Code. *And a Vulcan wrote the program that's interpreting it,* he reminded himself.

Oblivious to Kirk's impatience, the computer continued, "Paragraph 6: No law enforcement agent or other person acting in the capacity of a law enforcement agent shall invade or cause to be invaded the mental privacy of any innocent Federation citizen or other sentient being while in pursuit of suspects for whom a search warrant has been obtained under the provisions of Section 183, Subsection A, Paragraph 5.

"Section 243, Subsection A (Telepath's Rights), Paragraph 1: No law enforcement agent or other person acting in the capacity of a law enforcement agent shall compel any telepath to use his or her telepathic gifts against his or her will for any reason.

"Paragraph 2: No law enforcement agent or other person acting in the capacity of a law enforcement agent shall compel any telepath to invade the mental privacy of any Federation citizen or any other sentient being for any purpose, including justifiable searches as defined under the provisions of Section 183, Subsection A, Paragraph 5."

"Enough!" Kirk scowled in exasperation. Trust a Vulcan to write a program with a fascination for reciting the entire Federation Code! "I just wanted an answer to a simple question."

"There are fifteen other references in the Federation Code that pertain to the question you asked."

"That's all right. Cancel request. I seriously doubt that listening to the Federation Code is going to catch a murderer for me." Kirk reached for his coffee cup and settled back in his chair to do some hard thinking. What clues would Hercule Poirot need to solve this murder? How would Sherlock Holmes unravel this case? And without their all-too-fictional help, how was *he,* Captain James T. Kirk, going to catch the spy that had invaded his ship?

Chapter Eight

JOACHIM MONTOYA stormed around the work area of his quarters, venting his fury in a string of colorful oaths that threatened to corrode the bulkheads. Zayle and Vreblin moved their chairs closer to the walls to keep out of the commissioner's way until his temper cooled. Norris, sitting behind the table, ignored Montoya's outburst and continued to run his dispatches through her computer. In the adjacent sleeping area, Simons feigned sleep and watched the scene through barely open eyes.

Montoya picked up a compact datapad from the table and shook it violently. "I ask you—*would I say this?*" he demanded of the room at large. "'These events have shown the Kaldorni ambassador to be an arrogant and obstinate individual with no intention of negotiating any binding agreement with the Federation or with the Beystohn Planets. I therefore conclude we have no option but to terminate these discussions forthwith.' Would I say that? Just because we've had a temporary misunderstanding?" His face flushed a deep red. "So who the hell sent that message, anyway?"

Norris retrieved the datapad from Montoya. In two-column format, it showed two versions of

Montoya's morning dispatch to his supervisor. One column was a copy of the dispatch he had recorded and given to Simons to carry to the *Enterprise*'s communications officer. The report summarized the difficulties they were having, but emphasized Montoya's conviction that the negotiations would resume shortly. Privately, Norris thought Montoya's optimism was premature, but she also knew that his unflagging determination that negotiations *would* succeed had brought worse fiascoes to acceptable conclusions. His anger was as much at the suggestion of quitting before he had explored every option for reopening negotiations as it was at having his dispatches rewritten.

Norris read the altered dispatch again. It presented the same facts, but interpreted them much differently. The atypical conclusions of the counterfeit had alerted Montoya's superior, and he had asked for confirmation of the message. When the second transmission did not agree with the first, he sent Montoya copies of both dispatches. After almost blowing out the bulkheads when he first read the forgery, Montoya had cooled down enough to call his aides together before his temper again approached the flash point.

"Joachim, who handled the tape besides yourself?" Norris asked.

Montoya whirled to face her, his body taut with anger. Then her question registered, and he froze in the center of the room. His forehead wrinkled in concentration. "I wrote the report after breakfast. Then we were scheduled to discuss your transcript analysis, so I asked Cecilia to take the tape to the communications officer." He spun around and crossed to the room divider in three quick strides. "Cecilia, what did you do with that tape after I left?"

Simons stirred and raised her head, blinking as if just awakened. "What, Yonnie?" she asked in a drowsy voice.

"The computer tape with my dispatches. The one I gave you this morning. Tell me everything you did from the time I gave it to you until you sent it off."

"It was right there on the desk." She covered her mouth to stifle a yawn. "I left it there while I took my shower and got dressed, then I took it with me when I went to breakfast. After that, I went to the bridge and had the communications officer send it off. Is anything wrong?"

"Yes, something's wrong! The message Rayleigh received is not the one I recorded."

"I don't see how that could be." A bewildered frown creased Simons' forehead. "The tape was in our quarters or with me the whole time. Unless—" Her eyes widened. "You don't suppose someone slipped in here while I was in the shower, do you?"

Norris watched Simons, feeling a prickle of suspicion grow as the woman talked. Simons' act was good—very good—but it didn't ring true. *She's lying,* Norris thought. *Her story doesn't fit.*

"I have no idea!" Montoya's temper was again approaching its eruption point. "But I didn't record that damned message!" He whirled to face Norris. "What does your computer say about the tape?"

"I think it was altered." Norris tried to sound as uncertain as she dared. "With your permission, I'd like to see if the ship's cryptography banks have a program that can confirm my suspicions."

"Do it!"

Norris pulled the tape from the computer, grabbed the datapad, and hurried out the door. She knew that Montoya had been using the new Kreylor multilevel tapes, which retained everything recorded on them until they were purged by a special command. If someone tried to erase or write over data without the command, the information was dumped to a storage level.

Norris' computer showed two generations of tampering, but she did not want to discuss her findings with Simons in the room. Also, to decode the inactive blocks, she needed the *Enterprise*'s multichannel analyzer. She could identify a copy of Montoya's original dispatch on one of the tracks, but her machine was not powerful enough to disentangle the layered messages on the rest of the tape.

Janara Whitehorse mapped imaginary mountain ranges across the ceiling over her bed. As a meditation exercise, it would not win approval with her Deltan instructors, but four *boretelin* tablets prevented her from achieving a proper trance. However, the horror and revulsion she still received as the aftermath of the security guard's murder disturbed her much more than the drug-induced mental numbness.

The *boretelin* allowed her body to rest, but it inhibited the meditation her mind craved. She had been floating in the borderland between waking and dreaming for some time when a knock on the door roused her.

"Who is it?" Her words sounded as blurry as she felt.

"Kristiann Norris. Would you mind talking to me?"

Janara levered herself into a sitting position, shaking her head to clear away the fog. "Come," she said to signal the computer. It unlocked the door and Norris entered.

"I hope I'm not interrupting you, but you were so helpful earlier, and I have another problem my computer can't handle. I'll go away if you're busy, but I thought instead of bothering the captain, I'd at least ask you first. Unless you're not feeling up to it . . . after what happened."

"What—? Oh, that." Janara had difficulty following Norris' rapid changes of subject. "Something attacked a security guard in Auxiliary Control. I heard his mental screams when the assailant struck." Janara closed her eyes for a moment, fighting to suppress the memory. "It happens sometimes."

"I heard about the attack. The officers are trying to keep it quiet, but everyone is talking just the same. It sounded pretty gruesome."

"Rather," Janara agreed in a dry tone. "As for the computer work, you'll have to talk with the captain— or at least *Shan* Tenaida—anyway. They've put a lock on the computer and are releasing programs on an individual basis. . . . They'll probably require someone from the ship to do the work for you. Why don't you explain your problem, just in case?"

Norris outlined what she needed. As she listened, Janara noticed how many sensitive details Norris omitted while still covering the significant facts. To Janara's particular amusement, Norris projected her distrust of Montoya's wife without mentioning Simons' name. Someday, Janara decided, her ability to convey a message by implication would earn Norris an important position.

"I think this should go straight to the captain in private," Janara said when Norris finished. "*Shan* Tenaida is clearing programs for the crew, but you don't want to explain this where everyone on the ship will hear you. Also, you'll need Captain Kirk's authorization before you can touch the programs you need."

She activated the intercom. Uhura answered her.

"Where's Captain Kirk?" Janara asked. "I need his authorization for a program clearance."

"He's here on the bridge. You can talk to him now."

Norris shook her head emphatically. Janara nodded her understanding and asked Uhura, "Could he meet me in my quarters? It's extremely sensitive."

The intercom went silent. A few seconds later, Kirk reopened the channel.

"Lieutenant, would you explain yourself a little more clearly?" Kirk's voice held a dangerous edge. In the best of times, he disliked mysteries and, at the moment, he already had several months' worth.

Janara picked her words carefully. "Miss Norris has requested further assistance from the *Enterprise*'s computers. An altered message was sent through the ship's communications system. I thought you should know."

"Thank you. I'll be down immediately."

Less than two minutes later, Kirk barreled into Janara's quarters. His face had a deadly serious cast, and he questioned Norris until he had learned everything she knew.

"What I'm going to tell you now," he said, staring at each woman in turn, "is not to go outside this room. I'm telling you because you've guessed part of it already, and I don't want you discussing your speculations with anyone. Is that clear?"

Both women nodded.

"There's a spy on the ship who's been disrupting our operations and who may be trying to sabotage the negotiations. Those dispatches, Kris, are the first direct evidence linking the spy to your mission. I'll have to keep the tape after Tenaida analyzes it."

"I'll need Commissioner Montoya's permission for that. His dispatches are restricted communications."

"Anything that goes through the communications system of my ship is my business—especially when it's been altered. Tell the commissioner that, then bring the tape to the bridge."

"Right away." Norris collected the tape and her datapad, and left to find Montoya.

Kirk paced the length of the room. Now that he had a chance to speak with Janara, he was unsure how to make his request. "Lieutenant Whitehorse, Lieutenant Tenaida says you are a strong telepath. I was wondering—that is, I wanted to ask if you would use your ability to help us identify the spy."

Janara closed her eyes, fighting panic. The thought of closer contact with the being that had killed Yendes terrified her. "*Shan* Tenaida must also have told you most telepaths don't enjoy looking into other people's minds."

Kirk nodded.

She watched the subtle play of his facial muscles, seeking a measure of his desperation. "I'll consider it, Captain, but it's not something I will do willingly if there are any alternatives."

"Very well, Lieutenant. I'll remember that. However, in return, will you consider the damage the spy could cause if we don't catch him immediately?"

"Yes, sir." Even in her bleary state, the elegance of Kirk's trap impressed her. If she refused to help catch the spy, she opened herself to the horrors of his next attack. Whether or not she agreed to Kirk's request, her mental tranquility would be compromised.

Taking her silence as a refusal, Kirk strode from the room, grateful the trip to the bridge allowed him to release some of his frustration. He could order Janara to use her abilities to search for the spy, but if she refused, any action he took against her insubordination would only intensify her determination to resist.

Federation law would support her refusal, even if Kirk's motive was to save lives. Since he had no viable options, Kirk found himself hoping that Janara would agree before he resorted to issuing a direct order. If Janara thought about the situation, perhaps she would see that they had no choice.

As the door closed, Janara slumped against her pillows. She needed rest more than ever, but the events of the last hour had given her much to think about. Also, she had to get her programs cleared so she could continue with the Shansar problem. Dr. McCoy had declared her unfit for duty, but she did not plan to let that interfere with solving the troublesome equations. But before she could finish organizing her evening's activities, Janara was asleep.

n'Gelen l'Stror Klee sat cross-legged on the floor of his cabin, contemplating the Representation of the Unities. He had placed it on the wall, establishing this space as their Fortress of Life, when he and his wives had first entered the rooms. Symbolizing the spiritual dimension of Kaldorni life, each family's Representation was unique, created by the head of the clan—its form visualized after the weeks of ritual purification and fasting that the World's-Center Rite comprised. Klee's Representation, an abstract design of reds, rose-pinks, and brownish black, served as the meditational focus for him and the extended family that looked to him for both spiritual and secular guidance. Every member could recite the vision that had revealed the Representation to Klee, and all had committed to memory the significance of each shape and color.

Klee shifted position restlessly. He was unable to enter the flow of the Universal Harmonies as meditation before the Representation should have allowed. The disharmonies of this mission were multiplying, the wrongness expanding to engulf his family and his world.

His eldest wife knelt beside him. "You are not in Harmony with the Universe today." Her voice was low and sweet.

"I am not. Discord exists because I have failed to protect those under my care. My grave error is affecting the success of my mission and the fate of our planet. I must atone for it, but I cannot see the beginning of the discordance." He raised his right shoulder, held the gesture for several seconds. "How can one restore the Harmonies if the origins of the Discord are not known?"

She rested her hand against his cheek. "Redress those discordances you see now. Later, other Disharmonies may be revealed, and those may be corrected then. Where no reparations are made, the Discord spreads until no remedy is possible."

He took her hand in his, stroking it while he assessed her words. "You are most wise, Eldest Wife. I thank the Universe that you are not among the ones to be taken from me." He tightened his fingers around hers. "It is not that I would fight against the Way-of-Things, but how I dread what I must do."

She touched her forehead to the floor, accepting her duty. "We will prepare for the ceremony. Go now and do what you must."

Joachim Montoya raged through his quarters, taking target practice at the furniture with stray pieces of clothing. The temper tantrum did not improve the situation, but it was a small outlet for his fury. His mood had deteriorated when Norris had requested permission to leave the altered dispatch tape with Captain Kirk.

"Oh, Yonnie, I feel so terrible." Simons' voice caught in her throat, trembling as if she were about to cry. "I can't believe someone would change your dispatches while I was taking my shower." When he looked in her direction, she shifted position to emphasize the full silhouette of her breasts, but tears were gathering in her eyes. "I feel so guilty."

With an effort, Montoya put a rein on his temper. He went to the bed and took her in his arms. "It isn't your fault. It would have taken a professional to do it without being caught."

She burrowed her head against his shoulder. Montoya felt his desire starting to build as she pressed her body against his. It would be so easy, he thought, to forget his problems and spend the afternoon pleasing his wife.

Simons gave him a look calculated to arouse Methuselah. "I was afraid you were mad at me for letting it happen."

"Of course not." He felt strangely detached, as if his physical reactions belonged to another man. Something teased his mind. First his anger, and now the lust Simons engendered, threatened to send it back into his subconscious. Her fingers traced molten patterns across his chest and her lips left fiery brands

162

along his collarbone. The tide of lust threatened to drown him—and the half-formed idea snapped into focus: Cecilia was trying to distract him. Her approach was plausible enough to work, but Montoya survived by his ability to penetrate façades. A diplomat could not allow anyone, even his wife, to interfere with his job.

Nor did Montoya believe in coincidences. And the attempted seduction while he was still furious over the forged dispatches was a startling coincidence.

He grasped Simons by the shoulders and pushed her away. "I'm going for a walk. I want to sort this out, and I won't be very good company until I do."

"If you must." She again sounded ready to cry.

"I must." He was through the door before she could stop him.

Montoya found Captain Kirk on the bridge. He had just finished his shift and was turning the conn over to the second officer.

"Commissioner Montoya, what can I do for you?" Kirk's voice was almost cheerful, reflecting his satisfaction with the uneventfulness of his afternoon.

"I was hoping you could answer some questions for me, Captain." Montoya shifted his weight from one foot to the other, unable to hide his uneasiness. "My aide told you about my dispatches."

Kirk nodded, waiting for Montoya to get to the point.

"Could you tell me what time they were sent?"

Kirk turned to the communications officer. "Mr. Laysa, would you—"

"Aye, aye, sir," she answered before Kirk completed the order.

"What else can we do for you, Commissioner?"

"I'd like the answer to that question first."

"Twelve thirty-six," Laysa said.

Montoya did a double take. That was almost four hours after he had given the tape to Cecilia. "I believe, Captain, I need some other questions answered." He ran a hand through his graying hair. "I gave the dispatches to Cecilia about eight thirty. She said she took a shower before she came to the bridge. Can you verify her story?"

"Lieutenant, check the power usage logs for the commissioner's quarters and see how long the shower was running."

"Aye, aye, sir."

"Was there anything else you needed?"

"If it's not too personal, I wanted to ask when and where you knew my wife." At Kirk's frown, he hastened to add, "I don't mean to pry into your personal life, Captain. I am merely—as Kris Norris would put it—playing a hunch. I don't mean to offend."

After a moment, Kirk went to an unoccupied station and retrieved the log of the *Aeolus*. He recorded the data and handed the tape to Montoya. "That should answer your questions. Anything else I told you would be too subjective to be of value." With that, Kirk strode off the bridge, leaving Montoya to stare at his receding back. Tenaida and Brady exchanged worried looks, wondering at the change in Kirk's mood.

A moment later, Montoya left to find a quiet place to view Kirk's log extract.

By midafternoon, the antidote had relieved the Kaldorni's symptoms, and McCoy released the women from Sickbay. Normally, he would have kept his patients under observation for another day, but he felt they would recuperate faster among their own people. Also, in spite of the thermal blankets, the women found the temperature in Sickbay uncomfortably cool. However, McCoy was reluctant to set the environmental controls any higher because his staff didn't appreciate the tropical heat.

Ambassador Klee arrived at McCoy's office five minutes after the doctor had released Klee's wives.

Klee shifted his weight from one foot to the other, waiting for the doctor to speak first.

McCoy pushed aside his notes on the autopsy and motioned Klee to sit down. "What can I do for you, Mr. Ambassador?"

"I would ask if the Doctor McCoy would honor this humble servant by sharing food with him and those that dwell with him. The honored Captain Kirk is also to be invited. It is desirable to express thankfulness for what you have done to save my people. Also, I would be less than I already am if I failed to expunge my debt to you in the manner of my people."

"Mr. Ambassador, you don't need to thank me. I'm just glad we solved the problem so quickly."

"It would be a great privilege if the doctor and the captain would allow this humble servant to acknowledge the debt that is between us."

"Then we'd be delighted to accept the invitation. What time do you want us there?"

"My eldest wife indicated she would be prepared for the honored guests at 1900."

"We'll be there."

Klee stood. "If the doctor would excuse me, my wives have need of my presence to prepare for the ceremony."

"Of course, Mr. Ambassador." McCoy called up the file for his autopsy report. Klee's words did not register for several seconds. "Ceremony? What ceremony?" He looked up from the screen, but Klee had already left. McCoy sighed in exasperation, but decided the answer could wait. If he and Kirk had needed to make special preparations, the Kaldorni would have told him. He picked up his notes, hoping to finish the report before he went off duty.

He had added two paragraphs when a voice interrupted him. "Doctor, do you have a few moments? I need to talk to you."

McCoy scowled at the interruption, then felt all

thoughts of work leave him when he recognized the woman in the doorway. "Come in, Cecilia." He smiled and pointed at the empty chair.

Simons closed the door behind her. "I'm not interrupting anything, am I?"

"Just paperwork. Having it interrupted is a relief. What can I do for you?" McCoy put the computer on standby.

Simons melted into the chair. "Captain Kirk ordered me to stay away from Janie. I wanted to know why he would do that."

Watching the play of staged emotions flicker across Simons' face, McCoy realized that she would never accept the captain's restrictions, and the doctor wondered if anything he could say would convince her to obey Kirk's order. "Medically, there's no reason she can't see you." *Other than a mild concussion and assorted scrapes and bruises,* McCoy thought. "However, she's been working too hard, and I ordered her to get some rest. It sounds like the captain extended that to exclude visitors." He shrugged. "You'd have to ask him. We haven't discussed the matter."

"I thought he would have confided in you."

McCoy struggled against the grin that quirked the corners of his mouth. Simons' probing was far from subtle. "The captain is under no obligation to explain himself to me. If you want to know his reasons, you'll have to ask him."

"I was hoping you could help me, Leonard. Captain Kirk and I aren't communicating very well." Simons sighed, and her expression became a study of bewildered motherhood. "I know my daughter and I don't get along the way we should, but I *do* try. It's just that, for as long as I can remember, she's gone out of her way to be as difficult as possible."

McCoy felt himself sliding into the aura of plausibility Simons was weaving. He caught himself, swallowed the words of sympathy he had almost spoken, and framed a more rational response. "Your daughter is an adult. She has the right to live her own life. What you see as willfulness is how she defends her choices."

"The Deltans are giving her no choice. They're forcing her back to that planet so they can brainwash her. Freedom has no place in how they live. Everything is dictated by clan, family, tradition, and duty." Simons gave a short, bitter laugh. "Where's individual freedom in that?"

McCoy shook his head. "The Deltan way of life is old and complex. It may seem easy to some outsiders, but I know it isn't, even for those born to it. However, Delta Four has produced many scientists and philosophers whose achievements are honored throughout the Federation. A culture that produces such people can't be all bad." He let that argument sink in, then tried a different tack. "Have you considered this? On the *Enterprise,* your daughter encounters more different races and lifestyles in a week than many people see in a lifetime. However she makes her decisions, she *doesn't* lack information."

Simons' face darkened with anger. "That's not what I was worried about, Doctor. But I'll think about it anyway." She shoved herself out of the chair and stalked from the room.

McCoy slumped in his chair, suddenly feeling his age. He was getting too old to handle spoiled passengers with gossamer diplomacy. And, especially, he was getting too old to deal with women who made him feel like the king of the universe one minute and a useless fool the next. A veterinary practice on a remote agricultural station was sounding more and more attractive. McCoy grimaced, realizing that fantasy would not finish the work he had in front of him. With a sigh, he reactivated the computer and returned to the autopsy report.

Commissioner Montoya sat at attention. He gripped the edge of Captain Kirk's worktable, resisting the urge to prowl the perimeter of the room. Kirk, his hands resting on a noteboard, sat behind the table with his Deltan science officer hovering at his shoulder like a bodyguard. Montoya had not expected the scientist; he had braced himself to confront the first officer's boyish exuberance, but Brady's duties had kept him elsewhere.

Montoya broke the silence. "I read through the records from the *Aeolus* that you gave me, Captain Kirk. You were the victim of some pretty bad luck."

Kirk shrugged, pretending a casualness he was far from feeling. Montoya's opening told him that the commissioner would not readily accept any criticism of Simons. "The *bad luck* was too convenient for my taste. Such things are rarely accidental."

"I don't believe in coincidence either, Captain, but I would hesitate to condemn anyone on such flimsy evidence." After reading the report, Montoya felt Kirk had not handled the situation well, and that the illness he had blamed on Simons was obviously a cover for his own incompetence.

Kirk sensed the strength of the commissioner's skepticism. He shoved the noteboard across the table. "In any case, Tenaida translated your tape. If I were you, I'd watch whom I let near my dispatches. The next person might recognize your Kreylor multilevel tapes and purge the storage blocks when they rewrite the message."

"I beg your pardon?" The change of subject caught Montoya off-guard.

"Mr. Commissioner," Tenaida said, "if you will look at the analysis, you will see what the captain means. I believe the third level on the tape contains your original dispatch."

Montoya skimmed the text and nodded to confirm the Deltan's statement.

"That was replaced by a second message. This one reported the same facts, but interpreted them differently, which made terminating the discussions the only reasonable option."

Montoya identified the forged message and nodded again.

"Now we come to the interesting part of that block. Following your dispatch is a second report. Because the *Enterprise's* computer had to send it, we've determined the transmission vectors for the message. However, we have not yet decoded the text, and we may not be able to. It appears to be in a moving-cipher code that requires knowledge of both the substitution tables and the frequency with which they are shifted. The third unit on that level is a program to erase the memory tape and restore the text of your dispatch, which was saved in the overwrite program. The surface track is, of course, the copy of your original message."

"And this reprogramming was done while Cecilia was in the shower." Montoya stared at Kirk; his voice was heavy with skepticism.

"Someone took a long shower this morning, using as much shower time as most crew members use in a week. Furthermore, the computer in your quarters was used for about two hours, but it wasn't tied into the ship's memory, and everything was erased before the unit was turned off." Kirk ran a hand through his hair, looking for a way past Montoya's disbelief. He could see the commissioner's hostility etched in the harsh lines around his mouth, and he knew Montoya would reject everything he said if Kirk accused Simons directly. "The computer usage time is consistent with someone writing and recording a program, then dumping the working files. But your wife would have known if someone used your computer. She wasn't in the shower *that* long."

"What are you implying, Captain?" A deadly edge crept into Montoya's voice.

"One of two things, Mr. Commissioner. Either your wife lied about the shower and rewrote your dispatches herself, or the person using your computer was someone she expected there."

"I was with my aides all morning. No one else should have been in my quarters."

"In the last few days, we've had trouble with some of the ship's personnel appearing to be in two places at once."

"I'll ask Cecilia, then. That would explain things."

"A logical question, Captain. If I may?"

"Yes, Tenaida?"

"How would someone know when to come to the commissioner's quarters to rewrite the dispatches?"

Kirk rubbed the back of his neck, trying to loosen the tensed muscles. "An excellent point, Tenaida. Do you have any ideas, Commissioner Montoya?"

"None, Captain. No one should have known."

"That doesn't change the fact that someone did. Tenaida, can we prevent an encore?"

Tenaida leaned forward, concentrating on Kirk's words and trying to guess what the captain was implying. "I think we can catch anyone who tries it again. However, it will require some thought. I must be certain I have anticipated all possibilities."

"Good. Consider that a top priority." Kirk turned to Montoya. "Commissioner, until we catch this spy, I would feel better if you would allow me to assign some of my security personnel to personally protect you and your wife."

Montoya stared at Kirk in amazement. "You want your people to follow me and my wife everywhere we go?" He shook his head. "That is totally unacceptable, Captain. I will not be kept under surveillance as if *I* were the guilty party. Your guards will serve both of us better by trying to capture the real criminal."

"As you wish, Commissioner. However, may I ask that you—and only you—handle your dispatches until we catch the spy? And, please, don't discuss this with anyone. Not even your wife, since your quarters may be monitored."

"Bugged? I want something done about it at once!"

Kirk shook his head. "Knowing the spy may be

watching your quarters is to our advantage. When we figure out how to trap him, we'll use the bug against him. If we look for it now, he'll know we're suspicious."

Anger and reluctance chased each other across Montoya's face. "I suppose you're right, Captain. If that's the best you can offer, I've got work to do."

"I'm sorry we don't have instant solutions, Commissioner, but catching spies is not what we're trained for. We're doing the best we can."

"I understand, Captain." Montoya's tone was laced with suspicion. He rose and headed for the door with quick, angry strides.

"He did not believe you," Tenaida said after the door closed behind Montoya.

"No, he thinks we're hiding something. And he's convinced that I'm making unjust accusations against his wife." Kirk sighed, feeling his frustration winding into a hard knot in his stomach. "Tenaida, how do you manage it? This business has got me tied up tighter than a Mertrovia'an's tail in mating season, and you're as calm and unperturbed as ever."

The Deltan circled the table and sat in the chair Montoya had vacated. "Perhaps it is my mental training. From earliest childhood, we of Delta are trained to channel our emotions so they will not disturb us when we cannot act upon them."

"I wish I had some of that training right now."

"It would take years to master, Captain. However, there is a simple technique you could try. Think of yourself as a rock, and the annoyances as the rain. The rain flows over the rock and is absorbed by the soil. When the storm passes, the water is gone, but the rock is still there."

"A rock in the rain. I like that." Kirk closed his eyes for a moment and focused on the image. Some of his tension seemed to slide away. He would have preferred seeing the spy confined to the brig, but Tenaida's image seemed to help. "Back to business.

171

What's the probability that Simons altered the dispatches?"

"Eighty-seven-point-three percent, assuming she does not know the spy we are looking for."

"And if she does?"

"In that case, she either altered the tape, or knew with certainty that it was altered."

"Could she be Admiral Chen's spy, Tenaida?"

"I think not. Her records show no unusual abilities of the kind we have postulated that the spy must possess. In particular, she shows no technical skills of the level required for advanced biocosmetic work. Also, I have traced her activities, albeit with difficulty, for most of her life. Someone apparently has taken great pains to hide the computer records of Simons' movements, which tactic would require a thorough knowledge of computer programming.

"When the records are deciphered, they show that many interesting coincidences follow her, but I find no pattern of direct action—especially not direct, violent action. Certainly, her records show no correlations to events like Ensign Yendes' murder."

Kirk snorted. "We could argue that, Tenaida. However, what was that you said about computer programming? Anything like the examples showing up on our computer lately?"

"That connection never occurred to me." Tenaida looked stunned at having overlooked something so obvious. "I'll look into it immediately. Captain, may I ask what was on the tape you gave Commissioner Montoya?"

"Extract from the log of the *Aeolus*. If you've been tracing Simons, you know which one."

"Indeed. If you'll excuse me, I have work to do."

"Of course, Tenaida. Oh, by the way, don't work too hard to catch the person who's messing with the commissioner's dispatches. If we give Simons enough rope, I'm sure she'll hang herself."

"I beg your pardon?"

"An old human expression, Tenaida. It means, if she thinks we don't suspect her, she'll get careless and make a mistake. Then we'll at least know what game *she* is playing."

"That seems reasonable, sir. If we are too stupid to catch the flaws in her story, she'll assume we won't catch later mistakes, either."

Kirk nodded. "So we ignore her until she steps into our trap. And hope the other spy gets caught with her—since they seem to be working toward the same goal."

"I see. I'll be in my quarters working on the problem, if you need me."

"Carry on, Tenaida."

After the Deltan scientist had left, Kirk threw himself on the bed. Somewhere there had to be a fast, simple solution to this increasingly messy situation. If only his tired brain would tell him what it was.

The buzzer woke Janara from an uneasy sleep. She pushed herself upright, rubbing her eyes. She was groggy, both from the drug and from being awakened suddenly. "Come."

The door slid open, admitting Simons. Her mother looked contrite, and Janara was immediately on guard. Simons wanted something, and she wanted it bad enough to put on a major performance to get it.

"I came to apologize for what happened the other day," Simons said without preamble. "Dr. McCoy said you could have visitors, so I came to tell you that I've thought things over, and I shouldn't have lost my temper."

"It always seems to end that way, doesn't it?" Janara searched Simons' face. Her expression was controlled and gave no hint of true repentance. The *boretelin* gave Janara a welcome immunity from hearing her mother's thoughts, but the drugged slowness of her mind placed her at a disadvantage in the conversation.

Janara knew the apology could not be genuine, and even if it were, she realized it had come years too late. She no longer had anything she wished to say to her mother.

Simons perched on the foot of the bed. "I don't want to see my little girl trapped on a world where sex is constantly demanded, but no one knows anything of love."

Janara swallowed a sour grin. The sexual openness of Deltan society and the Deltan ethic against manipulating others for personal gain limited what someone like Simons could do among Deltans. Simons' opinions were biased by her prejudices. "You make it sound as though Deltans are trained to emulate Orion slave women. I assure you that is not the case. Besides, I experience more than enough emotion here on the *Enterprise.*"

"Honey, you don't even know what it means. Let me show you what it's like to be a real, *human* woman."

Janara bit her tongue to hold back a bitter reply. Some of her earliest memories were of Simons' violent emotions. By the time Janara was old enough to understand her psychic abilities and begin to control them, she loathed her mother's turbulent passions and all the benefits Simons claimed for them. Finally, shaking with the effort of maintaining her control, Janara found a neutral answer. "I am not you, Mother, and I must live my own life. Your choices may be right for you, but they aren't for me."

Simons flushed with anger, but held her position on the foot of the bed. She forced a cloying smile. "Let's not fight about that now, darling. We can talk about something else, can't we?"

"What should we discuss?" Janara heard the change in her mother's tone—Simons was coming to the purpose for the visit.

"Well, there's everything that's been happening on the ship. Yonnie's fit to be tied over the problems with his negotiations, and he's off at all hours conferring with his aides. And now, to top it off, our computer terminal is down, and Captain Kirk won't send someone to fix it."

Janara lifted an eyebrow in a gesture copied from Spock. Vulcan gestures were the only thing that irritated her mother more than Deltan mannerisms, and Janara hoped Simons' annoyance would lessen her caution. Janara's instincts told her Simons was lying, but even when she concentrated, her head was too fuzzy from the *boretelin* to register her mother's duplicity.

"Could I borrow your computer terminal for a while, darling? I wanted to record messages for some friends. If you don't mind, that is."

"I don't mind." Janara watched the tension leave her mother's posture. "Unfortunately, the captain's blocked off the entire computer system, and I haven't got my console unlocked. Also, you'd have to clear your programs through *Shan* Tenaida."

"What do you mean? Why's that?" Simons' body snapped as tight as a drawn bowstring.

"I don't know. They said there was a system glitch. Someone has to check each program separately."

"That'll take forever. I just want to send some messages. Surely you can arrange that much for your dear mother."

"'Fraid not. I can't even use my own programs until I get them cleared."

"I *will* talk to the captain!" Simons stood, squaring her shoulders with angry determination. "Surely *he'll* let me use the computer for what I need to do."

"Don't count on it, Mother." Janara's voice stopped Simons halfway to the door. "Captain Kirk isn't very fond of you these days."

Simons whirled around. "How do you know that? Have you been trying your nasty Deltan mind-reading tricks on *him?*"

Janara laughed, enjoying the feeling of being at the

warp buoy ahead of her mother. "I've seen his face when your name is mentioned. You are *not* one of his favorite people."

"We'll see about that." Simons stomped out the door.

Janara dropped into her pillows and threw an arm over her eyes. For the only time in her life, she regretted not knowing what her mother was thinking. Simons would never go through such an elaborate charade just to record a few messages. If she wanted access to Janara's computer console, her reasons must equal the effort expended on the performance. If Simons needed to use the computer that badly . . .

Once the thought occurred to her, Janara could not dismiss it. Finally, she reported the incident to Captain Kirk. Afterward, she felt unaccountably relieved. She stretched out, closed her eyes, and was soon fast asleep.

Kirk and McCoy met outside the Kaldorni ambassador's quarters. The doctor was fidgeting with the collar of his dress uniform. Kirk shuddered, feeling a sympathetic tightness around his own neck that had nothing to do with the cut of the uniform. If he let himself think about it much longer, he knew he would develop as strong an aversion to dress uniforms as McCoy. "What's the matter, Bones? This uniform was your idea. Are you having second thoughts?"

"As a matter of fact, yes!" McCoy gave his collar a second tug. "I was just remembering how hot those women wanted my Sickbay."

Kirk laughed. "You remember the old saying, Bones —when in Rome . . ."

"Yeah." McCoy shrugged. "The ambassador was very anxious to give us this thank-you dinner. He seemed to think he owed it to us."

"Then, in the interests of diplomacy, perhaps we shouldn't keep him waiting. I wish I knew a little more about Kaldorni customs, though."

They entered, pausing at the door while their eyes adjusted to the dim lighting and their bodies to the oppressive heat. The temperature in the Kaldorni's rooms was nearly the maximum the *Enterprise*'s environmental equipment could produce, and McCoy was reminded once again of the temperature in the ship's sauna.

Klee bowed to greet them, his movements accompanied by the jingling of the jewelry that covered his chest. His crimson robes were lavishly embroidered with metallic thread and decorated with gemstones. "Welcome, honored guests, to our humble lodgings."

Kirk and McCoy exchanged glances, uncertain of the proper etiquette for a formal Kaldorni evening. "The pleasure is ours," Kirk replied.

Klee's wives entered the room. In unison, they gave McCoy an elaborate bow, followed by a different, but no less complex, greeting to Kirk. Three of the women wore dark brown robes and black, heavy veils, while the other three were dressed in rose-colored outfits and translucent veils. Kirk was surprised to see their faces. The robes were richly embroidered and trimmed with a deep red that matched the ambassador's robe.

"If the honored guests would come this way—" The women formed a corridor leading away from the door, and the ambassador escorted Kirk and McCoy into the cabin's workroom. The standard furniture was gone. In its place, several sumptuous rugs were spread in a circle. Perfumed candles burned on every counter top, casting a mellow radiance that the room's artificial lights could not match. Kirk gave mental thanks to whoever had recorded the Kaldorni's ceremonial use of candles in the information the ship had received; without that warning to reprogram the room sensors and the air reprocessors, he shuddered to think what this display would have done to the *Enterprise*'s alarms and safety system.

"The place of honor for the Doctor McCoy and the

Captain Kirk is beneath the Representation of the Unities." Klee gestured for them to kneel on the rug under the large wall hanging. Kirk looked at the tapestry, admiring the abstract design and warm colors. The Kaldorni's clothing, he realized, reflected the design in the wall hanging.

McCoy knelt, struggling to fold his legs beneath him. By the time Kirk found a comfortable position, the ambassador was seated opposite them. The three women in the rose outfits knelt between Klee and the two humans, but the other women disappeared, leaving half of the circle empty.

They returned a moment later with a bronze tray holding a ceramic figurine. It was about a third of a meter high and intricately carved. Through the many openings, Kirk saw the vermilion glow of coals burning in the heart of the statuette. The figure reminded him of the fire-god figurine he had once seen in Spock's quarters. The women placed the tray before Kirk and McCoy and retreated to the other room.

"This is the Center of Harmonies," Klee said. "It will witness this ceremony and record that all is properly observed." He stretched his arms over his head and bowed until his forehead touched the floor. The women copied him, and after a slight hesitation, so did Kirk and McCoy.

Klee then led the women in a sustained recitation in the Kaldorni language. Antiphonal progressions of questions and answers alternated with unison chants until Kirk felt his pulse slip into the rhythms set by the Kaldorni voices. At times, the women in the other room intoned a counterpoint to the dominant cadences.

After a while, Kirk found himself wondering how long the ritual was going to take. He kept thinking of all the things he should be doing to catch the spy, and worrying about what the intruder was doing while he was trapped here in a hot room by the Kaldorni love of ceremony.

When the chant finally ended, the Kaldorni unfolded from their prone positions. Kirk gritted his teeth and struggled to lift his torso; he found that, after remaining prostrate for so long, his muscles were reluctant to move. McCoy, he noted sourly, sat up easily, and Kirk vowed to get even with the doctor later for showing up his captain.

The brown-robed women returned carrying brass trays heaped with food. The other women took the platters and knelt in a semicircle in front of Kirk and McCoy. One at a time, each woman extended her arms and offered her tray to the captain. While Klee explained her gift, each woman bowed deeply, first to Kirk and then to McCoy.

"This is Joy-of-Morning. She brings you sweetness of spirit and willing eagerness in all things. This is symbolized by the fruits and flowers she gives you." The woman's willowy grace enchanted Kirk. A small smile briefly lit her heart-shaped face as she presented the tray.

"Shade-in-Sun is the quiet one. She brings you calmness of temper and a steadiness for work. This is symbolized by the cheese and the meat she brings." Kirk felt himself sliding into her wide, misty eyes. She broke the contact and stared at the floor for the rest of the presentation.

"Fire-in-Night is the restless one. She is much skilled in the musical arts and knows many ways to delight the senses. This is symbolized by the candies and pastries she bears." With liquid, hummingbird movements, the woman offered her tray to Kirk. Her swift smile was molten and sensual.

"Now, most honored guests, it is required that you consume a mouthful from each tray, and present to your servants a selection from that tray."

Kirk nodded to show he understood. He chose a small, bluish red fruit and shared it with McCoy. It was both tart and sweet, and the juice ran down his face. He wiped his mouth with the back of his hand.

When he gave fruits to each Kaldorni woman, they ate with dainty bites. Kirk repeated the ritual with the meat and the pastries.

As they finished, the brown-robed women appeared with a tray of eating platters. Joy-of-Morning took the tray, knelt before Kirk, and offered it to him.

"Our honored guests may now select platters and fill them with the foods of their choice. After that, the others will follow."

Kirk took the top platter and loaded it with food; McCoy took smaller servings. When they had settled back to eat, each of the rose-garbed Kaldorni women filled a plate and returned to her original place in the circle. The brown-robed women carried the food to Klee. He thanked them and loaded his platter to overflowing. Only then did the three women fill platters for themselves and retire to the other room to eat.

They all ate in silence, broken only by the jingle of the Kaldorni's jewelry. After a few bites, Kirk understood why Ambassador Klee was so overweight—the food was delicious! Kirk wondered why all the Kaldorni were not more obese—he knew he would overindulge if he were served a steady diet of such food. For a while, the captain forgot his impatience with Kaldorni formalities and enjoyed his meal.

McCoy, watching him eat, made a mental note to give him another detox pill when they left. One capsule should have counteracted the trace substances in the Kaldorni food that were harmful to human metabolism, but Kirk was eating too much.

When everyone had cleared their plates—except for the ritual amounts of fruit, meat, and pastry that were fed into the Center of Harmonies—the brown-robed women removed the remnants of the feast. They returned with two hyaline goblets and a tall flask made of interwoven multicolored glass ropes. The tallest woman unstopped the flask and half-filled the smaller cup with the deep green liquid. She set the chalice in front of the ambassador and stood behind him with her dark-robed co-wives.

Fire-in-Night heated the flask over the Center of Harmonies until the liquid turned a pale blue. She filled the larger cup and offered it to Kirk with a deep bow.

"The most honored captain should drink deeply of the Fire-of-Life, and then give the honored doctor and each of his humble servants a taste of the Fire. After this, he may finish the cup."

Kirk sipped cautiously. The drink was warm and had a pleasant smoky aftertaste. He took a larger swallow before passing the cup to McCoy and the three Kaldorni women. When the last woman had taken her ritual mouthful, Kirk drained the cup.

Klee picked up his own drink, swallowed the liquid in one gulp, and inverted the cup on the floor. "I have now paid my debt to those I can no longer protect, and have passed their guardianship over to one who has proven himself more capable of their care. May the Balance of the Universe be restored, now that I have atoned for my failure to fulfill my responsibilities, and may my honor be sufficient to achieve the great mission my people have required of me."

At first, Kirk heard only the finality in Klee's voice that released him from the interminable formal evening. Then he realized Klee intended something more than an elaborate farewell to his guests. "What? Wait a minute. What did you say?" A dawning realization began to spread in Kirk's mind.

McCoy, realizing that his subconscious had suspected the purpose of the ceremony from the start, struggled to suppress a grin.

"The medicine of your dependent, the honored Doctor McCoy, cured these women where the methods of my people could not. You have proven yourself more worthy to care for them than their former husband." Klee sounded ready to break into tears.

He looked at Kirk wistfully. "A person with as

much status as the honored captain should have enough wives to reflect that status. May the venerable captain cherish and care for his new wives, and may they serve him well, as long as he preserves his Harmony-with-the-Universe." With that, Klee climbed to his feet and led the three brown-robed women from the room. Kirk was surprised that the squat Kaldorni could move so quickly.

He stared at the women kneeling before him. His wives? Kirk shook his head, trying to clear it. *That wine must have been stronger than I thought. I couldn't have heard him say that!* He looked again at the women, and decided his ears had not deceived him. McCoy, kneeling beside him, was having trouble containing his amusement.

Honor, duties, responsibilities—he tried to remember the words Klee had used, so he would have the appropriate ammunition to discuss the situation with the Kaldorni. Before he found an argument he thought might stand a chance, the women took charge. They rose to their feet and began tugging on his arms.

"Come." "Home go." "Captain home." They repeated the phrases as they pulled him toward the door. Finally, he yielded and took them to his quarters. With luck, the Universal Translator would allow him to straighten this out.

As they walked down the corridor, McCoy's broad grin only emphasized the impossibility of the situation. "You seem to be enjoying this," Kirk grumbled, making a sour face.

"You mean, you-all aren't?" McCoy gave him a wide-eyed, innocent look. "I thought having several wives was the ultimate spaceman's fantasy. Now you'll never have to worry about not getting enough exercise."

Kirk scowled. "You're forgetting that even the cargo handler on a garbage scow likes to choose his partners."

McCoy's grin widened. "I haven't forgotten. But the ambassador must not have heard." They stopped at the door of Kirk's quarters. "I have some things to do in Sickbay. Enjoy getting to know your new wives. And don't forget to take another detox pill."

"Right." He watched McCoy disappear down the corridor, plotting how to get even with the doctor for his amusement. It did little to help his mood when it occurred to him that, by any logic *he* knew, the women should have been McCoy's. Shaking his head, he showed the Kaldorni women into his quarters. His first plan was to convince them to return to the ambassador.

After an hour of discussion in his quarters, he gave up. All three women insisted it was their duty to care and provide for the honored Captain Kirk, whose servant, the honored doctor, had saved their lives with his medical skills. Kirk's arguments made them weep and beg him to tell them how they had displeased their worthy husband, but nothing he said could make them return to Ambassador Klee's quarters. Defeated, Kirk adjusted the temperature as high as it would go and ordered extra blankets for the women. Then he settled himself for a long and uncomfortable night in the chair by his worktable.

Chapter Nine

"MAY I BE PERMITTED to sit here?"

Kristiann Norris swallowed a mouthful of her breakfast. "Speaker t'Stror, of course, have a seat. I haven't seen much of you lately."

"I have been performing atonements for not perceiving my master's orders as he wished." t'Stror slid into the chair. "He has been involved with family concerns and has only just now ordered that I inquire if there is a way to correct the disharmony I have caused."

"Which of the ambassador's orders did you misperceive?"

"He instructed that I should explain That-Which-Is to the commissioner so he might understand the ways of our people. I was hasty in my judgment that I could find no way in which to do this. It is now the command of my master that I see if the Commissioner Montoya would find it no loss of honor to forgive the error of this unworthy servant and allow my ambassador to explain the concepts I could not."

Norris bit into her toast and chewed slowly. When she thought t'Stror had waited long enough, she answered. "I can't promise anything until I talk with Commissioner Montoya, but I believe he will consider reopening the discussions. If you will wait here, I'll talk it over with him."

"I will be most impatient in anticipating a response that will restore my good favor in the eyes of my master."

"I'm on my way, then." Norris hurried to her quarters and asked Montoya, Vreblin, and Zayle to join her at once. The previous evening, an annoyed Montoya had told his aides that Kirk suspected there was a listening device in his quarters. Norris was grateful for an excuse to hold the meeting in her quarters—without Simons lurking in the background.

Within five minutes, the three men had arrived. Montoya was last. "What's this about?" he demanded as he came through the door.

Norris grinned, anticipating the effect of her news. "I just talked with Speaker t'Stror in the messroom. He asked if we would consider reopening the discussions. He said he had *misperceived* the ambassador's instructions, and had been required to *atone* for his errors. He was ordered to learn if you would forgive his error and allow Ambassador Klee to explain the concepts t'Stror was unable to get across."

"I think we can arrange that," Montoya said with his first real smile since the Kaldorni delegation had walked out of the briefing room. "However, we don't want to appear too eager. What exactly did t'Stror say?"

Norris repeated the conversation. As she finished, Montoya glanced at his chronometer. "I think he's waited long enough. Tell him we'll consent to meet with Ambassador Klee in half an hour in the briefing room." Montoya's triumphant smile widened, and his eyes took on a mischievous twinkle. "Let's see what we can get away with. Tell t'Stror we will forgive his errors more quickly if he convinces the ambassador to let us use our Universal Translator. To minimize further misunderstandings, of course."

"Of course." Norris chuckled with delight. The Universal Translator was the perfect concession to demand from the honor-conscious Kaldorni. She left the three men planning their next move while she delivered Montoya's message.

Kirk leaned back in the chair, nursing his third cup of coffee. Half his breakfast remained on the plate. After spending the night sleeping at his worktable, he felt tired and groggy and not the least bit interested in food. It had been a relief to escape for a quiet breakfast without the Kaldorni women.

McCoy joined him as he refilled his cup for the last time.

"You really enjoyed seeing me get stuck with all those women, didn't you, Bones?"

"I'm sorry, Jim. I just never thought of you as the marrying type." Although he managed to keep his expression neutral, McCoy's eyes twinkled with amusement.

"And just what am I going to do with them now? If you think there's room in my quarters for three wives, you're sadly mistaken."

McCoy gave him a sympathetic smile. Although the officers' cabins on the *Enterprise* were large in comparison to those on a scout ship or cargo vessel, McCoy could not imagine sharing his quarters with three other people. And a commanding officer's need for privacy in his off-duty time was even greater than a doctor's. "I don't know what you're going to do. I'm not a diplomat, remember. Why don't you put Brady and Tenaida to work on it? If they can't come up with something, you may have to resign yourself to married life."

"Speaking of those two, I'm supposed to meet with them shortly. I'd better get moving." Kirk pushed himself to his feet, summoning the energy he knew he would need today.

"Me, too. Stop by my office later if you need some friendly advice."

"Thanks, Bones. I may take you up on that."

Shaking his head, McCoy watched the captain leave. Kirk looked very tired. Diplomatic missions were not his favorite, but this one, with its additional problems, was weighing heavily on him. And his Kaldorni "wives," McCoy suspected, were not going to make the situation any easier.

Kirk, Brady, and Tenaida sat around the table in the briefing room. The three of them seemed lost in the large room, but until Kirk persuaded the Kaldorni women to leave, his own cabin was too crowded to work in. Kirk fiddled with his empty coffee cup while Tenaida summarized the detective work he had done the previous evening.

"So you think Simons is one of our unauthorized computer programmers?" Kirk asked when the Deltan finished talking.

"The probabilities are—"

Kirk shook his head and held up his hand. "It's too early in the morning for that, Tenaida. I trust your probabilities, so log them in the computer, and tell me your conclusions." Kirk rubbed his gritty eyes. He felt as though he hadn't slept in a week, and he wondered idly if there was a corollary to Special Relativity that required time dilation effects to work selectively on sleepless nights. "I could sure use another cup of coffee now."

"If you would prefer, we can postpone this until you get some more—"

"No, the doctor would say I've had enough already. Continue with your report."

"Though I can't be certain that it was Ms. Simons who reprogrammed the vari-grav control unit or added the subroutines to the Kaldorni's food synthesis program, the skills required are similar to those needed to alter a person's history in computer records. Therefore, the probabilities are that those changes were made by Ms. Simons or by someone who knows her well. She may have an accomplice, although as yet I have no evidence to prove such a person exists."

"No, you're wrong." Brady leaned forward, his body taut with conviction. "Remember the message added on to the commissioner's dispatch tape. That went to someone, and Simons is the most likely suspect for sending it."

Tenaida's eyebrows drew together into a solid line. "True. However, we don't know who got the message, or what it contained. It might be completely unrelated to these matters."

"Want to bet?" Brady's eyes were uncharacteristically serious.

"Have you made any progress on decoding the message or determining its destination?" Kirk asked.

"No." Tenaida frowned. "The coding structure doesn't follow any standard pattern, and the computer hasn't determined the basis for the encryption schedule yet. The coordinates suggest it was sent to a vessel located beyond our sensor range."

"I knew you were going to say that," Kirk grumbled. "It goes without saying that they don't want us to know they're there."

"That *is* a safe assumption."

"If someone on the *Enterprise* is transmitting to them—" Kirk's eyes widened with sudden hope. "Could they be transmitting back? Mr. Brady, have Communications check, will you?"

Brady nodded, but the intercom whistled before he could say anything. Kirk reached for the control pad.

"Kirk here."

"Captain, Commissioner Montoya wanted you to know that the Kaldorni have reopened the negotiations."

"Thank you, Uhura. Would you send Janara White-horse down here immediately?"

"Aye, aye, Captain."

"Kirk out."

Brady's face wrinkled into a half-frown at the captain's apparently irrelevant order. Tenaida's face lit up with curiosity. Kirk gave them little time to think about it. "With most of the Kaldorni in one place, we'll try to find the wolf in sheep's clothing."

"I beg your pardon, Captain?" Brady asked.

"The spy."

"*Shan* Janara may not wish to search the Kaldorni's minds," Tenaida said. "And you cannot order her to conduct such an investigation without violating the Federation Telepathic Rights Statutes."

"I think Lieutenant Whitehorse will be delighted to do it, when I explain things properly." Kirk's mouth tightened with determination.

Tenaida frowned at the implied threat in Kirk's words. The Deltan realized he still had much to learn about humans. Quite apart from the difficulty of conducting such a search without violating Federation law, Kirk's proposal created a tricky maze of ethical questions. The door buzzer interrupted Tenaida's thoughts.

"Come," Kirk said. Janara entered the room.

"Lieutenant Whitehorse, I asked before if you would help us identify the spy aboard the *Enterprise.*"

Her body went rigid with suppressed emotion. "Captain, I detest close contact with other people's minds, and I protest your efforts to force me to conduct this search."

"Lieutenant Whitehorse, I can appreciate your feelings, but we're after the being who killed Ensign Yendes. Do you *really* want to let that thing continue to roam the *Enterprise?*"

Janara seemed to shrink into herself. The silence stretched as she examined her alternatives. "However, your logic is inescapable, Captain. What would you have me do?"

"We think the spy is one of the Kaldorni. The negotiations are about to resume, and I want you to replace Yeoman Menon, who's recording the sessions. From her station, you can examine the Kaldorni and see if our spy is there."

"One of the Kaldorni?" The question was more curious than surprised.

"Yes. We think the spy is hiding among the ambassador's party and using his position as a cover for his activities."

"Her." Janara's voice was flat. "I believe I know who the spy is."

"What?"

"Captain, do you remember the problem Ms. Norris was having with her translating computer?" When Kirk nodded, Janara continued, "The machine was consistently assigning a female voice to an apparently male Kaldorni. At the time, Ms. Norris and I decided the problem was caused by an unknown peculiarity of Kaldorni biology. However, on the basis of what you've just said, I believe the one called t'Stror is the spy."

"t'Stror? He's the ambassador's right-hand man." Brady's voice rose in disbelief.

"That could explain the trouble Commissioner Montoya is having with the negotiations," Tenaida said.

"It could, at that." Kirk paused, evaluating the new information. Unfortunately, it did not *prove* that t'Stror was the person they wanted. "Lieutenant Whitehorse, would you still report to the briefing room? We need to be sure t'Stror is the spy before we arrest him—I mean, her." Kirk shook his head in frustration. "Whatever the correct gender, would you confirm that t'Stror is the spy?"

Janara stared at the wall behind Kirk. The briefing room was austere and impersonal. In contrast to the bland setting, Kirk's determination to achieve his goals blazed like a supernova. Once Kirk had decided her telepathic abilities could help him and his crew, Janara realized, nothing she—or anyone else—could say would deflect the captain from his chosen course.

Even Federation law, Janara suspected, was an annoyance for him to circumvent, if it interfered with his ability to protect his crew. Janara shuddered at the thought of deliberately contacting the alien presence she had sensed aboard the *Enterprise,* but realized circumstances made refusing Kirk's request almost impossible. Even as she acknowledged this, she knew she could not yield the principle that justified her initial refusal. Bowing her head, she said, "Under protest, Captain, I will do as you ask."

"Your objections are noted, Lieutenant White-horse. And thank you."

Janara accepted his words with a tight-lipped nod and left the room.

"How did you know she would agree?" Tenaida asked.

"The look on her face after Yendes was killed. I figured another murder would be the more painful option for her. I just had to state my case in those terms."

"Your analysis was correct, but I don't understand how you reached your conclusion. Our people are conditioned from birth to abhor intruding on another being's privacy."

"I simply chose the only remaining logical alternative to our problem," Kirk answered with a slight grin that faded almost instantly. "Right now, I've got a new problem I need some help with."

"Captain?"

"I think I'm married. The Kaldorni, on the other hand, *know* I'm married. You two have to find me a way out of it."

Brady opened his mouth, but the expression on Kirk's face convinced him that not even friendship would save him if he wasn't careful. His jaw snapped shut. Swallowing once, he tried for a neutral tone. "You're married, Captain? How did that happen?"

"I'm not exactly sure, but—" Kirk described the previous night's events, trying to remember every detail, whether it seemed important or not.

"That's it. They're in my quarters now, and I spent the night in the chair. Damn uncomfortable place to sleep, too." He rubbed the small of his back to ease the stiffened muscles.

"Three of the Kaldorni ambassador's wives?" Brady scratched his head, amazed. The women had kept to their quarters since coming aboard, and the ship's grapevine was rife with speculation over their isolation. A puzzled look crossed Brady's face as he tried to evaluate the effect this development would have on their dealings with the Kaldorni.

"I didn't ask for any jokes, Mr. Brady." Kirk realized he was overreacting, but Brady's expression reminded him of the third-rate comic whose act consisted of an hour's repertoire of Starfleet jokes. "You've got to get me out of this!"

"According to Federation law," Tenaida said, "a marriage ceremony is legal and binding if the participants accept it as such. By taking part in the ritual, it is presumed that you accept its validity."

"But, Tenaida, nobody told me it was a marriage ceremony until it was over. Nobody in the Federation even knew what their marriage ceremony was, until they sprang this on me. There has to be a way to get me out of this. I don't want three wives! Besides, do you know how hot they've got the temperature in my quarters? A Vulcan might enjoy it, but another hour of it will kill me!"

"Captain, I am certain the environmental controls cannot be set to lethal temperatures."

"Well, it feels like it. I'm depending on you to find me a way out of it."

"Tenaida says it's legal, Captain. Besides, have you considered the repercussions of telling the ambassador you don't accept the validity of his ceremony?"

"What if I stay married? He expects me to treat them the way a normal Kaldorni husband would. And I haven't a clue how to do that."

"It *is* a delicate problem in diplomacy, sir." Tenaida canted his head to the side. "I will research the legal and cultural ramifications and see if I can find an answer to your dilemma."

Kirk sighed. "Thanks, Tenaida. Talk with Kristiann Norris, while you're at it. She's been studying the Kaldorni for Commissioner Montoya, and maybe she can help."

"All right, Captain. I'll start immediately."

"Thanks, Tenaida. A lot." Kirk stood, arching his back to loosen the cramped muscles. "I'm getting that other cup of coffee now. Does anyone want to join me?" Both Brady and Tenaida refused, insisting they had work to do.

Kirk played with his coffee cup, wishing he had gotten more sleep. Even if McCoy let him borrow his quarters, he doubted a nap would give him any more rest. Besides, a captain should be an example for his crew. Kirk sighed and drained his cup.

"Oh, Jimmy, how nice to see you. Do you mind if I join you?" Cecilia Simons stood at the end of the table.

"I was heading for the bridge."

"I wanted to talk over old times with you. If I didn't know better, Jimmy, I'd think you were avoiding me."

Kirk forced himself to smile. "On a ship this big, the commanding officer has many duties."

"Surely you must have some time for yourself—and me."

Kirk took a deep breath to calm himself, and immediately regretted it. Her perfume was overpowering, drowning him in its cloying fragrance. He shook his head to clear it. "There's more to the captain's job than you would think. Right now, I am very busy."

"Tell me what it's like to be a starship captain, then. I'm dying to know everything you've been doing."

"Not right now, Ms. Simons. I'm due on the bridge." He stood, taking his cup to put in the recycler on his way out.

"Jimmy, could you do me one little favor?" Her voice was low and sultry, calculated to make any man beg to please her. Kirk felt the hackles rise along the back of his neck.

"What's the favor?" he asked, fighting against her strange allure. *How does she do it?* he wondered.

"I wanted to record some messages in my free time." She gave him a diffident smile. "I mean, since I can't visit with Janie—"

"Yes, continue." Kirk's voice was cold.

"Anyway, I wanted to write some messages—" She slid her food tray onto the table and moved closer to him. Her hand caressed his throat in rhythm with the thunder of his pulse. He swallowed hard, uncomfortably aware of how close to him she was standing. Then he remembered Tenaida's instructions to be "as a rock in the rain." He visualized himself as a stone, inert and unyielding, and felt the pressure of Simons' sex appeal lessen.

"—and I couldn't get any of the computer consoles to work for me. When I asked, everyone said your science officer had cut off access to the computer, and I'd have to get a security code from him." She shrugged, acting bewildered. "He said he wasn't authorized to give out codes to passengers."

"I'll talk to him about that," Kirk said.

"Jimmy, could you *please* give me the code? I don't want to talk to him again. He scares me. I'm afraid he'll do something to me."

Tenaida won't, but I may! Kirk shuddered with the

force of his anger. He plucked her hand from his shoulder. "Ms. Simons, I told you I didn't want to hear any more of your anti-Deltan remarks. As for your computer access, I put Tenaida in charge of assigning the codes, and you'll have to get yours from him. However, I'll tell him to have it ready when you ask."

"Very well, Captain." Dismissing Kirk, Simons threw herself into a chair and began eating her breakfast. Her anger showed clearly in the tight lines around her mouth. Kirk took one final look, noticing the wrinkles around her eyes and how she tried to disguise her age with makeup. When her attention was focused elsewhere, it was difficult to understand why she was so irresistible. He turned away, eager to escape before she thought of anything else she wanted from him.

Janara checked the indicators that reported the status of the recording equipment in the briefing room. Two units ran at all times, and a backup recorder was ready, if needed, to replace either of the primary units. She felt conspicuous, as though she had no right to witness the negotiations.

She concentrated on the people seated around the table and tried to suppress her revulsion for such telepathic probing. To isolate the spy, she had to lower her mental defenses, becoming vulnerable to stray projections. Although she tried to focus on the briefing room, Janara caught flashes of the crawling sexual heat she associated with her mother's attempts to suborn some hapless male. As it had since childhood, exposure to her mother's tactics induced a violent attack of nausea. With an effort, she brought her stomach under control, fighting her instinct to retreat into catatonia. She rechecked the Kaldorni in the room, but t'Stror was still absent. Janara wished he would return, so she could determine if he was the spy. None of the Kaldorni in the room had a mental signature even close to that of the savage predator she feared.

To control her agitation, Janara started some calming exercises to keep her mind detached and receptive. Once she reassembled her defenses, Janara knew she could never force herself to lower them enough to identify the alien.

When the contact came, she was unprepared for it. One moment, she was checking the recording equipment and trying to ignore the thoughts of a passing crewwoman. The next thing she knew, the giant cat was inside her skull, shredding her brain with its claws. Janara lashed out in fear and pain. The mental projection retreated in surprise, and Janara slammed her shields into place. She envisioned a polished metal wall encircling her mind, and the cat's renewed attack bounced off without touching her.

With difficulty, she focused on the scene in the room. While she was fighting off the telepathic attack, t'Stror had entered and was now talking with the ambassador. Janara opened a crevice in her mental wall, probing for t'Stror's mind.

The second attack was as vicious as the first. Janara reinforced her defenses, hoping they would repel the assault. When the mental pressure abated, she realized t'Stror was staring at her. The hatred on his face matched the savagery of the telepathic attack. Janara forced herself to look away. Every muscle in her body was shaking.

Chief Engineer Montgomery Scott grumbled about the ship's incompetent dietitian as he checked the information on his reader board against the equipment displays. The waste recovery system could not handle the discrepancies in Leftwell's parameters for the Kaldorni food program. The incorrect input settings had overloaded the trace element processors, crashing the entire subsystem. Scott was still muttering about the abuse to his machinery when the room lights brightened, then every indicator on the main panel went red.

He hit the intercom switch. "What's happening?"

"There's a rupture in the fuel flow. The magnetic field collapsed and the portside engines dropped off line."

"On my way." The noteboard hit the counter and bounced to the floor as Scott ran for the turbolift. He skidded into the main control room as the power levels dropped to zero.

"Emergency power!" He grabbed the edge of the counter and hooked his foot under the top rung of the ladder to anchor himself against the sudden loss of gravity. While he slapped all the override switches he could reach, Layne's hands flew over the panel, cueing in the sequencing commands. The gravity generators gave a stomach-twisting pulse, then settled back to half power as the system switched over to batteries.

The intercom sounded before they finished shifting to the backup systems. "Scott!" Kirk yelled. "Why did you cut power from the warp engines?"

"We dinna do it, Captain."

"Bridge monitors show the warp engines were taken off line by someone in Engineering."

"I'll check, Captain. But I dinna authorize it. Scott out."

"We thought you went to check the dilithium converter assemblies. Dettner went to help you," Layne said.

"Thank you. I'd better get down there."

Scott tripped over something at the base of the ladder. He leaned down and turned the body over. Even in the red glow from the emergency lighting system, the deep gashes showed through the dark blood on Dettner's face. Scott shouted up to Layne, "Get a medical team. And Security, on the double."

"What is it?"

"Someone's attacked Dettner. Probably whoever

took out our engines. Get that security team!" Scott looked around, searching for any sign of unauthorized personnel. No one was in sight. He shook his head, realizing anyone who knew enough about the *Enterprise* to take the engines off line also knew enough to do it from the maintenance section.

"You're not going after the intruder, are you?" Layne asked.

Next to the ladder was an equipment locker. Scott took out the largest wrench he could find and hefted it. "Aye, I am." The idea did not make him happy. "We canna leave any stranger with our power systems for any longer than we must."

Scott crossed the engineering room, pausing to check the dilithium assemblies. They were untouched. Behind him, he could hear Layne sending for assistance. He reached the maintenance section, but the door was locked from the inside. Swearing to himself in Gaelic, Scott removed the access panel and entered the override code.

The door slid open, revealing a complicated array of equipment, monitors, and subsystem modules. The ship's functions were controlled by panels in the main engineering room, but for the ship's safety, every aspect of the engineering and life support equipment could be independently monitored and adjusted by equipment in the maintenance section.

The intruder was in the far corner of the room. A man of Scott's height and build, wearing a blue-gray Engineering uniform, hovered over the regulator unit for the warp engines. The flickering indicator lights threw sinister patterns across his cheeks. Scott ran forward. The man looked up, and Scott froze. The resemblance was so exact that the engineer felt he was looking in a mirror.

The intruder yowled—a chilling sound more appropriate to a Koorane nightstalker—and charged. His fist caught the chief engineer in the face. Scott lost his balance and fell, hitting his head against the edge of a counter. The intruder turned, shoved home several switches on the control panel, and ran for the access hatch to the lower decks.

The room spun around Scott. He struggled to rise, but had only reached an unsteady sitting position by the time the security men and the first officer found him.

"Did you see the intruder?" Brady asked.

Scott felt the back of his head. His fingers came away bloody from a small cut. "Aye. I thought I was looking at myself," he said.

"What?"

"He looked more like me than my own twin brother."

"How close did you get to him?"

Scott glanced at the blood on his fingers. "Close enough."

Brady stared at Scotty, bewildered. Kirk had seen the spy trying to impersonate him, but they all had been convinced that the disguise would not pass close inspection. How could the intruder have fooled the chief engineer at such proximity? It made no sense. The skills and equipment required to produce such a perfect impersonation were monumental. "Is this where you found him?"

"Aye, but I dinna ken how long he was in here before we caught him. We'll have to check everything before we know."

"Then do it, Mr. Scott. We have to find all the tampering. The warp engines are down, and Commander Sulu reported peculiar energy readings when he tried to bring the impulse engines up to full power."

"I'll get started right away."

"You'll do no such thing, Scotty. At least, not until I've checked you over." McCoy advanced on Scott, his medical tricorder poised for action.

"Doctor, you heard what Commander Brady said. Our power systems are out. I don't have time to play games with you and your medical gadgets."

"I'll relieve you from duty, Mr. Scott. I have the authority."

"Do it after I get the warp engines on line again." Scott pulled himself upright and keyed a diagnostic sequence into the console.

McCoy ran the tricorder over the chief engineer's body, checked the readings, and scowled. "You've a nasty bump on your head, possibly a concussion. But if you'll report to Sickbay when you get the engines fixed—or if you experience any dizziness—I won't drag you in now."

"Thank you, Doctor." Scott turned away, immersing himself in the *Enterprise*'s power systems. He was so busy he did not even notice when McCoy left.

Brady followed the doctor to the door, his expression tense with worry. "How serious is his injury? Will it affect his work?" He kept his voice low to prevent Scott from hearing his question.

"It shouldn't. He'll have a bad headache, and his head will be sore for several days, but it's not as bad as I told him." McCoy slung the tricorder over his shoulder. "If it was, I'd haul him into Sickbay in spite of the engines."

"Thank you, Doctor. If you'll excuse me, I'll go help him." Brady retraced his steps, his silhouette outlined by the multicolored indicator lights on the control consoles. McCoy gave the blinking panels a final look and headed for Sickbay. Dettner needed surgery to repair the deep slashes on his face.

Srrawll Ktenten prowled the quarters assigned to her alterbody, t'Stror. She flexed her fingers, feeling the thickened nails, and fought the instinct to transform into something more able to eliminate danger. The predatory forms of her homeworld were worse than useless. No one would mistake a savage, catlike *phena* or a powerful, wolflike *talbera* for one of the *Enterprise*'s regular crew.

She snarled under her breath. Her own careless-ness had cost her a flawless cover. She should never have believed the Simons *vrith'k* when she said her Deltan cub was harmless. Ever since boarding the *Enterprise,* Srrawll had felt the mind-hunter pulling in her thoughts. Though Srrawll was not, in the strictest sense of the word, telepathic, her race had evolved on a world populated by telepathic predators. Survival depended on detecting an attacker's use of telepathy.

Srrawll threw herself at the bed and curled up in a ball. To save herself and prevent the aliens from stealing her homeworld, her next move must be planned and executed meticulously. She closed her eyes, surrendering to a vision of a mature *kenda* tree with a comfortable nest in the hollow of a forked branch. The air was warm and scented with summer flowers—and there was nothing larger than a fright-ened *karra* within a long run in any direction. After a few moments, she leaped off the bed. Such homesick self-indulgence would not repel the invaders nor would it solve her immediate problem. She must control herself, must examine her options and plan carefully. The safety of her world depended on her, and she could not afford another mistake.

Kirk was outside the briefing room door when the negotiations recessed for lunch. He waited for Ambas-sador Klee to come through the door. "May I have a word with you, Mr. Ambassador?"

Klee dismissed his aides and gestured for his honor guard to follow him at a distance. "I am going to have my luncheon repast with the women who are my wives. Offense is not intended when I ask you to talk as I go to my quarters."

"None taken." They began walking slowly down the corridor. Kirk adjusted his strides to match Klee's pace.

"Are your new wives a pleasure in the hours that you spend with them? I have tried to train them always to delight the wishes of their husband."

"Mr. Ambassador, that's what I wanted to talk to you about. I don't feel right taking your wives from you."

"But it is correct that you should have them, honored Captain. Your esteemed servant was able to heal them after the rituals of our people had failed. It is proper that they should belong to the man who is able to protect them."

Kirk shook his head. "You are guests on my ship. It's my duty to care for everyone aboard. No special thanks are needed."

"It is also a matter of my honor that I cannot remain married to those I cannot protect. I have no honor if I do not permit these women to dwell with the man who can provide for them what I cannot."

"That's the point, Mr. Ambassador. I'm a ship's captain. All I have is my Starfleet salary and a few personal possessions. There's barely enough room for me in my quarters, let alone three other people. I don't have any way to accommodate your wives properly."

"Most respected Captain, the women we are discussing are now *your* wives. It is not proper that you should diminish their honor by calling attention to their previous, unworthy husband. However, as captain, do you not have the ability to command anything you desire? Certainly, you should be able to order for your wives the living space they require."

"Uh, right," Kirk stammered, taken aback by the ambassador's immovable certainty and utterly unsure how to get around it. The conversation was not going at all as he had planned. He was still looking for a new way to phrase his objections when they reached Klee's quarters.

"If the honored captain will excuse me, I must now

attend upon my wives." The ambassador bowed slightly and extended his arm in farewell. Kirk did his best to repeat the gesture as Klee disappeared into his cabin. How, Kirk wondered, was he ever going to persuade the Kaldorni to take back his wives? His arguments were useless against Klee's talk of honor and obligations.

"All right, Tenaida—explain how the intruder got into the computers *this* time." Kirk heard the edge in his voice and realized his frustration from the interview with Klee was spilling over into this discussion.

The Deltan dropped a plastic disk onto the table. Kirk frowned. The Engineering access key carried the operating codes for the computer-controlled stations in the Engineering section. Anyone with that key could completely disable the *Enterprise*.

"The intruder attacked Lieutenant Dettner and used his key to get into the Engineering control system. When I designed the new security program, I didn't consider stolen access keys."

"Or that the spy would know enough to steal one."

"True. Until this action, the intruder hadn't shown such detailed knowledge of the ship's operations."

"Maybe someone told him. Or maybe he hid out in Engineering long enough to pick it up. The question is: how bad was the damage, and how do we keep him from doing it again?"

"I've assigned passwords to restrict the access keys. I also designated codes for the medical department's keys, although it would be more difficult to disrupt the ship with the programs controlled through the medical keys."

"And how bad was the damage this time?" Kirk asked.

Tenaida called up Brady's damage report on his screen. "The initial power surge overloaded the warp drive regulator units and fused half the control circuitry. Commander Scott is still assessing the minor problems. He'll log those and report progress of the repairs on the computer later."

"In other words, Scotty said, 'Don't bother me, I'm fixing my engines.'" Kirk gave Tenaida a strained, lopsided grin. "How long will the repairs take?"

"Mr. Scott estimates he will need twenty hours to replace the control circuits. And another ten to bring the system up to operational specifications."

"*Thirty* hours?" Until the repairs were completed, the *Enterprise* was helpless—a sitting duck for any threat that came along. "Did you get all the intruder's programming out of the control systems?"

"I don't know, Captain. I disabled the segments I found, but Commander Brady and I should examine all the programming in the Engineering control systems."

Tenaida hesitated uncharacteristically for a moment. "And, Captain—there's something else I think you should know."

"Yes?"

The Deltan twisted the stylus in his hand, fidgeting from nervous tension. "Word has spread among the crew that the three Kaldorni women are staying in your quarters. I have heard—jokes—about it. Captain, it is not good for your image to have them there."

"Don't tell *me* about it! I thought I'd given that problem to you to solve. Haven't you or Commander Brady come up with anything to get me out of the marriage yet?"

"I regret that we have not yet formulated a viable plan."

"Well, if you get any ideas, let me know immediately!"

The intercom whistled. The captain tapped the pad. "Kirk here."

"Captain, someone just found a body on the shuttle deck. It's one of the Kaldorni."

"On my way. Kirk out."

Kirk thought the turbolift would never reach the

hangar deck. He sprinted toward the crowd gathered behind the box-shaped shuttle and saw that the body was sprawled on the deck, tangled in the brightly colored and highly decorated Kaldorni robes. The clothing was nearly intact, but the limbs and facial features had been burned past any hope of identification. In spite of the ventilation system, the stench of the charred flesh hung in the air. Kirk felt his stomach heave with revulsion. He forced himself to look away from the body. On the deck half a meter away, a carrying pouch had spilled its contents on the floor. Among the items, Kirk saw an identity disc.

"Whose is that?" Kirk pointed to the plastic counter.

Security Chief Chekov stepped around the body, picked up the disc, and handed it to the crewwoman who was recording the scene. She slipped the disc into her tricorder. "Identity disc belongs to k'Vlay t'Stror, of Ambassador Klee's staff, from the United Worlds of the Kaldorni Systems."

"What?" Kirk seized the tricorder to verify the identification. The disc was t'Stror's.

McCoy worked his way over to Kirk. "What is it, Captain?"

Kirk pointed to the body. "Autopsy that as soon as Security is through. I need to know the cause of death and what burned the face and extremities like that. Also, compare the physiological parameters with the identity disc we found."

McCoy glanced at the body, grimaced, and looked away. "Is there anything else you want, while I'm performing miracles?"

Kirk shook his head. "We thought we'd found our spy. But the identity disc says that's him on the floor."

"I'll get on it right away." McCoy looked at the security chief, his eyebrow raised. When Chekov nodded permission, McCoy gestured to his assistants to load the body onto a stretcher.

Kirk followed McCoy out the door. Tenaida fell in step with him.

"Have you identified the intruder?" the Deltan asked.

"Lieutenant Whitehorse spent the morning in the briefing room. She said that her predatory alien was Speaker t'Stror."

"It appears that Speaker t'Stror is dead."

"Or we're supposed to believe he's dead. McCoy will find out the truth."

"I don't follow your reasoning."

Kirk felt the weight of his responsibilities drag on him. As captain, his decisions affected the lives of everyone on his ship. And once again, the spy had outmaneuvered him. He scowled in frustration. "Murder is rarely logical, Tenaida. But I'll bet the intruder thought we were getting too close, and decided to change identities by 'murdering' himself. What I haven't figured out is how he's going to pull off the masquerade."

Tenaida was silent until they reached Engineering. From the way the young Deltan's eyebrows were twitching, Kirk knew he had given Tenaida a lot to consider.

Montoya was talking when Kirk entered the briefing room. He waited until the commissioner noticed him. "Captain Kirk, can we do something for you?"

"I have a message for Ambassador Klee. I regret it's not a pleasant one."

"You will speak to me this message that you have," said the aide seated at the ambassador's left. Kirk could not remember the man's name. "I function temporarily as mouthpiece while the Speaker t'Stror meditates upon the imbalance of his overzealousness."

"My message is that one of your party has been murdered. The identity disc with the body belonged to Speaker t'Stror. May I extend my deepest sympathies to the ambassador and the rest of your party on the loss of your companion?"

Kirk's words sparked an extended discussion in clipped, guttural Kaldorni. Two of Klee's aides appeared to be offering contradictory advice. When they had finished arguing, Klee turned to Kirk. "There will, of course, be reparations."

"I beg your pardon?"

"It is said that the captain is responsible for all that occurs upon his ship. Therefore, it is the carelessness of the captain that has caused the loss of this valuable servant. As a man of honor, the estimable Captain Kirk will wish to give to us the life of one of his servants who is equally valuable."

"Servants?" Kirk shook his head. "I don't own the life of anyone on this ship. I cannot do as you request."

"We do not *request* this, and all we see obey your commands as master. We have observed the way of your ordering your servants and the value of the duties that they supply you. It is our opinion that there is one among your servants who is seen by us to be of greatest value. The insult to our people may be appeased by the life of the one you call Tenaida."

"His life is not mine to give. He is a free man."

"This cannot be. Free men give orders, not receive them. Until reparations are made, we cannot continue in conference with these others from your people. When your honor is restored, we will talk again." The Kaldorni marched from the room.

Kirk dropped into a chair. "How did I put my foot in it this time? I'll never understand those people."

"Captain, would you tell us about the murder?" Norris smiled at Kirk. "Please?"

He rubbed his forehead, trying to make sense of the chaotic situation. "You people are the experts on the Kaldorni. Maybe you *can* help figure this out."

Two hours later, Kirk felt qualified as an authority on the Kaldorni and on Kaldorni psychology. However, he still did not understand the Kaldorni interpretation of the *Enterprise*'s command structure that had led them to choose the Deltan Science Officer-in-Training as the ship's most valuable officer. Nor did he know how to convince Ambassador Klee that he had no power to surrender Tenaida as a compensatory payment for the death of Speaker t'Stror.

Chapter Ten

"ALL RIGHT, BONES, what did you come up with?" Frowning, Kirk closed the door to McCoy's office. He turned a visitor's chair to face the doctor and slid into it.

Seeing the expression on Kirk's face, McCoy realized something must have happened since Security found the body. "You look like you've got another problem, Admiral."

"You can say that again! On top of everything else, the Kaldorni are demanding Tenaida's life as reparations for t'Stror's murder."

"Would it help if it wasn't t'Stror?" McCoy looked smug, pleased with the results of his foray into forensic medicine.

Kirk stared at McCoy, scarcely believing he'd guessed right. "You're sure?"

McCoy gave an emphatic nod. "The body isn't t'Stror's. The blood type, the antigen matches, even the body mass is wrong. The murderer tried to destroy all the identifiable features, but every test I can run on what's left proves it isn't t'Stror."

"Then who is it?"

"A Kaldorni. I don't know which one." McCoy shrugged, and some of his satisfaction vanished. "We've gone through our medical records on the ambassador and his staff, but they didn't tell us much."

"What about the support files for their identity discs?"

"Invasion of privacy. You'd have to ask Ambassador Klee or clear it through Starfleet Command, the Diplomatic Corps, and the Federation Council."

"I could try, but I don't think we can afford to wait that long. And if I asked the ambassador—assuming he'd talk to me about it, which I doubt—we'd alert the spy that we're onto him. Maybe Tenaida can get around the safeguards."

McCoy fiddled with his stylus to cover how uneasy his next information made him feel. "There was something else. The body was loaded with Trisopen-5."

"Trisopen-5? That's nasty stuff. How much?"

"Enough to make him remember his entire life in vivid detail. I'd say the murderer pumped his victim dry of information before killing him."

"The spy. It's got to be. We thought he was masquerading as t'Stror. He must have guessed we'd caught him."

"So he used the truth serum on another Kaldorni, killed him, and assumed the identity of the murdered man. It would fit the facts, though I don't see how he expects to pull off the masquerade for long." McCoy shuddered, appalled at the killer's cold-blooded planning.

Kirk nodded. "It doesn't seem likely, but he's apparently used mind control on some of us, so maybe he thinks he can use it on the Kaldorni to hide the substitution. Or, maybe he's been using some type of mental manipulation all along to cover the flaws in his disguises. Otherwise, even with the most advanced biocosmetic fabricator he could steal, I don't see how his impersonations could be *that* good."

"He's been pretty successful so far," McCoy answered pointedly.

"True, but this does solve one of our problems: If

one Kaldorni killed another one, they're both the ambassador's responsibility because he selected his aides and is accountable for their actions. Bones, do you think that will get Tenaida off Klee's hook?"

McCoy doodled a pattern on the desktop. "It might. It's certainly worth a try." He shoved a datapad across the desk to Kirk. "He should have this autopsy report, since the victim was one of his people."

Kirk picked up the report. "I don't know if this will work, Bones, but I'll give it my best shot. Klee seems to think I'm his equal since he gave me half his wives."

"Good luck, Captain."

"Thanks, Bones." Kirk looked at the noteboard in his hand. "I think I'll need it."

Tenaida loaded the tray with vegetables and cheese. After several hours of unsnarling the programming bugs in the Engineering control systems, he planned to eat a light meal and meditate before working out to relax himself.

"May I speak with you, Mr. Tenaida?" Simons glided across the room. She stopped in front of him and fluttered her eyelashes in a manner that Tenaida recognized as one that humans regarded as seductive. "Captain Kirk told me to see you about getting access to the computer. I'd like to send messages to some friends." She gave him a helpless little smile. "There's not much for me to do, since my husband is working so hard."

"Indeed." Tenaida set his tray on a nearby table and gripped his hands behind his back to control a sudden tremor. Simons' proximity created spontaneous reactions in certain extremities. He dug his fingernails into his palms, telling himself that he was imagining things because he was tired. As a Deltan bound by his oath of celibacy, he should not be thinking of such matters. And as a Deltan trained to control his reactions around less sexually advanced races, he should not be experiencing such sensations. Gritting

his teeth, he struggled to assume the Vulcan poker face
that his immediate superior used.

"Which programs do you require?"

Simons regarded him with wide, innocent eyes. "I
really don't know, Mr. Tenaida. I usually just use
Yonnie's, but he's been too busy to tell me which ones
I need. Could you just give me his access code? I
mean, if it wouldn't be too much trouble?" She rested
a hand lightly on his shoulder. Tenaida's arousal
increased.

"Madam, you must have your own access code. If
more than one person uses a given code, the computer
will cancel it and erase any information it protects."
He took a deep breath and tried again to quell his
physical reactions. His body resisted, acting as if
governed by an external force. With a start, he realized what was happening: on a primitive, almost
unconscious level, Simons was a telepath. And she
wasn't a typical Deltan or Vulcan telepath—she was
one of the rare few who could impose her will on
others. At the moment she was projecting intrusive,
overpowering lust, hoping to distract him enough so
that he would give her the access codes she wanted.

"Can't you do anything so I can send my messages?" She moved closer and stared in his eyes. The
sensuality she projected became even stronger.

Tenaida picked up his tray and jerked free of her
clinging hand. "I'll compile a list of the programs
you'll need. When I'm done, I will assign you an
access code and clear the programs for that code. You
will be given the list when I have finished it."

"Would you do that for me?" she asked. "Could you
do it now? I'm sure the computer console in my
quarters is free. Yonnie is off somewhere having a
meeting with his aides."

"I cannot work on it immediately, as I have a prior
obligation." He bolted for the door, carrying his
dinner. Behind him, he heard her whisper a vicious
"Damn!"

In his quarters, Tenaida set the food aside while he struggled to reassert control over his body. Simons' mental assault had ripped through the delicately balanced restraints that governed his life. After his mind and body calmed and he organized his findings, he knew Kirk would be interested in his discoveries about Cecilia Simons.

However, at the moment, Tenaida's concern was less intellectual. Simons had triggered his mating instincts, and his body was throbbing with desire. However, on a human ship, he could not allow his physiology to follow its natural course. The long hours of lovemaking would overload the *Enterprise*'s air purification system with Deltan pheromones.

Tenaida shuddered, remembering his last leave on Delta Four and the two weeks he had spent becoming reacquainted with his three cross cousins and their soul mates. By the time he had left, they had become so close, so united in mind and body and spirit, that the merest brush of a fingertip was enough for them to share a deep emotional and mental intimacy. After a melding like that, what Simons suggested was the foulest perversion he could imagine. Tenaida fought his body, struggling to bring his erratic hormone levels under control. When he had calmed, he headed for the gym, hoping a vigorous workout would bring his troublesome physiology back under his conscious control.

Kirk knew little of the etiquette for visits among equals on the Kaldorni homeworld, but after some thought, he decided human customs would serve for the occasion. The Kaldorni women watched him curiously as he smoothed the imaginary wrinkles from the braid on his dress uniform but, observing his preoccupation, concluded they were not invited to share this ritual.

The dietitian had provided a drink that tasted almost like Kentucky bourbon, but contained nothing more harmful to Kaldorni metabolism than alcohol. Kirk was exceptionally pleased with the container fabricated to hold the liquor: a rainbow-tinted glass bottle that changed colors as it was rotated.

After checking and rechecking his preparations, the captain confirmed the meeting with Ambassador Klee. The door of the Kaldorni quarters whisked open at Kirk's first knock. As he entered the dimly lit room, Klee greeted him with a slight bow and a sideways roll of his head. Kirk did his best to copy the greeting.

"Honored brother, you grace our humble living space with your presence."

"The honor is all mine, to be allowed to share your company." Kirk extended the bottle. "May I present you with a small gift to express my pleasure. It resembles a beverage popular on the human homeworld." Smiling, Kirk gave the bottle to Klee.

In the room's corners, the extra heaters Scotty had found somewhere were operating at maximum, maintaining the temperature in the Kaldorni's quarters in spite of the power restrictions elsewhere on the ship. The temperature made Kirk wish for a tall glass of iced tea, but he knew he would have to settle for something else because the caffeine it contained was toxic to the Kaldorni. Much to Kirk's relief, Klee produced glasses.

"Would it be pleasing to the honored captain to share in the drinking of his gift? It would be my privilege to serve him if he would take a sitting position on the rug."

Kirk followed Klee into the central living area and sat beneath the large wall hanging. He would have preferred a chair, but there were none in the room. Klee joined him, handing Kirk a large, square glass of the synthetic bourbon. There was a long pause while they sipped their drinks. Kirk schooled himself to patience, knowing he had to follow Kaldorni custom here even though his own preference dictated immediate action.

"It is extremely rare to find a being from your Federation who is willing to conduct his affairs in accordance with the Harmonies of the Universe. The Captain Kirk is to be congratulated upon his skills as a human being."

Kirk gulped his drink in surprise. With his struggle to understand anything about the Kaldorni, such a compliment was the last thing he had expected from Klee. "One learns from one's instructors, and I've had a good teacher."

"The respected captain does his humble servant too much honor. There was a matter you said must be discussed before we arranged the matter of the reparations?"

"Yes. Dr. McCoy has completed his autopsy on the dead man." Kirk told the Kaldorni of the doctor's findings.

By the time Kirk had finished, Klee's face was a study in confusion. "Is there a significance to this story that I am failing to perceive? How is it that you can display so much certainty that the body does not belong to the man who is missing?"

Kirk considered his options. He was uncertain how Starfleet would react to his telling the Kaldorni about the spy—knowing Chen, he suspected she would disapprove strongly—but under the circumstances, the risk seemed justified. Klee listened, rocking back and forth with intense concentration. He made no protest and seemed to follow the logic behind Kirk's conclusions.

"If I grant the truth of this, it is needful that I accept the blame for what has happened because I failed to detect the disharmony of an outworlder among my aides." His face creased with a perplexed frown. "As yet, I see no proof that this thing is true. How can I make a determination on what I am told when both occurrences are so disharmonious? The Harmony of the Universe rests in the balance of its truths, but there is no harmony in any of this.

"And what does the honored captain propose to do for reparations? From either of these disharmonies, I am now missing the services of my most valued aide. The Captain Kirk cannot restore what is lost, but honor demands that he submit to me the life of his most valued assistant.

"It is not known how that one can replace the aide lost to me through the carelessness of the Federation's servants, but it is to be hoped that he will be trainable. It is most certain that the skills he gives to the venerable Captain Kirk are highly needed to protect those that serve me against the dangers of your greatly perplexing Federation."

At the word *trainable,* Kirk felt relief wash through him. When Klee had demanded Tenaida's *life* in reparations, he had meant the statement literally. Also, Kirk realized, Klee had chosen Tenaida as Kirk's *most valuable servant* solely on the basis of the work he had seen Tenaida do. The outline of a solution began to take shape.

Kirk drew a deep breath, struggling against his urge to rush now that he saw the pattern for solving his dilemma. "If you failed to detect the spy among your aides, wouldn't that carelessness negate the later carelessness of my people?"

"It has not yet been proven that this disharmony existed first. No explanation has been offered that will cover the impossibility of this stranger looking so much like one of my own that even I, the Protector of my Clan, cannot distinguish this strangeness. If the Harmony of the Universe is to be restored, the known discordances must be atoned for. Reparations for alleged disunities cannot be contemplated until the imbalance is proven."

"Until we determine what actually happened, wouldn't it increase the disharmony to demand reparations? What if you were to receive payment for an act that was your fault?"

Klee, obviously troubled by the implications of

Kirk's question, took a long time to answer. "A disunity exists. I seek to balance it in the only way that appears reasonable to me. If I do not protect the Harmonies of my people, I will be judged unworthy to guide them in their search for Balance."

"You've asked for Tenaida's life, but he's the person on the *Enterprise* who is best qualified to determine which of the possible—disharmonies—is the true one. Would you suspend your claim to his services until the matter is settled? Then we'll know who's responsible and what reparations should be paid."

Klee took even longer to consider this strange suggestion. Kaldorni custom contained no provisions for delaying reparations. Finally, Klee seemed to melt into himself with resignation. "It is not possible by the ways of our world to address disharmonies such as those you propose. Since the disunity cannot be balanced without creating another, finding the solution to this would seem the way the one called Tenaida can best serve the interests of my people.

"It is not my wish to appear rude to my honored guest, but I would meditate now that I might select a clearer path through the disharmonies you have brought me."

"I'm sorry my information was so disturbing, Mr. Ambassador. If you'll excuse me, I'll leave now. Perhaps we can talk again later."

Klee gave Kirk a deep bow, then prostrated himself before the wall hanging. He ignored Kirk as the captain let himself out of the rooms. Once in the corridor, Kirk leaned against the wall, savoring in equal parts his feeling of relief and the cooler temperature outside the Kaldorni's rooms. He had accomplished most of his objectives, but the strain of guessing the proper formalities had drained him. After a few moments, he headed for McCoy's quarters. He sorely needed to talk to someone who did not practice circumlocution as an art form.

* * *

Janara Whitehorse was certain working in her quarters was a direct violation of Dr. McCoy's orders. On the other hand, what the doctor could not see would not bother him, and Janara found the Shansar equations more relaxing than several other activities McCoy would have allowed. Tenaida's suggestions had pointed to a solution for the major difficulty. With that resolved, the rest of the model was falling into place. She had been absorbed in the equations for several hours when the door buzzer interrupted her concentration.

"Come."

Tenaida entered the room. She looked at him curiously, wondering why he had not called her before coming. The man moved toward her with a predatory, feline power foreign to the Deltan.

"Do you want something?" His actions seemed abnormal, alien. She slipped her hand over the intercom button and waited for his next move.

"You." He closed the distance between them and grabbed her by the shoulders. She punched the intercom to "Transmit" as he hauled her from the chair and crushed her into a bodylock. With the first contact, the savage, saber-toothed cat exploded into her mind, stripping away her defenses. Her consciousness cringed away from the mental onslaught. She struggled against the physical hold and tried to regroup her defenses on the psychic level.

The intruder flipped her against the wall as easily as if she were a toy. She slid to the floor, half-stunned by the impact, but used the brief time her assailant was not touching her to reinforce her mental defenses. Hampered by his Deltan form, the spy tried to kick Janara. She saw the blow coming and lashed out at her attacker's other leg. Thrown off balance, the intruder fell heavily, but rolled away before Janara could land a karate chop on his neck. The spy regained his feet and was circling warily, looking for another opening, when someone pounded on the door.

"Open. Security." The man's voice was muffled by the door.

"Come," Janara gasped. Her left side felt as if every rib had been broken. Her assailant, snarling savagely, ran for the bathroom to escape through the adjoining cabin.

The security team split. One man followed the fugitive while another raced down the corridor to intercept him. Janara heard a voice call for the doctor before she lost consciousness.

Janara moaned and tried to block the bright lights from her eyes. Pain lanced through her shattered collarbone and broken ribs.

"Lie still and don't move." Dr. McCoy's voice seemed to come from a great distance. Janara opened her eyes cautiously. The doctor's pale face and dark hair took shape against the blinding background. He smiled to reassure his patient. "Captain Kirk needs to talk to you now. I'll fix those bones as soon as he's done."

"Understood," Janara whispered. "May I see *Shan Tenaida*, too?"

"That's up to the captain."

Janara closed her eyes. She heard McCoy speak to Kirk, but the captain's reply was drowned by a woman's shrill protest coming from the adjoining room.

"What do you mean—let that Deltan *animal* see my daughter, but not her own mother? Hasn't he already done enough? He nearly killed her, and you're going to let him in there to finish what he started? He belongs in the brig, not running around loose assaulting people. When their hormones are acting up, they're capable of anything!"

"Madam." Kirk's voice was flat, betraying his thinning patience. "If you don't leave immediately, I'll put *you* in the brig. The rest of your allegations aren't proven, and there's no positive identification of the attacker. You may discuss visitors' privileges with Dr. McCoy after your daughter comes out of surgery."

Simons started to protest, but Kirk cut her off. He beckoned to a guard who had helped carry Janara's stretcher to Sickbay. "Escort Ms. Simons to her quarters, and see that she gets there." The man nodded. Simons looked from Kirk to the burly guard and left quietly.

Kirk called Tenaida to Sickbay. While he waited for the Deltan to arrive, he hovered behind McCoy, trying to interpret the readings on the monitor panels. "How bad are her injuries?"

McCoy set the large scanning unit for another pass over Janara's torso. The computer added the new data into the image, emphasizing the splayed cracks in the ribs. "She's in a lot of pain, and I need to fix those broken bones as soon as Christine gets the operating room ready."

"I won't take long, Bones. But the security men are positive her assailant was Tenaida, so I have to get her statement."

"You don't think he did it? You're out of your mind!"

"I don't know, Bones. At first, we were operating on the assumption that the spy could control minds and make people do things they wouldn't ordinarily do. Then Scotty saw his double in Engineering, so we know the intruder is also a master of disguises. That means I need to know everything I can about this attack. Was it Tenaida? Or someone that just *looked* like Tenaida? I've got to know what I'm up against."

McCoy scowled. "That's a problem."

"That's an understatement, Bones."

Tenaida entered the room. His damp face was deeply flushed, his breathing was rapid and shallow, and there was an uncontrollable tremor in his muscles. For a moment, McCoy wondered if Tenaida could have been the attacker. He inhaled deeply and concentrated on his own reactions, but he felt no more than the usual physiological warmth he experienced when he was exposed to Deltan pheromones. That made Simons' suggestion of attempted rape due to hormone imbalance extremely unlikely. However, something had happened to deeply upset the young Deltan. While Kirk questioned Tenaida, McCoy went to the dispensary to get him a mild tranquilizer.

"Where were you for the last hour, Tenaida?" Kirk's tone was grim.

"I was in the gym, practicing heavy gravity movements."

"Was anyone else with you?"

"Not that I saw. However, the exercise logs will confirm my activities."

"I hope you're right." Kirk told Tenaida what had happened, then pointed through the door into the examining room. "Dr. McCoy said she wanted to talk to you."

Tenaida stopped inside the door, studying the slight form on the bed. When he moved to her side, she seemed even more frail and delicate than she had from across the room. A sudden rage shook him at the sight of her bruised face, and he fought the urge to inflict the same damage on her assailant.

When Janara sensed his presence, her eyelids fluttered open. She tried to speak, but the pain kept her from taking a deep enough breath. Her hand stretched toward his, begging him to grasp it. He looked at her, torn by a flood of unexpected emotions. He tried to sort them out: tenderness, protectiveness, an overwhelming need to lose himself in her thoughts and feelings. *This is what my cousins give to their soul mates. I shouldn't be feeling this.* He forced the emotions down and clasped Janara's hand.

With the physical contact, he sensed the images in her thoughts, which were blurred by the painkiller Dr. McCoy had given her. She reached for the dark, cool textures of his mind, letting herself drift among the surface patterns of his awareness.

Then she was gone, leaving behind a sense of her caring and her impressions of the being that had attacked her. He probed the memory, shuddering involuntarily as the image of the savage saber-toothed cat erupted in his brain.

"Tenaida, what is it?" Kirk's voice penetrated his concentration. The Deltan shook his head, trying to bring himself back to reality. He forced his fingers open and laid her hand gently on the bed. His whole body was trembling, and the wetness on his cheeks was not sweat. He took a deep breath and met Kirk's concerned look.

"She gave me her perceptions of her assailant and her memories of the attack. If you will excuse me, Captain, I need a few minutes to examine the information."

"Wait for me in McCoy's office," Kirk ordered. "Then we'll collect Commander Brady and go somewhere where we can talk." He turned to Janara. "Who attacked you?"

"Alien. Not . . . Tenaida." She spoke in a faint whisper, and Kirk had to lean over to hear her words.

"Are you positive?" Kirk knew he could not afford a mistake. Even though McCoy was hovering at the door, impatient to begin surgery, he had to be sure of Janara's statement.

"Not . . . Tenaida." Her whisper was definite, and Kirk knew he had not misinterpreted her response. He straightened.

"Your patient, Bones." He strode from the room.

"Well, Tenaida?" Kirk threw himself into the chair before the worktable in the Deltan's quarters. Behind him, Patrick Brady lounged against the wall, trying to conceal his tension with a casual pose.

Tenaida sat opposite the captain, stiffly erect in his chair. "The assailant projected the image of a large predatory felinoid into *Shan* Janara's mind during the attack. It would appear that was to keep her from defending herself against the physical assault."

"I'd say the plan very nearly succeeded," Kirk said.

"Yes. But why should the intruder attack her now? She's reported similar mental impressions since the Kaldorni came aboard."

"The spy has decided Lieutenant Whitehorse poses a threat to him. But—what is this spy? The security team reported they chased you—you, Tenaida—from the lieutenant's quarters. At that point, they had the turbolift on security override. No matter how good the spy is at mind control, your—body—could not have gotten from the crew quarters down to the gym in ten minutes without using the turbolift. I'd say that effectively rules out the mind-control hypothesis and every variation of it that we might consider."

"Agreed, Captain. The exercise logs will show I was in the gym when the attack occurred. It is equally unlikely, given *Shan* Janara's efforts to defend herself, that the intruder's disguise could have remained intact. Biocosmetic appliances are notoriously fragile during the first forty-eight hours after application, and such a violent struggle should have damaged or dislodged a significant percentage of the intruder's disguise."

"Does this mean what I think it does?"

Tenaida nodded. "For the spy to create the difficulties we have been experiencing, I believe the intruder has the ability to alter its body shape at will. When someone has appeared to be in two places at once—they were. The spy has been assuming our forms to disrupt the ship's operations."

"A shapechanger?" Kirk examined the idea. It explained a lot, but he had never heard of any creature who could do what this one apparently could. In particular, the ease with which the alien assumed new identities was hard to believe.

Brady straightened his posture as he considered this

concept. "Are such complete transformations physiologically possible? You're talking about a thorough duplication, even to the point that key physical parameters are reproduced. Like voice patterns."

"To account for the observed facts, the creature would have to have the shapechanging ability I have just postulated. In which case, we are dealing with a previously unknown race."

Kirk nodded. "I'll accept that. But back to the attack. Why now? Do you think the spy noticed Lieutenant Whitehorse in the briefing room this morning?"

"That's possible." Tenaida frowned. "That would require the spy to be telepathic—actually, that ability is probably necessary to carry off these impersonations. At the very least, I would assume sufficient psychic abilities to sense when a disguise is not sufficiently convincing."

"But how telepathic is that? The intruder obviously doesn't know everything about us. And why did he impersonate you for the attack?"

The lines around Tenaida's mouth deepened. "I don't know. Insufficient information."

Kirk frowned. Tenaida's unspoken thoughts hung in the air, almost as if they were in mental contact. Each of the three men knew that events were rushing toward a climax. Kirk felt an almost tangible aura of danger gathering around them. Somehow, he needed to regain control, to get the upper hand in the situation—for once, to be waiting when the spy made his next move. "A trap. We need some kind of trap."

Tenaida took a deep breath. "The bait must be something the intruder will find irresistible."

Brady stepped forward, "He seems to have a taste for Deltans. You could confine Lieutenant Tenaida to the brig. It's a good place to spring a trap."

"Yes." Tenaida stared at the corner of the worktable, refusing to meet Kirk's eyes. "Perhaps you should confine me to the brig, as Ms. Simons suggested."

Kirk grimaced at the idea of considering anything

from that source. "Let's leave that for a last resort. Anyone in the brig is a sitting duck."

"A *sitting duck*, Captain?"

"A—a target that isn't moving—one that's very easy to hit. The spy would know exactly where to find you, but you wouldn't have any way to defend yourself without giving away the trap."

"I'll keep that in mind." Tenaida fell silent.

Brady moved to Kirk's side. "Captain, if you don't mind, I'd like to run some simulations on this shapechanging idea. See if I can come up with its operational parameters."

"Sounds like a good idea, Mr. Brady. Let me know what you come up with."

"I promise, you'll be the first to know." Brady stepped back, resuming his place against the wall.

Tenaida shifted nervously in his chair. "Captain, may I change the subject?"

"What's on your mind, Tenaida?"

"I may have discovered something important about Commissioner Montoya's wife." Tenaida described his meeting with Simons, complete with a clinical account of his own reactions, and finished with his conclusions about her telepathic abilities.

"Subconscious projections of intense lust. Sounds unbelievable?" Kirk's face took on a far-off, thoughtful expression. "But it explains a lot. She was always so desirable that it was almost impossible to see beyond that."

Tenaida seemed genuinely puzzled. "It's irrational to spend one's entire life coercing other people to do things against their will and that lead to results harmful to them."

"Irrational. But human." Kirk frowned as a new perspective occurred to him. "Who?"

"I beg your pardon?"

"I assumed she did it solely for her own amusement. But with that ability, she would make a formidable operative for someone. If everyone is watching

225

her sexual exploits, no one will take anything else she does seriously." Kirk rubbed his forehead, trying to focus his tumbling thoughts. The idea, once formulated, had an inevitability he found compelling. Simons' act was too good, too well-rehearsed, to be played for low stakes. He shook his head in disbelief. "An interplanetary playgirl and spy. I thought such things were the product of bad fiction."

Brady shook his head. "You're speculating."

Tenaida seemed perplexed. "There's no evidence to support that position, Captain."

Kirk shrugged. "Call it a hunch, Tenaida. If we start looking, I'll bet we'll find enough facts to convince even you."

"Wouldn't our time be more profitably spent trying to trap the murderer?"

"Perhaps." Kirk shot a speculative look at Tenaida. "On the other hand, we might get lucky and catch both at the same time."

"Perhaps." Tenaida's tone was heavy with skepticism. Kirk's optimism asked more of the universe than the Deltan believed it would deliver.

Simons kicked her shoes at the far wall of the room and threw herself on the bed as hard as she could. She balled her left hand into a fist and pounded the pillow. The action barely diminished her anger, but her quarters lacked a more suitable punching bag.

Damn this job! And damn her restrictive position as Montoya's wife! And, especially, damn anything that put her within a megaparsec of her ungrateful, telepathic, and all-too-Deltan daughter! As long as Simons was not around the girl, she could forget she had a daughter. For that matter, Simons was sure Jane-Anne was equally grateful not to be reminded of her mother.

With her anger somewhat abated, Simons stretched out on the bed. Something about that last scene in Sickbay nagged at her subconscious. What was it? She ran the scene back in her mind: her protests against Tenaida, Kirk's anger at her words, his order to forcibly remove her. What was it he had said—that the assailant had not been positively identified, in spite of the eyewitness reports from the security men? Unless—

Snatches of overheard conversations and hints of information dropped by Montoya's aides reorganized themselves in Simons' brain. Someone else on the *Enterprise* was working her territory, and that person had a better cover than hers. She ran through the possibilities and realized suddenly who the spy was.

Simons bounced off the bed, and pulled her collapsed suitcase from the closet. The miniaturized phaser was hidden in the base, so she was able to retrieve it without re-expanding the case. She put the weapon in her pocket and returned the suitcase to the closet. One Kaldorni had differed from all others. If Simons' guess were correct, her competitor would be no more successful at hiding that difference in his new identity than he had been in his old.

She was smiling to herself as she left her quarters. With luck, the Kaldorni ambassador would be so incensed at losing another aide that he would terminate the negotiations immediately. If not—well, at least Simons would be able to operate without tripping over someone else's mistakes. The sooner she concluded this mission, the sooner she could get off the *Enterprise* and away from Montoya.

She went to the lounge for a cup of coffee while she waited to spring her trap.

Srrawll Ktenten prowled her quarters, snarling at the transcriber. It took an eternity to produce the hard copy that Ambassador Klee had requested. "s'Flen, do this. s'Flen, fetch that." Srrawll snarled again. From the standpoint of rank and privileges, k'Navle s'Flen had been the logical choice when she needed a new Kaldorni identity to replace t'Stror's. But s'Flen was not a member of the Clan Stror, and Ambassador Klee distrusted him accordingly.

His true function on the negotiating team was to prevent Klee from concluding an agreement that would give Clan Stror an advantage over rival families. And—much to Srrawll's disgust—s'Flen's major duties were errand running and operating the transcriber. The last piece of paper popped out of the machine. She gathered the sheets together and knocked them on the table with more violence than was needed to align the edges. With the transcript ready for the ambassador, she paused to calm herself and double-check her Kaldorni disguise before venturing into the corridor.

When s'Flen knocked on the door, Klee was talking with his wives. Much to Srrawll's relief, the ambassador took the papers without inviting s'Flen to join his family for the evening ceremonies. There were, after all, advantages to not being of Clan Stror. After a day of being Klee's errand boy, Srrawll needed the freedom to roam the ship, seeking the critical vulnerability that would topple her enemies and save her world.

She paused outside s'Flen's quarters, but could not force herself to reenter the room. First, she decided, she would get something to eat. The crew would not expect s'Flen to understand their language, and she might overhear something that would tell her how to eliminate the troublesome Deltans.

Her lips drew back from her teeth, and she barely suppressed the yowl that rose in her throat as she remembered how the little mind hunter had foiled her plan to dispose of both Deltans in one move. If the security men had arrived a minute later, the Whitehorse *tavra* would have been dead and the Tenaida nuisance confined to the brig for murdering her.

She entered the recreation lounge and thrust s'Flen's diet card into the food dispenser. The selector pads absorbed her savage keystrokes as she ordered the least obnoxious of the Kaldorni slop that the card prescribed. When the panel slid open, she took the tray to an empty table along the far wall.

"May I join you?"

Srrawll looked up. Cecilia Simons stood beside the table. Of all the humans she did *not* want to see—! One of the benefits Srrawll expected from disposing of the t'Stror identity was not having to service Simons' sexual appetites in exchange for the information the woman provided. Unfortunately, acting rude to the *vrith'k* was not in character for the diplomat s'Flen. "It would be my honor to with the reverent lady Simons speak."

Simons placed her coffee cup on the table and slid into the chair. She flipped back the long sleeve of her dress, revealing the phaser she held in her hand. It pointed at Srrawll, and Simons' hand was trunk-steady. "You can drop the awkward sentences, t'Stror. I know you speak better English than that."

"t'Stror is dead. Known am I as k'Navle s'Flen."

"Nice try." Simons' mouth split in a predatory grin. "But your walk gives you away. All the other Kaldorni move as little as possible, and that with obvious difficulty, because of the ship's heavier gravity. You try, but anyone with eyes can see how easily you move. I wonder why Captain Kirk hasn't noticed yet."

"What you are talking about, I understand not." Even to her own ears, Srrawll's protest sounded weak.

"But Captain Kirk would. Should I call him? And a security team?" Simons moved the phaser a few millimeters. Srrawll followed it with her eyes, barely restraining herself from swatting it out of the woman's hand. She knew Simons would be able to fire before she could reach the weapon.

"What is it you wish of me?"

"Talk. I want to know what you're up to. I think we're working toward the same goals, and we could profit by combining our forces."

"I do not know what it is you mean, but if you will conceal again your weapon, I will consent to whatever discussion you feel is appropriate to the situation."

A satisfied smile spread across Simons' face. "Act naturally and finish your food, then we'll adjourn to the briefing room where the negotiations are being held. Don't try any tricks, because I don't intend to let you pull a double cross."

"I lack understanding of what causes you this worry, but it will be as you say. One hopes this discussion will relieve the discordances that disturb your Harmony."

"I'm sure it will." Simons glided to the coffee dispenser for a refill. Srrawll watched her, snarling under her breath and wishing for a whisper-gun to throw a dart into the arrogant human's back. No double cross, indeed! Srrawll added another name to her list of nuisances scheduled for elimination.

Chapter Eleven

"DOCTOR, MAY I ASK Lieutenant Whitehorse a few more questions about her assailant?"

Chapel looked up from her computer screen. Even in the quiet of Sickbay, Tenaida's approach had been so silent that Chapel had not heard him. "I'm sorry, sir. She was extremely restless after surgery, and Dr. McCoy ordered a sedative."

"You don't agree with those orders?"

As she tried to decide how to answer, Chapel drummed her fingers on the counter. McCoy would consider discussing diagnoses with someone outside the medical department insubordination—or worse. However, Tenaida was the one person on the ship who would understand her concern. "I'm no expert on psi-related disorders, but I spent six months working with Tai Jorrel when he was rehabilitating the children from the Zebulon-Theta disaster." Chapel fell silent, remembering.

The initial surveys of Zebulon-Theta had detected no native life forms larger than a coyote. After reviewing the surveys, the Federation had established a research station on the planet. Six months later, the outpost's record logs began showing evidence of mental instability among the research personnel.

Ninety percent of the humans on Zebulon-Theta were dead before someone discovered the planet's secret: it had once been populated by a race of long-lived, powerfully telepathic beings. The last of these creatures were still on the planet, profoundly insane and craving death.

A handful of children survived the Zebulonis' racial suicide, but they were deeply traumatized by the psychic overload, which provided a catalysis for their own latent abilities. Intensive psychotherapy and massive doses of psi-suppressant drugs had been required before the children could function again in normal society.

Chapel shook herself mentally, returning her attention to the present. "What Lieutenant Whitehorse needs is a psi-suppressant, but the ship's dispensary doesn't have any that are safe to use on Deltans."

"I see. Would you be able to use *boretelin* under the present circumstances?"

Chapel searched her memory. It had been several years since she had worked with the Zebulon-Theta survivors, and it took her a moment to place the drug. "Tablets, right? Do you have some available?"

When Tenaida nodded, Chapel continued in a more confident tone, "Few interaction problems with other drugs, targets specifically to the psi-centers, no side effects. It's ideal."

"I'll bring it at once." Tenaida left as quietly as he had arrived.

While she waited for Tenaida to return with the medication, Chapel went to Janara's room to examine her patient. Janara was in good condition, except for another set of cuts and bruises. McCoy had fused the broken bones and closed the major wounds. Now, Janara needed rest so her body could repair the damage the *Enterprise*'s medical services could not.

Tenaida returned with the *boretelin* and gave the bottle to Chapel. After giving Janara a mild stimulant, she shook two tablets from the bottle and set the container on the counter beside the bed. When Janara stirred, Chapel slipped an arm around her shoulders and helped her into a half-sitting position.

"Here, swallow these," Chapel ordered in a low voice, holding out the *boretelin*. Janara stared at the tablets, her head swaying with groggy confusion, until she recognized the medication. She fumbled the tablets out of Chapel's hand and into her mouth. Chapel held a glass of water for Janara while she drained it, then eased her under the blanket. Janara was unconscious almost before her head reached the pillow.

Chapel straightened. "It'll be at least an hour before the sedative wears off enough for her to talk. You can ask your questions then."

"Thank you, Doctor." Tenaida turned and was gone, leaving Chapel alone with her patient.

The day's events had driven all thought of his Kaldorni *wives* from Kirk's head until he entered his quarters. The stifling heat reminded him he had yet to find a way of returning the women to Klee, but before he could retreat to safety elsewhere, the Kaldorni women surrounded him. They led him across the room and pressed him against the pillows they had piled on the bed.

Kirk was too tired to oppose three determined females, so he settled back without protest. Shade-in-Sun removed his boots and uniform, while Joy-of-Morning brought slippers and a light robe for him. Both were decorated with ornate designs that matched the women's own clothing. Looking at the decorations, Kirk decided his *wives* had learned the quartermaster functions of the ship's computer entirely too quickly.

He had just found a comfortable position after donning the robe when Fire-in-Night appeared with a tray of food. She presented it to him with an elaborate bow and then balanced the tray across his legs. Stepping backward, she stood beside the bed, waiting for commands. Joy-of-Morning brought a decanter and a matching wine goblet inlaid with a complex pattern. Fire-in-Night held the glass while Joy-of-Morning poured the wine. When it was full, Fire-in-Night offered it to Kirk with a liquid bow and a sultry smile.

Kirk took the wine, struggling to hide his impatience with the elaborate formality—this round was being played by Kaldorni rules. He reached for his detox pills, washing one down with a mouthful of wine before he started on the food. The meal consisted of spiced meat and vegetables served over a cooked grain. The combination of flavors and textures was unusual but pleasing. When Kirk had emptied the bowl, the women offered him fresh fruit and sweet cakes to finish the meal.

Kirk pushed the tray aside, hoping he had eaten enough to compliment the women's culinary skills. He pantomimed for the Universal Translator. Shade-in-Sun handed it to him and he thumbed it on.

"That was a very good meal. I thank you for it." He tried to speak slowly and to give his words the sense of ceremony the Kaldorni expected.

"It honors us to serve our most worthy husband. Is there anything else you require that Shade-in-Sun can provide you with?"

"Yes, I'd like some information." He paused a moment, wondering where was the best place to start. "What would happen if I sent you back to your planet by yourselves? It's not that I don't appreciate you," Kirk added hastily when the women started to cry, "but living like this, crowded into the captain's quarters on a starship, is no place for ladies like you."

Shade-in-Sun dashed her hand across her face to wipe away her tears. She fired a series of questions to the other women, speaking so rapidly the Universal Translator could not keep up with her. Her co-wives answered in the same staccato dialect, and the overlapping speech from the three threatened to overwhelm the computer. Kirk turned the machine off, hoping the women would tell him their conclusions when they finished talking.

After what seemed an interminable debate, the women fell silent and Shade-in-Sun faced Kirk. He reactivated the translator. "We do see the logic in our honored husband's statement that his room is most crowded, but as captain of this ship, our husband has the power to command that his lodgings reflect his more important status. We wonder why it is that our husband has not already done this."

Kirk groaned, wondering how he was going to convince these women of the difficulties inherent in their suggestion. By Starfleet standards, the cabins in the *Enterprise* were quite large. On a smaller ship, a cabin the size of Kirk's quarters would have accommodated nine officers on rotating three-man shifts.

Here, the space was assigned to his exclusive use. However, to increase his living space would necessitate major remodeling of the adjoining cabins and moving half of his senior officers to new quarters. Kirk shuddered to think how most of them would feel about the idea. "It's hard for me to explain," he said, "but the captain's quarters can't be enlarged that easily."

Shade-in-Sun looked skeptical but continued. "My co-wives and I agree it would cause us great sorrow never to see our homeworld again. However, if we go there with no husband or clansman to protect us, there would be small enjoyment of the little time we would have."

"Why?"

"There are many dangers on our world, and everyone must have a protector to shield them from harm. A husband defends wives, children, and perhaps even his younger brothers or cousins.

"Throughout one's life, one grows in strength and wisdom and is better able to determine what the Harmonies of the Universe are. But there are always those who are discordant and who seek to disturb anyone they can touch. Without the protection of a husband and his clan, a woman has little chance of surviving the discordant ones. Is this not how it is with your people?"

Kirk wiped his forehead, feeling hotter than ever. "Adults in our society are expected to take care of themselves."

"But then how do you achieve Harmony with the Universe, if there is no one to guide your searching?"

Kirk started to say most humans never considered the subject, but then he saw a way out of his dilemma. "Our people look for harmony in other ways. Would you explain the duties of a Kaldorni husband so I don't accidentally destroy your Harmony?"

Shade-in-Sun bowed to him. "Our husband is most wise." The women clustered on the bed, explaining to Kirk the duties expected of a harmonious Kaldorni husband.

Kirk escaped to the refuge of the lounge to mull over what the Kaldorni women had told him. On their violent, danger-filled world, protectors for the weaker members of the society made sense. What he would never understand was the complex web of ritual and obligation that formalized relationships in the culture. While he worked to unravel the puzzle, he listened with one ear to a duet between Lisbeth Palmer of Communications and a botanist he could not immediately place.

Kris Norris, wandering past the room, heard the music. She glanced through the door and saw Kirk. On impulse, she walked over to him and pointed at an empty chair. "Is anyone sitting there?"

"No." Kirk smiled at her. "I can't promise to be good company this evening though."

"A hard day? Goodness knows, I can sympathize with that, considering ours."

"I was working on an unresolved problem—by

trying not to work on it. Is anything happening with the negotiations?"

Norris shook her head. "I don't expect much before morning. Joachim asked if we could negotiate around your alleged lack of honor and harmony, and I expect Klee will suggest that we discuss the possibilities in more detail. And so on, until we reach a consensus for reopening the formal talks."

Kirk started to tell her about McCoy's autopsy and his own talk with Klee. Chekov entered the room and stopped beside Kirk. "Captain, may I have a word with you?"

"Business?"

Chekov gave a brief nod.

Kirk stood. "You'll have to excuse me yet again, Kris. A captain's work is never done."

She grinned back. "What can I say? A diplomat's job is only slightly better."

Kirk laughed and followed Chekov from the room. In the corridor, he moved up and fell in step with his security chief. They were silent until they reached Chekov's office. "All right. What is it?"

"I was looking at the recordings from the monitors we installed outside the quarters assigned to the Kaldorni. After listening to Commander Brady's hypothesis, I assumed t'Stror was altering his form and that he had disguised himself as t'Stror before coming aboard the *Enterprise*."

"The body Security found on Starbase 15 was probably the real t'Stror."

"That would appear to be a reasonable hypothesis. At any rate, I assumed that any distinguishing characteristic that separated t'Stror from the other Kaldorni would identify him in his new disguise."

"I agree. Did you find something?"

"I think so. I would like you to judge for yourself what I have here."

"By all means."

Chekov activated the computer console and then

stepped to the side to let Kirk watch the display. Scenes of Kaldorni in the corridor played across the screen, including several shots of t'Stror. "Captain, do you see how easily t'Stror moves? All the other Kaldorni have trouble walking in our gravity, and they say they find it difficult because it is so much heavier than what they are used to."

"t'Stror told me he had made several trips off planet and enjoyed the change." Kirk stopped, shaking his head to clear it. "What am I saying? That was the spy talking. But could it have been the real t'Stror's opinion on the subject?"

"I don't know. However, I would like to show you some other recordings. This one was made this morning, just before everyone was going to lunch." The screen showed two Kaldorni entering the turbolift. One walked easily and supported the other, who moved as if heavily drugged. With a start, Kirk realized the clothes on the dazed man were the same as those on the corpse found on the hangar deck only a short time later—they were watching the murderer lead his victim.

"That looks like enough evidence to accuse someone of murder. Do you know who?"

"I think so. I searched this afternoon's recordings, and have identified which one of the ambassador's aides I think the intruder has replaced. However, Captain, I wanted you to confirm my conclusion before I took further action."

"All right, Mr. Chekov." The computer cycled through the Kaldorni's movements during the afternoon. Kirk watched the sequence three times before he said anything. "There isn't much doubt, is there?"

"I did not think so, Captain. However, I did not want there to be any chance of error."

"Who is the spy now, Lieutenant? Do you have a name?"

"If my information is correct, he is the one called k'Navle s'Flen. He has a very high position in the ambassador's party. However, he belongs to a rival clan and Ambassador Klee does not trust him."

"I see. Now that we've identified the spy again, what should we do about it?"

A frown creased Chekov's forehead. "According to Federation law, you cannot put one of the ambassador's aides into detention unless Ambassador Klee waives diplomatic immunity for him."

"That's going to be troublesome. Unless—" A satisfied grin spread over the captain's face. "If we convince Ambassador Klee the person we want is an impostor, he should be willing to let us make the arrest."

"I do not see how you expect to accomplish that, Captain."

"I can't, but McCoy can. He's got the body of the real s'Flen down in the morgue. Now that we can tell him what to look for, I'll bet he can make a positive identification of the body within an hour. When we have his results, we'll tell the ambassador."

"Do you want me to put a guard on s'Flen?"

The thought was tempting, to always have the suspect within sight of someone Kirk trusted, but he forced himself to reject the idea. "No. If we gave s'Flen his own personal watchdog, it would tip the spy off that we've figured out his disguise. However, you'd better keep extra teams patrolling the corridors until this is cleared up."

"I hope that will be sufficient, Captain."

"So do I, Mr. Chekov. So do I. And if you'll excuse me, I'll get McCoy started on that autopsy. Get those extra guards posted as soon as you can."

"Immediately, sir."

The briefing room door whisked shut behind them. Srrawll whirled around, but the phaser had reappeared in Simons' hand. *Not yet, then,* Srrawll thought. The Kaldorni shape could not withstand the phaser fire. She concentrated, rearranging the cell structure across her chest and abdomen. The asbestos-like hide of the adult fire-fury would not repel a sustained burst of fire, but it would give her the critical seconds needed to reach Simons when the opportunity came. Srrawll clenched and unclenched her fists, feeling the fingernails strengthen and sharpen.

"Why don't you explain who you are and what your purpose is? I'd also like to know how you manage to change identities so easily." Simons gave Srrawll a frigid smile and wiggled the hand that held the phaser. "For starters, that is. And if you don't talk, I know some tricks with a phaser that aren't in the owner's manual."

Srrawll eased into a chair without taking her eyes off the weapon. "You were told correctness before. I am the ambassador's aide that is known as k'Navle s'Flen. It is not within my understanding to know why you suspect me of being a different thing."

A pitying smile spread across Simons' face. She shook her head. "Try again. You're really not that good a liar, t'Stror."

"The one called t'Stror is no more. The men of Captain Kirk found his body on the hangar deck. Why do you insist that I am that person?"

"The way you walk. The way you talk. Little things like that." Simons' smile widened and became more predatory. "Have you ever seen the damage a phaser will do to naked skin when it's set for narrow beam and one-quarter power?"

"I do not understand why it is that you continue to threaten me. What is it I have done that has menaced you?"

"You know as well as I." Simons' finger twitched on the firing stud. "Of course, if you're telling the truth, we could call for the ship's security people—to see if you really are the person your identity disc claims you are."

Protect! Protect! The urge crashed over Srrawll like a

cloudburst. Images of her warm, dark jungle flooded her mind. She fought the compulsion to rip out the woman's throat since Simons would expect such a reaction from a cornered opponent. Srrawll forced herself to slump in apparent defeat. Struggling to avoid the defiant snarl that bubbled in her throat, Srrawll asked, "What do you wish for me to tell you?"

"How about your identity and the nature of your mission?" Simons allowed a small smile of triumph to play across her face.

Srrawll studied her opponent, waiting for success to make Simons overconfident. Gathering herself for the spring, Srrawll slid lower in her chair. When she spoke, however, she kept the proper tone of defeat in her voice.

"We call our planet The World. It has no other name that has meaning to us. I am here to protect The World from those who would rob us of it." Her head sank into her chest in despair. "I have failed. You may use your weapon now."

"No." Simons shifted her phaser, aiming for a crippling shot at Srrawll's shoulder. "That's a start, but you can tell me more than that."

Srrawll uncoiled her legs and sprang in a powerful leap, striking at Simons' phaser hand. The weapon discharged, but the beam's main force was absorbed by the fire-fury skin across Srrawll's chest. The shapechanger's claws slashed the tendons in Simons' wrist, sending the phaser flying toward the wall a dozen paces away.

The momentum of the leap carried them both to the floor. Srrawll pinned Simons flat and covered her mouth with one hand. She pulled a syringe from her carrying pouch and injected Simons, waiting for the Trisopen to take effect before loosening her grip. A sound halfway between a purr and a snarl gathered in her throat.

"Why?" Simons' voice was weak and blurred from the drug.

"I don't owe the enemy any explanations. But in a few minutes, you won't remember it anyway." The shapechanger's lips stretched into a defiant snarl. "I do it to save my world. The fat ones come to steal it or fight over the theft with others as bad as they. If I knew how, I would kill all of them, just so they would leave my world alone!"

"That's nice." Simons' eyelids drooped as she slid into the drug-induced trance.

The spitting, snarling cat smashed through Janara's mind, ripping away the layers of drugged unconsciousness. McCoy's sedative was wearing off, but its action still interfered with the *boretelin* Chapel had given her. She struggled to block the cat from her awareness, but its attack grew stronger. She moaned and tried to open her eyes. Her eyelids felt as if they were made of solid lead, but with effort, she forced them apart.

At first, she did not recognize where she was. Even with the subdued lighting, she knew she was not in her own quarters. As the room came into focus, she identified the medical equipment and patient monitors, but could not remember how she had gotten to Sickbay. She tried to recall the events of the past few hours, but she was too groggy and the details refused to come.

As the savage cat renewed its psychic attack, Janara reached for the bottle of *boretelin* tablets. Her hand clutched it as if it were a lifeline. She shook out several pills and gulped them down, struggling to hold the cat at bay until the drug took effect.

Slowly, the cat faded to a darkness as black as its hide. The last thing that registered on her consciousness was the pain of phantom claw gashes across her torso.

Montoya looked up from the computer screen as the door closed behind his wife. "It's getting late. I was starting to wonder if something had happened to you."

"I was walking around." She dropped onto the bed, looking distraught and helpless. "That Deltan animal beat up my poor little Jane-Anne, and Captain Kirk won't let me see her. Her own mother!" She blinked several times, trying to hold back the tears that filled her eyes.

Montoya turned off the computer and crossed the room to join her. He put a comforting arm around her shoulders, holding her close. "I'm sure Captain Kirk has his reasons, but if it will make you feel better, we can go to Sickbay now and talk to the doctor. That way, you'll at least know what's going on."

"Do you really think they'd tell us anything?"

He looked at her pale, woebegone face and smiled tenderly. "You're her mother, aren't you? The captain was probably trying to say you'd be in the doctor's way while he was treating her. I'm sure they'll let you see her now, if she's awake."

"At this time of night?" Her voice cracked, and she looked away to hide her tears.

"I thought you said she worked the night shift." Montoya kissed her forehead. "Besides, if Dr. McCoy is as good as everyone says, Jane may be out of Sickbay by now."

"Do you really think so?" She looked up at Montoya, blinked her eyes several times, and swallowed hard before she spoke. "Could we go right now? I would feel so much better if I just *knew* how she was."

"I think we can manage that." Montoya stood and pulled her to her feet. She leaned against him for support as they left the room.

Chapel looked up from her terminal as two people entered Sickbay. Commissioner Montoya stopped beside the admitting station. "My wife is concerned about her daughter. We hope you can give us some information, and possibly allow Cecilia to see the girl."

Chapel stood. Montoya was not particularly tall, and Chapel's uniform boots gave her an additional advantage. She used it to emphasize her words. "I don't have the authority to allow visitors. Dr. McCoy left strict orders that Lieutenant Whitehorse was to see no one."

Simons sniffled. A large tear coursed down her cheek. "Is she in such bad shape that even her mother can't see her?"

"I don't know why Dr. McCoy said no visitors." Years of reassuring patients made it easy for Chapel to hide that lie. She summoned her most reassuring smile and continued, "The last time I checked her, she was resting comfortably. You don't need to worry on that count."

"Doctor, could we see her for a few moments? I'm sure that would relieve my wife's mind considerably."

"I'm not authorized to overturn my superior officer's orders in that matter." A trace of annoyance crept into Chapel's voice. "However, if you insist, I'll ask Dr. McCoy whether he wants to make an exception to his orders."

"We would greatly appreciate that, Doctor."

Chapel gestured toward the outer office. "If you will please wait in the other room, I'll try to find Dr. McCoy." When Montoya and Simons were seated, Chapel called McCoy, who was washing up after running additional analyses on the dead Kaldorni.

McCoy scowled when Chapel told him Montoya and Simons were in Sickbay, but while Chapel talked, he returned the body to the mortuary locker and traded his surgical whites for his regular uniform. When Chapel signed off, McCoy called Captain Kirk. He waited in the corridor until the captain arrived.

McCoy and Kirk entered Sickbay together. Montoya planted himself in front of McCoy. "Doctor, my wife is concerned about her daughter. Is there any way she can see her?"

Kirk stepped forward. "Commissioner, those orders are mine. They are for Lieutenant Whitehorse's protection."

"Surely you don't suspect the girl's mother of threatening her safety?"

Kirk glanced at Simons. She seemed strangely quiet. Uneasy but unable to isolate the cause, Kirk focused his attention on Montoya. "Commissioner, at the moment, everyone on this ship is under suspicion. Too many strange things have been happening."

"I still don't see—"

"Excuse me, sir," Chapel said, interrupting Montoya. "Captain, would you allow the commissioner's wife to see her daughter if you and Dr. McCoy were in the room?"

Kirk gave the idea a moment's thought and nodded grudging assent.

"But only for a moment," McCoy said. "She needs rest and shouldn't be bothered with visitors." He started toward Janara's room. Kirk followed them, frowning with concentration. It was not his imagination—there was something different about Simons' behavior.

"What?" McCoy rushed to his patient. The diagnostic panel displayed a mass of confused readings. Janara was drugged, but McCoy did not recognize the effects of any medication he knew. He moved closer and his foot kicked something. Leaning over, he picked up a small, square, rough-textured bottle. Its top was missing, and it held four or five brown, oval tablets. McCoy frowned, unable to identify the pills. He glanced toward Kirk. "Jim, tell Christine to get in here at once."

"How long has she been like this?" McCoy asked when Chapel joined them.

Chapel looked from Janara to the diagnostic panel,

comparing the readings with the ones she had been monitoring just before Simons and Montoya arrived. She shook her head. "Not long. I was monitoring her from the other room."

She circled the bed and opened the control panel for the monitoring equipment. The diagnostics program registered a null output. When she got the same results a second time, Chapel snapped the cover shut. "The transponder circuit is malfunctioning. It isn't sending any warning signals to my console."

"What's going on?" Kirk demanded.

McCoy held out the bottle to the captain. "Lieutenant Whitehorse took an overdose of something. I don't recognize these pills."

Chapel straightened to attention, looking like a trainee waiting for a reprimand. "The pills are *boretelin,* a Deltan psi-suppressant. I thought it would be more beneficial than sedatives for her."

"Deltan?" Simons pushed her way into the group. "First, you let that animal beat her up, and now you let him poison my poor little Janie. I want that creature punished!"

"Ms. Simons," Chapel said, "the drug may be Deltan, but it's hardly a poison. And if anyone is at fault here, it's me. I left the bottle within reach."

"I want that Deltan *punished!!*"

Kirk's thoughts snapped into focus and he realized what was nagging at his subconscious. Simons' words and gestures were the same, but she lacked the overpowering sexuality he identified with her. While he tried to unravel the significance of that insight, Kirk went to the intercom and called Tenaida to Sickbay. When he finished, McCoy was still questioning Chapel about the drug.

"The function of any psi-suppressant is to block off the areas of the brain involved with the psi functions. *Boretelin* was formulated for use on untrainable telepaths. It can be administered at high dosages for long periods without side effects." Chapel scanned the diagnostic panel again. "As far as I know, the only effect of a large dose is unconsciousness, but I've never heard of anyone taking quite that much."

Footsteps sounded in the outer room. Tenaida walked through the door in time to catch the last of Chapel's explanation. "Doctor Chapel's information is essentially correct. There have been occasional reports of allergic reactions, but no other harmful effects have ever been observed." He raised an eyebrow in a questioning gesture when he saw the almost empty bottle in McCoy's hand, but he said nothing.

"He's lying!" Simons' voice rose in a despairing wail. "First, he beat her up and said he didn't do it, and now he's tried to poison her with a drug he says is harmless." Montoya had followed Tenaida into the room. Simons went to her husband and buried her face against his shoulder. "Yonnie, can you do something, if these people won't?"

Montoya's arm tightened protectively around her. "Captain, wouldn't it be wise to restrain the suspect until you investigate the matter? I think my wife has a valid point."

Kirk felt as though a trap had closed on him. He knew Simons' accusations were ridiculous, but he could not afford to antagonize Montoya by saying so. The captain looked toward Tenaida, wondering what he was thinking. The Deltan caught Kirk's eyes and nodded almost imperceptibly. Kirk remembered Brady's earlier suggestion to confine him to the brig as bait for the intruder. Though the idea still troubled him, he saw no other choice. "Very well, Commissioner. If that will satisfy you."

"Jim, you can't—" McCoy protested.

Kirk gave a shake of his head, hoping McCoy would recognize the warning. When the captain spoke, his voice sounded tired. "Not now, Doctor. We'll talk about it later." He cut off further protests by sending for the security guards.

"I want someone with Lieutenant Whitehorse at all

times. She's been having too many accidents lately, and it's about time we practiced a little 'preventive medicine.' Also, just to be safe, I'm posting a security guard outside the door until further notice."

McCoy started to object, but a second look at Kirk's grim expression changed his mind. When the security men arrived, Kirk had them arrest Tenaida. After politely but firmly removing Montoya and Simons from Sickbay, Kirk went to the brig, ostensibly to interrogate his science officer.

By the time Kirk reached the brig, Security Chief Chekov was waiting. Kirk jerked his head toward the office. "I'll be with you in a minute, Mr. Chekov." He turned to the two guards. "Johnstone, Ramirez—put Tenaida in maximum security. And guard that door until *I* bring your relief."

The guards exchanged puzzled looks. Access into the cell block was controlled from Chekov's office. Tenaida was calm, accepting his arrest with complete equanimity, making such extreme precautions seem unnecessary.

Kirk glared at the two guards to warn them that his orders were not to be questioned. Johnstone palmed the door lock and waited for Chekov to release the forcefield. They escorted the Deltan down the corridor, and they locked him in a cell behind another force barrier. When the door field was restored, Johnstone and Ramirez took up their places on either side of the opening.

"Captain, would you explain what is happening now?" Chekov asked, stepping into the corridor.

Kirk pointed toward the security chief's office. The room was small and sparsely furnished, with surveillance screens covering one wall. Kirk closed the door and pulled a chair around to watch the monitors on the security cells. Satisfied with his arrangements, he finally answered Chekov's question. "Bait. I think the spy was in the room when I arrested Tenaida. If so, she will attack now while she believes Tenaida is confined and unable to defend himself.

"I want your two best men to trade shifts on that cell. One of them should be there at all times. Don't let either of them leave this area or get out of sight of another guard for any reason until this is settled. Is that clear?"

"Yes, Captain."

"When your men arrive, I'll give them the passwords I'll use if I want to see Tenaida. Absolutely no one else is to go into the cell, unless they're accompanied by me. If someone tries to get in without the correct password, or if I'm not with them, I'm ordering the guards to shoot first and ask questions only after the person is under restraints. Even if the person looks like me."

"Do you really think the spy will try to attack Lieutenant Tenaida while he is in maximum security?"

"Tenaida and I discussed it, Lieutenant, and we think there's a chance. Besides, what have we got to lose? If the spy doesn't move soon enough, I'll let Tenaida out and hope we've got a better idea by then."

Chekov called in two more guards. Kirk gave them their orders and passwords, and took them to Tenaida's cell. "Remember," he said, repeating his orders for emphasis, "keep in sight of another guard at all times. Don't even go to the head by yourself. I don't want to give the spy any opportunity to replace you and attack Tenaida."

"We understand, sir." The looks of grim anticipation on their faces told Kirk how badly they wanted to get their chance at the spy. He hoped the intruder would make her move before a long vigil wore down the guards' fighting edge.

When Kirk re-entered the office, Chekov was examining his monitor channels. "Would Lieutenant Tenaida mind if we used the video monitors to watch the inside of his cell? And listened with the enhanced audio sensors?"

"Take any precaution you think necessary. The spy has the advantage—she knows right where Tenaida is."

"All right, Captain. We will use all our sensors at full sensitivity." Chekov began keying in the commands and Kirk escaped to the relative peace of McCoy's office in Sickbay.

Kirk stared at the wall, trying to isolate the thought that he could not—quite—drag out of his subconscious mind. If, as he suspected, the shapechanger had replaced Cecilia Simons before Simons and Montoya came to Sickbay, then where and when had the substitution occurred? And what had happened to the real Simons? That afternoon, both he and Chekov had thought the shapechanger was disguised as the Kaldorni k'Navle s'Flen.

He turned on the computer, worked through the security clearances, and called up the afternoon's recordings from the intercom monitors. After five minutes' search, he found Simons and s'Flen entering the turbolift on Deck Seven. Kirk scanned forward and found where they entered the briefing room, but Simons was the only person who left.

After calling for a security team to investigate, Kirk went to the briefing room himself. The armed guards went inside, but returned immediately, looking worse for the experience. "There's a body in there," Tiilson, a stocky blond ensign, reported. "It's not a pretty sight."

Kirk entered the room. Simons' nude body was sprawled on the floor. The torso had been sliced open by parallel gashes that ran from collarbone to pelvis. Blood covered the body and the surrounding floor. Kirk turned away, grimacing.

"Get a stretcher down here at once," he ordered. "We'll need an autopsy on that body. And search the room for any clues."

"Yes, Captain." Tiilson hurried to the intercom.

Kirk listened to the guard's agitated voice for a moment, then turned to his tall, dark-haired partner. "Keth, tell McCoy I want the autopsy report the minute it's ready. I'll talk to Commissioner Montoya now and will be available after that." He paused, glancing over at the corpse once more. "Have the doctor wake me up when the report is ready."

"Aye, aye, sir."

Kirk stared at the intercom, wondering how to tell Commissioner Montoya of his wife's death. Montoya would not take the news well, especially given the circumstances of the murder. Finally, Kirk hit the control pad. There was no good way to break the news, so he might as well quit procrastinating.

The voice that answered the call was blurred with sleep. "Montoya here."

"This is Captain Kirk. I'm sorry to disturb you at this hour, but something important has come up. Are you alone?"

"My wife is asleep, Captain. Can't this wait until morning?"

If I put it off, Kirk thought, *there may not be any morning for you.* "I'm afraid not, Commissioner. Could you come to Dr. McCoy's office at once?"

When Montoya answered, his voice sounded more awake. "Very well, Captain. I'll be there in a few minutes."

"I'll be expecting you. Kirk out." He slapped at the intercom pad. "Chekov? Kirk here. Put a triple guard outside Commissioner Montoya's quarters. If his wife leaves those rooms, arrest her immediately. Use extreme caution; she's to be considered armed and dangerous."

"Yes, Captain."

"On second thought," Kirk said, cursing himself for his stupidity, "pass Montoya through, but arrest *anyone* else that leaves that cabin."

"Acknowledged."

"Kirk out." He slumped in his chair, fiddling with the strap on his chronometer. *Five minutes,* he told himself. *If Montoya isn't here in five minutes, I'll have to assume he's been replaced, too.* He activated a medical scanner and linked its output to the computer, setting the system to warn him if the scan registered less than 95 percent correspondence with Montoya's identity files. The phaser in his lap felt comfortingly solid.

Montoya entered and took the seat Kirk offered. "All right, Captain, would you mind telling me what's so important it cannot wait until morning?"

Kirk glanced at the computer screen. It showed a solid 98 percent on all scans. Knowing he faced the real Montoya did not make it easier to choose the right words. "Half an hour ago, we found a body in the briefing room, Commissioner. We're certain of the identification; it was your wife."

"That's impossible. I left Cecilia in our quarters not five minutes ago."

"I'm afraid that was an impostor, Commissioner. When we found her, your wife had been dead for some time."

Montoya opened his mouth to protest, but no words came. His jaw muscles twitched convulsively, and his face took on a numb, bewildered look. "You've seen the body, Captain?" he asked when he could speak.

"Yes. It wasn't a pretty sight, but I'm certain of the identification." Kirk shuddered, remembering just how well he knew Simons' body.

"I would like to see her, Captain. I have to be sure."

Kirk searched Montoya's face for clues to his emotional state. He seemed in control, as calm as the proverbial stone Vulcan. How long that restraint would last, Kirk could not guess, but for the moment, he decided to play things Montoya's way.

"Very well, Commissioner."

McCoy was doing the autopsy when Kirk escorted Montoya into the ship's morgue. The doctor threw a sheet over the torso to conceal the deep wounds from Montoya. He stared at his wife's face for several minutes without registering any emotion. Finally he walked out of the room, his movements slow and wooden. Kirk heard him drop into a chair.

"Bones, do you have any preliminary results?"

McCoy gave him a disgusted look: the condition of the body should have been enough to tell Kirk what the doctor's initial findings would be. "Cause of death: loss of blood and internal damage. You saw those slashes. Also, she was given a massive dose of Trisopen-5 shortly before she died."

"Just like the other one." It gave Kirk little satisfaction to know the spy was being consistent. Also, with Simons dead, they might never learn what her interest in their mission had been.

"There's something I'd like to show you, though." McCoy switched on a display screen. "I did a full body scan. Notice the dark area behind the left ear."

"An implant of some sort?" Kirk asked. "It looks like one of the code-receiving chips Intelligence uses for their agents."

"It's similar, but I don't recognize the design and the neural connections are wrong. It isn't one that our people admit to using."

"Can you get it out so we can study it?"

"I don't know. I'll try, but I'd prefer to have Tenaida and Scotty help me with it. These infernal gadgets often incorporate self-destruct mechanisms."

"In that case, don't do anything for a while. Tenaida should be free to help you in an hour or so."

"Good." McCoy returned to work as Kirk left the room. He was analyzing the slashes, hoping to learn what had made them, and he wanted to finish the job as quickly as he could.

Kirk stopped beside Montoya's chair, waiting for the other man to notice him. Montoya raised his head, giving Kirk a dazed, hopeless look. "What will you do about the thing impersonating my wife?"

"With your permission, sir?" When Montoya nodded, Kirk called Security. "Tell the guards on Commissioner Montoya's quarters to arrest anyone inside." He turned off the intercom.

"Thank you, Captain. Is there somewhere I could be undisturbed for a while? I need to sort some things out." He stumbled over the words, stretching them out as if talking was too great an effort.

"Use Dr. McCoy's office. He's busy and won't need it for some time."

"Thank you." Montoya staggered out of the chair. His motions, like his words, were stiff and mechanical. He acted as though his brain had divorced itself from the rest of his body.

Kirk took Montoya to McCoy's office. Montoya seemed oblivious to his surroundings, but Kirk gave him a glass of McCoy's medicinal scotch anyway. For a moment, Kirk found himself wishing he could join Montoya and postpone his next unpleasant duty, but he knew he would be needed soon in the brig. Before he reached the turbolift, the intercom paged him.

"Kirk here."

"Captain, no one was in Commissioner Montoya's quarters. And the guards saw no one leave the cabin."

"Acknowledged. Kirk out." He looked nervously over his shoulder as he hurried into the turbolift. Somehow, the spy had outguessed them once again and had evaded the trap. She was loose on the *Enterprise,* and Kirk had no idea where to start looking.

Chapter Twelve

When Kirk called Montoya, Srrawll suspected someone had found the body in the briefing room. Leaving it there had been sloppy work, but removing the evidence without attracting attention had been impossible. She had considered disfiguring the body, but without a false identity to mislead the investigators, the effort would have been wasted.

Destroying the body with Simons' phaser would have been better, but to Srrawll's disgust, the device had been keyed to Simons. By the time Srrawll discovered that, the flesh of Simons' hand had cooled enough that it would not trigger the sensors in the phaser's handle. When she left the body in the briefing room, Srrawll had hoped it would not be found until morning. Once Montoya was sound asleep, she could drug him as Simons had done when she had slipped out at night. Then, using Montoya's form, Srrawll could execute the fat ones. When Kirk finally discovered who was responsible, the negotiations would be over.

Now, however, she could not replace Montoya. In the short time available to her, even with the Trisopen, she might miss critical information needed to carry off the sustained impersonation of so important an individual. She feigned sleep until Montoya left, then opened the cabin's air duct.

Concentrating carefully, she visualized the sur snake of her home jungles. After a moment, she felt her form shift, lengthening and stretching. And then she moved inside, feeling the walls of the air duct against her scales.

Kirk drained the dregs from his coffee cup and grimaced. With the best food synthesizers and technicians in the Federation at his disposal, he *still* could not get a good cup of coffee. He reached for the carafe to pour another cup, wondering whom he had to bribe to get something that tasted like the real thing.

"Assistant," he said to the computer. "Scan and evaluate Commander Brady's files on the shape-changer theory. Is such an entity possible?"

After a long moment, the computer replied, "Commander Brady's files contain much speculation but no data amenable to analysis."

"But could such a being exist?"

"Insufficient data. Commander Brady postulates an ability for total transformation of cellular material. However, he does not stipulate the time parameters of such a transformation, nor does he specify how much of this hypothetical creature's metabolism would be directed to fueling the transformation. Other factors needed for the analysis include the physical size of the creature and its biochemistry. Without such basic information, no meaningful analysis of this problem is possible."

The door buzzer interrupted Kirk's irritated reply. "Come," he called as he deactivated the computer.

With a swish, the door slid aside. Patrick Brady, looking tousled and rumpled, entered Kirk's office. He threw himself into a chair and reached for the other coffee cup. "Captain, if you had to have a meeting at this ungodly hour, at least you provided the amenities. Though I'm sure your chief surgeon wouldn't approve of you serving it by the pot."

Kirk shrugged. "Is the dress uniform for my benefit, or did I interrupt something important? Does it have anything to do with that ensign you've been admiring?"

"Captain!" Brady said with injured innocence. "I'll have you know I've been working so hard lately I haven't had time for pursuing said fair ensign. Do you always run such a sweatshop?"

He gulped a mouthful of his coffee and almost choked. "Where did you get this stuff? It tastes exactly like the witches' brew they serve on Starbase 34. And I have it on good authority the mess officer there uses the engineer's sweat socks to give it the proper punch."

"Maybe that's what they modeled our synthesizer program after. But the coffee's not what I wanted to talk to you about."

"I didn't think so." Brady dropped his joking manner. "What's up?"

Kirk described the events of the last hour, concluding with Simons' death and Tenaida's arrest. "So that's the plan. We're hoping the spy will make a move and we can catch her. Is there anything I've left out?"

Brady reached for the coffee. He lifted the lid, then swung his arm, emptying the carafe in Kirk's face. Kirk yelled as the hot liquid hit him. Brady launched himself at Kirk. He cleared the desk with ease, and his hands closed around Kirk's throat.

The attack took Kirk by surprise. He tried to twist away from his attacker and fell sideways out of his chair, pulling Brady down on top of him. Brady's hands squeezed harder, closing off Kirk's windpipe. But Kirk had not survived Finnegan's attacks at the Academy without learning a few things about gutter fighting. He slapped his hands hard against Brady's ears.

Brady grunted in surprise, and his hold on Kirk's throat loosened. Before he could recover, Kirk slammed one knee into Brady's crotch, then rammed both fists into his kidneys, knocking the wind out of him. Brady struggled to keep his hold on Kirk, but the captain grabbed his thumbs and jerked. There was a sharp crack of breaking bone. Brady yowled and scrambled to get his feet under him. Kirk kicked out with both legs. Brady flew backward, crashed into the wall, and slid to the floor, stunned.

Kirk pulled himself to his feet, gasping for breath. He slapped at the intercom pad. "Security. My office. On the double."

Brady let out another frustrated yowl and struggled to his feet. Before Kirk could move, he stumbled out the door. Kirk tried to follow, but by the time he reached the door, Brady was out of sight. Frustrated, Kirk leaned against the wall, trying to catch his breath.

The turbolift whisked open and four security men jogged up to Kirk. "Security reporting as ordered, sir."

"Search the area. The spy just attacked me, then escaped into the corridor. He's disguised as Commander Brady."

"Commander Brady? We'll find him right away, Captain." The security men split into two teams and began searching the corridors. Kirk leaned against the wall, still trying to gather his scattered wits. The attack had caught him completely off guard, especially since the spy's conversation had sounded so much like Brady's. Did that mean Brady had met the same fate as Cecilia Simons—or was the spy a very observant actor? And what was her next move?

As soon as he asked the question, Kirk began cursing himself for a fool. *Of course* the spy would head for the brig. Whatever she wanted with Tenaida, she would hope to accomplish by speed, to get to Tenaida while Kirk and the security men were busy elsewhere. Kirk hit the intercom switch. He warned Chekov of his suspicions and ordered him to find out what had happened to Patrick Brady. Then, still swearing under his breath, Kirk headed for the turbolift at a dead run.

Captain Kirk entered the brig and approached the two guards flanking Tenaida's cell door. Both guards remained impassive, one watching the corridor while the other kept his eyes on the prisoner.

Srrawll massaged the poison sacs at the tips of her fingers. "Let me in the cell with him," she ordered.

The guard inspected her. For a moment, she feared he had found a flaw in her impersonation, but he turned toward the forcefield control mechanism. With his hand poised over the touch pads, he said in a conversational tone, "'Tis a wee bit early for playing poker, is it not, sir?"

Srrawll blinked, wondering what to say to the irrelevant remark. When she hesitated, the second guard fired his phaser. She crumpled to the floor, knocked unconscious by the heavy stun setting.

The watch officer looked up when Kirk entered the guardroom. "Captain, I thought you just went in to talk to the prisoner."

"No, I—" A grin of triumph split Kirk's face. This time, he had guessed right! "We've got her!" He charged from the room and into the maximum security area, just in time to see his double collapse on the floor.

"Report," he ordered, skidding to a halt beside the guards.

"This person asked to enter Lieutenant Tenaida's cell. He didn't know the response to the code phrase." The guard repeated the poker question.

"It's later than you think, Mr. Kelowicz," Kirk replied. "Let's get Tenaida out of there and lock up our prisoner. Have McCoy send someone to collect physiological data on—whoever that is—before the prisoner wakes up. And put a guard in there with her. If she tries *anything,* stun her again. I want her to still be here when I return."

"Yes, sir."

They lowered the forcefield and carried Kirk's double inside the cell. With the spy locked up and under restraints, Kirk and Tenaida left the maximum security area. After telling Tenaida what had happened in the last few hours, Kirk sent him to Sickbay to help McCoy extract the implant from Simons' body. That left Kirk with nothing to do until the prisoner regained consciousness. He got another cup of coffee and settled into a chair to wait.

"Captain?"

Kirk pushed his head off the table and struggled to open his eyes.

"Captain, the prisoner is awake. Do you wish to question him now?"

Kirk straightened in the chair, stretching his back. "Yes, Kelowicz. I'll be there in a minute." He picked up his half-empty cup and downed the cold coffee in three gulps. Scowling at the bitter taste, Kirk left the cup on the table and followed Kelowicz to the prisoner's cell.

It was a shock to see himself strapped to the bunk. Extra restraints had been added, making it almost impossible for the prisoner to move. Seeing Kirk's expression, Kelowicz said, "Lieutenant Chekov ordered the additional restraints, sir."

"A wise precaution." He entered the cell. The spy glared at Kirk, putting all her hatred into the look. Kirk was grateful for the weapons held by the guards behind him.

"I am Captain James T. Kirk of the starship *Enterprise,*" the prisoner said. "You are an impostor and I demand to be released at once!"

Kirk moved closer. Even from this distance, he could detect no visible flaws in the impersonation. He shuddered, chilled by the uncanny resemblance and the eerie sensation of seeing and hearing himself. "The medical department examined you while you were unconscious. You are not, in spite of outward appearances, James Kirk. Who are you?"

The double tensed, testing the restraints. They tightened automatically, holding the captive's body firmly against the bed. "A prisoner of war. You have no authority over me."

"A prisoner of war?" Kirk's voice rose in disbelief. "You are a spy, a saboteur, and a murderer. So if you have anything to say for yourself, you'd better start talking."

The double clamped his jaws shut and turned his head toward the wall.

"All right, let's try this. If we don't find out anything more about you, we can't reprogram the food synthesizers to meet your dietary needs. You might have trouble finding enough energy to hold your borrowed form." Kirk turned and walked out, signaling the guards to restore the forcefield.

"It is not your plan to starve the prisoner, is it, Captain?" Chekov asked when he and Kirk were seated in Chekov's office. "That would be considered a very cruel and unusual punishment."

"Of course not, but what I said is partly true. We'll need information before we can program the food synthesizers properly. I'm guessing it must take a lot of energy to maintain an alien's shape, so I'm hoping the threat of starvation will encourage the prisoner to talk sooner." Kirk glanced at the monitor to see if his words had had any effect yet.

"I understand, Captain. We will continue to observe the prisoner, and we will notify you the minute anything changes."

"Carry on, Lieutenant." Kirk pushed himself out of

the chair and forced his legs to carry him through the door. He stopped at Sickbay for McCoy's report on Patrick Brady.

"A bad concussion, and assorted bumps and bruises." McCoy blocked the door to keep Kirk from moving to Brady's bed. "He'll be fine, but he needs rest. Same as you, Captain. Are you going to your quarters, or do I give you the bed next to Mr. Brady's?"

"I'll take my own, thank you."

"By the way, what happened to him?" McCoy nodded his head toward Brady.

"Apparently, the spy attacked him. Fortunately, she didn't have enough time to finish him off."

"What about you?"

Kirk shrugged. "We've caught the spy. Now I think I'll go sleep for a week."

"Just what I was going to prescribe."

With great effort, he made it to his quarters before collapsing from exhaustion. The Kaldorni women were asleep on blankets piled on the floor, so the bed was unoccupied. Kirk fell across it without bothering to undress. As his head hit the pillow, he recalled the double's words about being a prisoner of war. "What was that supposed to mean?" Kirk mumbled to himself. If it was important, he would figure it out in the morning. Right now, he was too tired to think.

The intercom buzzer woke Kirk. He shoved himself to a sitting position and looked at his chronometer: 0700. It was past time for him to be up, even if he had gotten only four hours of sleep. He rubbed his eyes and reached for the control pad.

"Captain," Tenaida's voice came through the speaker, "I thought you would like to know what we learned from the implant in Ms. Simons' body."

"Definitely, Tenaida. I'll be down in five minutes." Kirk bounced off the bed, suddenly feeling wide awake. Finally, he was starting to get some answers instead of only finding more questions. The room was oppressively hot, and he considered taking a shower. After a moment's thought, he decided to postpone it until after he had seen Tenaida. He traded the rumpled uniform he had slept in for a clean one, tugged a comb through his hair, and was out the door before the Kaldorni women had roused themselves from their makeshift beds on the floor.

At this hour, most of the crew were on duty, asleep, or eating, and the corridors were deserted. Kirk saw no one as he hurried to Sickbay. He charged through the door, out of breath from his haste. "Let's have it."

Tenaida handed him a noteboard showing the circuit schematics for the implant. The Deltan looked tired but his expression was confident, as if he were well-pleased with his results. "We were able to disarm the self-destruct circuits in the implant, so we could remove it from the body with its information intact. I dumped its data into our computer for analysis."

"And came up with what?"

"The implant was a cipher chip for Simons to encode and decode her communications with the people who hired her. We decoded the message she added to Commissioner Montoya's dispatch tape. It suggests she was working for Dalien Cenara."

"Dalien Cenara?" Kirk stared at Tenaida in disbelief, wondering if he had heard the Deltan correctly. Dalien Cenara was the most notorious underworld figure in Federation space. He controlled an immense organization and was involved in every illegal activity that would turn a profit. Rumor claimed that Cenara could find a person for any job—if the customer could pay his price. "Someone must have wanted something pretty bad if they went to Cenara for it. Do you know what her instructions were?"

"I infer her mission was to disrupt the negotiations. That would have led to war between the Kaldorni Worlds and the Beystohn League over the disputed planet."

"Then someone who would profit from the hostilities paid Cenara to sabotage the discussions." It was a grim, ugly, and all-too-probable scenario.

"That's my conclusion." Tenaida's mouth quivered in agitation. "Captain, there was something else about the implant."

"Ye-es?" Kirk drew the word out into a question, afraid if he pushed too hard Tenaida would not tell him what was bothering him.

"I am disturbed about how the implant was placed in the skull." Tenaida took a deep, shuddering breath. "It was totally encased by bone, and there were no insertion marks—Dr. McCoy believes that bone was grown around the unit and the plate grafted into the skull."

"If that's true, is this discussion heading where I think it is?"

Tenaida nodded, his mouth compressed into a harsh line. "It means that someone has greatly improved implant techniques. A device installed like Ms. Simons' is virtually undetectable to all but the most thorough medical scans. Furthermore, given the neural connections required for a person to operate the implant, it could not be removed from living tissue. To attempt to do so would immediately activate the self-destruct mechanism."

"Destroying the person, as well as the device." Kirk shuddered, thinking that someone had found an incontestable way to insure loyalty. "Federation Security will want to know about this as soon as possible. Dispatch your report to them, Priority One, when it's finished."

"Very well, Captain."

"To change the subject, where does our friend in the brig fit into this?"

"I don't know." A puzzled look spread across Tenaida's face. "How long do you intend to deprive the prisoner of food? If she's been eating the Kaldorni food, you can't expect her to take your threat of starvation too seriously."

Kirk gave Tenaida a sheepish grin. "I was improvising—and hoping she doesn't like Kaldorni food. What I'd planned to do was question her again this morning, and then see if McCoy and Leftwell have had time to work up her nutritional requirements from the medical exam the doctors did last night."

"I see. When were you going to conduct the interrogation?"

"After I've had a shower, breakfast, and enough coffee to keep me awake. Do you want to help with the questioning?"

"Definitely."

"Then meet me in the brig in an hour."

Janara opened her eyes and looked around the room, cataloging the monitors and equipment of a standard room in Sickbay. She focused her awareness inward, probing her body for new injuries. Her collarbone and ribs had been repaired, but she found a fresh assortment of bruises on her body. She ran a hand down her torso, half expecting to find a long knife cut.

The motion attracted Chapel's attention and she came to the bedside. "How are you feeling this morning?" she asked.

"All right." Janara checked herself again. The residual damage was minor and, for once, McCoy's sedatives had passed through her system without making her feel like one of the rock specimens in the lab. Even the predatory cat was seeking other game for the moment. "Actually, I feel quite good."

"That's great. Dr. McCoy said I was to feed you breakfast, and then he wants to talk to you." Chapel sent for her breakfast tray.

McCoy entered the room as Janara finished her cereal. After he had ordered Chapel to remove the tray, McCoy paced the room, avoiding Janara's curious look. When he realized what he was doing, he stopped beside the bed.

"I have some bad news," he said, trying to meet Janara's eyes. "Your mother was murdered last night."

"A knife," Janara said in a flat tone, drawing a line from her collarbone to her pelvis.

"More like giant claws." McCoy stopped when he realized what Janara had said. "How did you know?"

"I—felt it."

"Then you already knew your mother was dead?"

Janara shook her head, denying the specifics. "I knew someone was attacked. I didn't know who."

McCoy searched her face for any sign of emotional reaction. "You act as if it doesn't matter that your mother was killed."

"Should it matter, Doctor? Our relationship was due to an accident of biology, nothing more. Would you like me to cry for you?"

"No, but I don't think it's healthy for you to bottle up your feelings, either."

"What feelings do you mean, Doctor? I don't feel anything. Just tired . . . and empty." Janara closed her eyes and turned her head away. "If you don't mind, I think I'll take a nap."

McCoy waited for several minutes, but Janara ignored him. Finally, realizing Janara would not continue the discussion, the doctor left. There were limits to how much help he could offer to someone who did not want to accept it.

"Captain, it was the strangest thing! We were watching the prisoner on the monitor like Lieutenant Chekov ordered, and suddenly his—I mean, her—entire body started to melt and . . . and change shape. It took three or four minutes. You can see the final results of the transformation."

Kirk took a long look at the screen. The prisoner

was still strapped to the bunk, but a compact felinoid, definitely female, had replaced the duplicate James Kirk. She twisted against the self-adjusting restraints, and the motion drew the uniform tunic tight across four small, rounded breasts. Her nose was broad and flat, and her narrow, lipless mouth was twisted in a vicious half-snarl. Two pointed, triangular ears twitched in short, angry movements as she strained to hear any sound her captors made. The five centimeters of black fur on her head stood on end.

Her unblinking amber eyes stared toward the concealed video pickup, and Kirk wondered if she knew it was there. "Analysis, Tenaida?"

"If that's her true form, she doesn't belong to any race known to us."

"But is that her natural appearance? Could it be another disguise?"

"I don't know. However, *Shan* Janara consistently reported a black, catlike being. If her appearance is for our benefit, she would confuse us more by continuing to look like you."

"Then let's talk to her, because we're not going to get any more answers sitting here."

"Agreed."

Kirk signaled to the three waiting guards to follow him. He left one man outside the shapechanger's cell and took the other two men inside with him. The man already in the cell moved to the far wall. Each of the guards braced himself against a wall and trained his phaser on the prisoner.

The felinoid stared past Kirk. Only the increased twitching of her ears showed she had noticed him.

"Are you ready to talk yet?"

"Am not obligated to talk with murderers and thieves." She punctuated the words with vicious snarls.

"Murderers? What do you call killing my security guard? Or Cecilia Simons? Or the Kaldorni ambassador's aides?"

"Thieves and friends of thieves. They are not important."

"And what is important?"

"I defend my people. My solitude. I am prisoner of war because I failed."

"Where do you come from?"

"The World. Where else?"

"That's not particularly helpful. Many beings call their planets *The World*."

"Prisoners of war are not required to tell their captors anything. That is *your* law. My law says thieves must be killed like the animals they are."

"What does this have to do with the *Enterprise* or anyone aboard her?"

"The fat ones are thieves. You aid the fat ones, so you are no better than they. In war against the enemies of my planet, I kill all that interfere."

"Yagra," Tenaida said. "The prisoner is from Yagra IV."

"Is *not* name of The World!" She hissed and snarled, arching her body against the restraints that held her. Her struggle was so violent Kirk was afraid she would hurt herself.

"Is Yagra IV the name used by members of the Federation for the planet you come from?"

"Yes!" she answered between yowls and snarls.

"Captain, this changes the situation for the negotiations. The Prime Directive clearly prohibits colonial development under these circumstances."

"Yes, a native intelligent race on the planet negates both the Kaldorni and the Beystohnai claims to exploitation rights." Kirk was not sure if discussing the Prime Directive in front of the prisoner would persuade her to cooperate, but at the very worst, he did not see how she could become less compliant.

"Of course, we must prove the prisoner comes from that planet."

Kirk glanced at the shapechanger. She was listening intently to the discussion, but her expression was hostile. Clearly, she did not believe what he and Tenaida had just said. "How long will it take you to prove she comes from Yagra?"

"I don't know, Captain. I'll start on it at once."

"Unless the prisoner wants to tell us anything now—" The felinoid clamped her jaws shut when she saw Kirk looking at her. "—I think we'll continue this later."

The prisoner stared at the ceiling, pretending she had not heard anything Kirk had said. The captain motioned to the security guards, and two of the three men followed him and Tenaida out of the cell.

"May I see the patient, Doctor?"

McCoy looked up from his computer screen. He had not heard Tenaida approach. "I don't see why not. I'm keeping her here for observation, but she can have visitors."

"Thank you, Doctor."

Janara was sitting against a pile of pillows, with the computer screen in front of her. When Tenaida entered the room, she shoved the machine away with an annoyed grimace. "The doctor set this thing for 'read only,' and I haven't been able to counter the blocks. I'm getting tired of what little I can do."

Loose strands of dark hair framed her face and accented her smooth olive skin. Her expression softened as she forgot her irritation with McCoy. A wave of tenderness for the small woman washed through Tenaida, and he was overwhelmed by her beauty. *Why have I never noticed it before?* he thought. He swallowed, trying to bring his voice under control.

She shook her head and gave him a half-smile. "That's the nicest thing anyone has thought about me in a long time, but you know it isn't true."

"To me, it is," Tenaida responded. He swallowed and continued, barely able to keep his voice from shaking. "I would ask if there is a soul mate for you. She who was bonded to me died many years ago, and until now, I have not found anyone I would wish to take her place."

Janara sank into the pillows and closed her eyes. After a small eternity, her eyelids fluttered open again. Tenaida let himself drown in her gaze.

She smiled, breaking the spell. "There is much to consider in your proposal. It will give me something to do until the doctor releases me from his tender care. I had never thought to find one of my own kind to share my life."

Tenaida wrapped his hands around one of hers, holding it like a precious jewel. It was so small it seemed lost between his wide palms. At last, reluctantly, he laid her hand on the blanket. "I must go. The alien we captured is from the disputed planet, and the captain wants my advice on the scientific and technical aspects of the discovery."

"Tell me what's happened," she said, touching his hand. "It will help you organize your thoughts for the captain."

After a moment, he nodded in agreement. He told how they had captured the shapechanger and what finding a native intelligent race on Yagra would mean for the *Enterprise*'s diplomatic mission. When he had talked himself into silence, she suggested an idea he had overlooked.

He glanced at his chronometer, judging how long he had before Kirk would need him. "I must run some simulations on your suggestion, but I think you have solved our problem."

"I hope so. There isn't much else I can do from this bed."

"I'll ask the doctor to allow you full use of the computer, although he is most stubborn about such things."

"Don't I know!" Janara watched Tenaida leave with a soft smile on her face.

* * *

Kirk downed another mouthful of coffee and set the cup aside. Three hours of continuous subspace communications with Admiral Chen and the Federation Council's legal department had sorely tried his patience. The diplomatic briefing that followed had done nothing to improve his frame of mind.

"That's about it." He gave Kristiann Norris the noteboard with the last of the documents he had just summarized for her. "When Tenaida compared the prisoner's physiology to our files on Yagra IV, it confirmed her claim that she came from that planet. Since her race is obviously intelligent, the need for negotiations between the Kaldorni and the Beystohn League no longer exists."

Norris nodded. "The next thing we have to do is explain this to Ambassador Klee. He isn't going to be happy at losing those resources for his planet."

"Lieutenant Tenaida suggested a solution. We submitted it to the Federation Council along with a recommendation to permanently quarantine Yagra IV. We're waiting for the reply."

"What was *Shan* Tenaida's idea?"

"When we were called to Starbase 15 to pick up your party, we were working on the first phase of a routine exploration and mapping assignment. We had just finished scanning the Shansar system. It's a little farther from the Kaldorni Worlds than Yagra, which may explain why they haven't discovered it yet. There are no intelligent inhabitants in the system, and Tenaida reports the second planet is similar to the Kaldorni homeworld in climate and gravity. We proposed that the Kaldorni be given the exclusive right to develop that planet."

"That should satisfy Ambassador Klee, but what about the Beystohn League?"

"Conditions on the fourth planet in the Shansar system should be much more to their liking than anything on Yagra."

271

"Isn't it something of a coincidence that you just happened to have a solar system waiting to be parceled out?"

"Not really. There are plenty of uninhabited—and unexplored—planets in this sector. The *Enterprise* could have found something suitable with very little effort, although neither the Kaldorni nor the Beystohn League have the spaceflight technology for extensive exploration—yet. If there's any luck involved, it's that we didn't have to search for what we needed."

"And what about the prisoner? She may consider herself a hero protecting her world, but that doesn't justify her actions in everyone's eyes. Joachim, for one, wants to see her properly punished."

Kirk sighed, wondering if any answer would satisfy Montoya. The commissioner alternated between periods when he seemed functional and times when he refused to leave his quarters or see anyone. "I don't know what will happen there, Kris. The Federation Council will decide that." Before he could say more, the intercom sounded. He tapped the switch.

"Kirk here."

"Captain, we have a message for you from the Federation Council."

"What is it, Uhura?"

"The Council concurs with your recommendation to terminate the scheduled negotiations between the United Worlds of the Kaldorni Systems and the Beystohn Amalgamated League of Planets because of the identification of a native intelligent race on the disputed planet, Yagra IV.

"Further, given the nature of said race and their expressed desire to remain isolated, the Council provisionally accepts your recommendation to establish a quarantine, which will become permanent if approved by the resident sapient population of the planet.

"The prisoner is to be handed over to the authorities at Starbase 15, where she will be confined pending discussions with representatives of her homeworld to decide the appropriate punishment for her activities against individual Federation citizens.

"Proposal for the disposition of planets of the Shansar system to the Kaldorni Worlds and the Beystohn League is approved, if the respective negotiating teams can conclude appropriate treaties. Under the circumstances, Federation regulations against disclosing locations of Class-G exploitable worlds to governments with less than Class-VI spaceflight capabilities are waived. Detailed instructions will follow shortly. End of message.

"Also, Mr. Scott reports most repairs are completed and warp capability is restored."

"Thank you, Uhura. Tell Mr. ben Josef to set course for Starbase 15, and let me know when the next message arrives. Kirk out." He grinned at Norris, letting her see his pleasure at the Council's answer. "That's the word. Now you know as much about the situation as I do."

She stood, brushing the wrinkles out of her tunic. "Thank you, Jim. I'd better see if Joachim is ready to be briefed on this, and then I have to set up a meeting with the Kaldorni."

"I'll walk you part of the way." Kirk rose and moved to her side, offering her his arm. "Do you think the Kaldorni will accept our proposal?"

"They should. In their own way, they're reasonable beings."

Kirk entered the Kaldorni's quarters. Klee bowed to the captain. Kirk returned the greeting and seated himself on the floor. The short Kaldorni joined him.

"I've come to discuss the discord created when my security people did not prevent the murder of your aide, s'Flen," Kirk said.

"This discordance is a matter of the most concern. But the honored captain should know that my failure to detect the impostor among those that serve me is a matter of greatest shame to me."

"There is truth in your words, Mr. Ambassador. However, my superiors charged me with finding the intruder, so the disgrace at failure must be mine."

"It would seem your failure is indeed disgraceful. If you are at fault, you owe me reparations for the loss of my aide. It would also seem that your Commissioner Montoya wishes reparations for his wife because I failed to detect the discordance of an alien among those who serve me. The compounding of these errors is becoming more than the Harmony of the Universe can balance."

"May I suggest a resolution to the problem?"

"I will listen to your words and hope they may be as harmonious as the ones given my people by your commissioner."

Kirk felt the relief wash through him. If Klee liked the Federation's solution to the Yagra problem, he should approve the captain's next idea. "I will persuade Commissioner Montoya to waive reparations for the death of his wife if you will waive compensation for s'Flen."

After a moment, Klee extended his hands and bowed to touch his forehead to his palms. "I believe this can be made acceptable to my people."

"I also wish to give you a personal token of apology. I ask you to accept the right to care for my three wives. My honor owes you this additional apology because of my responsibilities to protect everyone on my ship. I hope you will receive the women and cherish them in the spirit of brotherhood and harmony that prevails between our peoples."

"If your honor demands this of you, I will protect

these women as long as I hold the strength to defend them."

"I thank you greatly, Mr. Ambassador. You have restored my harmony with the universe." With an overwhelming sense of relief, Kirk headed for his quarters to tell the women.

Epilogue

KIRK AND KRIS NORRIS leaned against the wall, watching luggage being loaded onto the transporter pad for transfer to Starbase 15. The Kaldorni had returned to the base half an hour earlier. And with their departure, the *Enterprise*'s official duties were over.

"Well, Jim," Norris said, "it's been an interesting trip."

"I'm sorry about that. I could have used a little less excitement."

"We have to take events as they come, I guess."

"Speaking of that, how is Commissioner Montoya handling things now?"

She laughed. "Actually, he's over most of the shock, and we'll have lots of work hammering out the final agreement with the Kaldorni. That's what he needs right now—something to keep him busy.

"What about you? Where's the *Enterprise* off to next?"

"Would you believe, to a detailed exploration of the Shansar system? The Federation Council wants more information, now that they've assigned development rights to the second and fourth planets. Since we did the preliminary scans, we got the assignment."

"That's good. Will you be stopping over on Starbase 15 anytime soon?"

"I don't know. It depends on our schedule."

"Anytime you're in my neighborhood, stop in. I'll buy you dinner, and I promise it won't be from a Starfleet regulation menu."

"I'd like that. Good-bye, Kris."

"Good-bye, Jim." She gave him an impish grin and stepped onto the transporter pad.

"Do I detect a hint of romance there, Captain?" Brady asked. Kirk jumped, startled for a moment that he had company.

"I don't think so. She's just a very nice lady—and a friend."

"I see you returned the Kaldorni ambassador's wives to him."

Kirk allowed a smug expression to spread across his face. "Once I explained it in the proper terms of *honor* and *harmony with the universe,* I think he was as glad to have them back as I was to give them to him. You don't know what a pleasure it is to have the temperature in my quarters set at a reasonable level again!"

"Speaking of warm climates, when is Mr. Spock due back?"

Kirk glanced at his chronometer. "Anytime now. He was supposed to be here half an hour ago, but Base Traffic Control said his shuttle had been delayed."

The door whisked open, and Tenaida and McCoy entered, almost colliding with Kirk and Brady. McCoy circled around to face the captain. "Jim, why didn't you expedite the rest leave I recommended for Janara Whitehorse?"

"What rest leave?"

"I can answer that," Tenaida said. "*Shan* Janara asked that the recommendation not reach the captain until we finished our work on the Shansar system."

"She needs rest. And time to adjust to her mother's death."

Tenaida shook his head. "I don't see why you think everyone should react to such an event by dissolving into a pool of useless emotions."

Kirk glanced at Tenaida, noticing his bland expression. He suspected the Deltan was not telling them something, but saw no way to find out what. "Bones," Kirk said finally, "I think you're outvoted this time. If Lieutenant Whitehorse wants to finish her investigation of the Shansar system, it sounds like the best prescription to me. But I promise she'll get her leave as fast as possible when I see the request."

"And what about you, Captain? This mission has been stressful for you too."

"I think I'll manage." Kirk gave Tenaida a questioning look. "Do you suppose, gentlemen, that we are fit for a quiet game of poker? Or does the doctor think it would be too strenuous, considering our current weakened conditions?"

While the transporter whined, McCoy glared at the three of them. As Spock materialized on the pad, the doctor announced, "In your *current weakened conditions,* I should confine the lot of you to Sickbay!"

Spock responded, "May I inquire as to what weakened conditions you are referring?"

"These men have had an extremely strenuous two weeks," McCoy announced with a theatrical flourish. "I can't begin to tell you how difficult it's been for them."

Spock lifted an eyebrow. "Indeed, Doctor. I was under the impression that the ship was undertaking a routine diplomatic mission."

Brady grimaced. Kirk chuckled at his expression and turned to Spock, shaking his head. "Just once, Spock—just once—I'd like to see what a *routine* diplomatic mission was like."

Spock's eyebrow rose even higher. "Then may I assume that the advice program you were testing proved useful?"

Kirk shook his head. "The program needs work, Spock."

"That is not unexpected. It was a very preliminary version."

Kirk allowed himself a grin. "Well, Spock, I hope your last two weeks weren't half as exciting as ours."

"I would not presume to make comparisons until I know what happened on the *Enterprise*. However, I have had an extremely stimulating leave. T'Slar of the Vulcan Academy of Sciences and her associates have made some astounding discoveries on the structure of the space-time continuum. Within the next twenty years, their theories will completely revolutionize our concept of space travel. And the Andorian group led by Tarlev of Gan—"

McCoy rolled his eyes and shot Kirk an exasperated glance as Brady looked on with amusement. Tenaida, however, listened carefully to Spock's monologue, committing each detail to memory.

Kirk grinned and gestured toward the door. "Gentlemen, shall we go mind the store?"

STAR TREK®
PRIME DIRECTIVE

JUDITH AND GARFIELD
REEVES-STEVENS

Starfleet's highest law has been broken. Its most honored captain is in disgrace, its most celebrated starship in pieces, and the crew of that ship scattered among the thousand worlds of the Federation . . .

Thus begins *PRIME DIRECTIVE,* an epic tale of the STAR TREK universe. Following in the tradition of *SPOCK'S WORLD* and *THE LOST YEARS,* both month-long *New York Times* bestsellers, Garfield and Judith Reeves-Stevens have crafted a thrilling tale of mystery and wonder, a novel that takes the STAR TREK characters from the depths of despair into an electrifying new adventure that spans the galaxy.

**"YOU HAVE BROKEN OUR MOST SACRED COM-
MANDMENT, JAMES T. KIRK—AND IN DOING SO,
DESTROYED A WORLD . . ."**

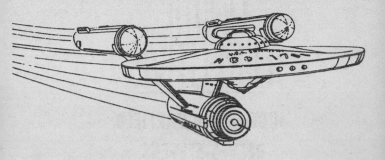

A mission gone horribly wrong—the *Enterprise* is
nearly destroyed as an entire planet is ravaged by
nuclear annihilation. Captain James T. Kirk is blamed
and drummed out of Starfleet for breaking the Federation's highest law: the Prime Directive. Kirk and his
crew must then risk their freedom and their lives in a
confrontation that will either clear their names or lead
to the loss of a thousand worlds.

In the third blockbuster Pocket Books STAR TREK
hardcover, Judith and Garfield Reeves-Stevens have
created the biggest, most exciting STAR TREK novel
yet . . .

Now Available in Hardcover
From Pocket Books

PRIME DIRECTIVE